Praise for Sarah Castille's
Barely Undercover

"There was no possible way I was putting this book down."
~ *Guilty Pleasures Book Reviews*

"Sarah Castille's second Legal Heat novel is a smoldering, emotionally intense story…"
~ *The Romance Reviews*

"There are plenty of sexy times with some light BDSM in there. James is a growly alpha which always does it for me."
~ *Fiction Vixen*

"This story was an amazing! […] Ms. Castille is a fantastic storyteller and I can't wait to read her next one!"
~ *The Book Tart*

Look for these titles by *Sarah Castille*

Now Available:

Legal Heat
Legal Heat
Barely Undercover

Barely Undercover

Sarah Castille

Samhain Publishing, Ltd.
11821 Mason Montgomery Road, 4B
Cincinnati, OH 45249
www.samhainpublishing.com

Barely Undercover
Copyright © 2013 by Sarah Castille
Print ISBN: 978-1-61922-270-0
Digital ISBN: 978-1-61921-823-9

Editing by Christa Soule
Cover by Angela Waters

This book is a work of fiction. The names, characters, places, and incidents are products of the writer's imagination or have been used fictitiously and are not to be construed as real. Any resemblance to persons, living or dead, actual events, locale or organizations is entirely coincidental.

All Rights Are Reserved. No part of this book may be used or reproduced in any manner whatsoever without written permission, except in the case of brief quotations embodied in critical articles and reviews.

First Samhain Publishing, Ltd. electronic publication: December 2013
First Samhain Publishing, Ltd. print publication: December 2014

Dedication

To Sharon, Rana, Adele and Tarick.

For listening to my stories and believing in me, no matter what path I choose to follow.

Chapter One

In a dimly lit back alley, a hulking man stalked through the shadows. The chains looped over his thick leather boots clanked with the thud of his feet on the cobblestones. The six glowing eyes of Cerberus, the three-headed guardian hound of Hades, glared into the darkness from the center of the patch on the back of his worn leather jacket.

As far as bikers went, he was pretty scary.

Lana Parker wondered what he would do if he caught her following him. The last private investigator his wife, Angel, had hired was still in the hospital. And after seeing the biker's picture, Lana had almost refused the case. It had taken her four years to escape her ex, bad-boy biker Levi Sullivan. The last thing she wanted was to get anywhere near another biker gang.

But Angel had changed Lana's mind. Determined to escape from the biker world, Angel had convinced Lana to take a case she ordinarily wouldn't have touched with a ten-foot pole. Having once been in the same position as Angel, Lana couldn't refuse.

She picked up her pace, trying to match the biker's long strides. The alley smelled of diesel, the crisp, sharp scent of the ocean and a faint whiff of piss and stale beer. For an instant, the smells triggered a memory. Another case. Another alley. Or was it this one? Two and a half years ago, she had been new to Vancouver and all the Gastown alleys had looked the same.

Her foot slid on the cobblestones. Loose gravel bounced off a nearby dumpster and clattered across the alley, the sound ringing in the quiet space. The biker stopped midstep. Lana froze.

For a long moment, he didn't move. Then his head jerked to the side, his long, blond ponytail brushing over the three noses of Cerberus. Not one of them sneezed. No doubt he was packing a couple of weapons inside that heavy leather jacket—weapons he could pull out and fire in a heartbeat at a young, financially strapped private investigator. The breadth of his body could not be solely attributable to the fast food and gourmet cookie addiction she had noted over the last week of surveillance.

His head swiveled, owl-like, over his shoulder. Even in profile, his face made her shudder. Long, sharp beak of a nose, thick lips, unforgiving chin. But it was the multitude of knife scars crisscrossing his broad face that bore testament to his violent life. Even Angel—who had promised Lana a 15 percent bonus for a picture of her husband *in flagrante delicto*—admitted her man was dangerous with a capital *D*.

Not just a man. Rex Morgan. Leader of Hades, British Columbia's most infamous motorcycle club. Murderer. Arsonist. Drug dealer. Thief. Litterbug.

Suspected adulterer.

And soon to be single...if Lana got the pictures Angel needed to secure custody of her daughter.

Lana plastered her body against the rough brick wall and breathed in soft, shallow pants. Kind of like sex. Not that she remembered much about sex, at least good sex. It had been two years since she'd been dumped by James Hunter, ruggedly handsome homicide cop, sex god and heartless bastard. The few guys she'd slept with since then had left her cold.

She shook her head to clear her mind. Why the hell was she thinking about sex now? And why did she have Heartless Bastard on the brain? Her subconscious seemed to have its own agenda tonight, and one that could get her killed if she didn't rein it in.

After one last sweep of his ponytail, Rex resumed his march down the alley, his long legs eating up the cobblestones until he reached a black metal door inset in the brick wall. He pulled a card from his pocket and ran it through the card reader. The door buzzed open and he disappeared inside.

Damn.

Lana bolted down the alley and grabbed the handle just before the door snapped shut. Her eyes swept over the entrance and she caught a flash of gold. She leaned in to examine the small, discreet plaque affixed to the wall.

Carpe Noctem.

Her heart sank. No wonder she had Heartless Bastard on the brain. They had met in this club during her first-ever investigation. Moonlighting as Carpe Noctem's head of security, the mouthwateringly sexy cop had caught her with her finger on the shutter release. He'd liked her sass. She'd liked his over-the-top, crusty-cop style. After the case was solved and the bad guys were in jail, they'd had a few drinks and night after night of hot, kinky, mind-blowing sex. Then—*poof!*—he was gone. Never to be seen or heard from again.

Heartless Bastard.

What if he was here tonight?

She hesitated for only a second before she stepped through the door. She couldn't let Angel down. And with a good disguise, no one would recognize her.

Twenty minutes later, Lana stepped out of the changing room and through the interior entrance of Vancouver's most exclusive sex club, unrecognizable, even to herself. Although there was little she could do with the riot of red curls running rampant down her back, a heavy coat of foundation and a light dusting of bronzer had banished her freckles and darkened her naturally pale skin. Fake eyelashes and miracle eyeliner had turned her big green eyes into smoky emerald pools, and a slash of red lipstick had given her a trout pout to die for.

Someone had left a pair of handcuffs in the changing room,

and she clipped them on to the belt of the risqué police officer costume she had tucked into her backpack for just this sort of emergency. Even if Angel hadn't warned her about Rex's penchant for sex clubs, Lana would have been tempted by the skintight, cleavage-baring, dirty-cop outfit she'd found in the costume shop. She was in law enforcement, after all. Sort of.

"Whit woo!" A short, skinny dude made a lewd gesture with his hips and motioned Lana over to his table. She tipped back her police hat and peered down at him through mirrored aviator sunglasses. Leather, chains and an overabundance of pink, spiked hair decorated his scrawny five-foot-and-a-few-inches frame.

"Really?" She rolled her eyes and sighed. She needed a real man. Big. Strong. Protective. Easy on the eyes. Dominant in the bedroom. Docile in the kitchen. Handy with a mop.

Heartless Bastard with a domestic side.

She searched the room, taking in the curtained alcoves hugging the curve of the wall, the tan leather couches and the new sparkly, red-tiled floor. No sign of Heartless Bastard. Her anxiety dropped a notch and she looked around for Rex.

Laughter and the clink of glassware drowned out the pathetically tame hip hop music buzzing through the speakers. Latex-, leather- and Lycra-clad bodies jostled for space on a dance floor near a roped-off area at the back of the club.

Taking a deep breath, Lana wove her way through the crowd, her fake handcuffs jangled on the hooks at the front of her barely there, strip-of-Lycra skirt. She wasn't as worried about flashing a cheek as she was about cracking a smile. Still, it was way more fun than being nude in the morgue. Her last case, investigating an undertaker's alleged infidelity, had given her a chill.

"Ooooh, Officer, I've been a bad, bad boy." A portly, balding man in a cheap brown suit snaked an arm around her waist and pulled her into his lap. The tiny skirt rolled to the top of her thighs, exposing her sparkle-studded G-string and the problem with eating too many donuts.

"Go tell your mama." Lana stomped a stiletto heel into his shoe and the tiny handcuff straps on her knee-high boots rattled in what she hoped was a menacing way.

Apparently not. He grabbed at her thighs and succeeded in snapping one of the garters attached to her black mesh stockings. "Whaddya gonna do, sunshine? I'm resisting arrest."

Stilling herself, Lana positioned her elbow to inflict the maximum amount of pain in his place of least resistance, and then remembered she was supposed to be flying under the radar.

"Resist this," she hissed. She angled her elbow down and shoved it between his legs only half as hard as she'd originally planned. The man exhaled a breath and doubled over. Lana slid off his lap and made a run for the bar, pressing a hand to the built-in bra cups on her corset as her almost-Ds threatened to escape.

"Hey, stop her."

Lana took a quick look back and ran smack into a solid wall of muscle. Rough hands gripped her shoulders, holding her tight. Her gaze locked on to a mini glowering Cerberus affixed to the front of a worn leather jacket.

Oh God. Rex.

"Where are you running so fast, pet?"

Lana jerked back, the deep growl from above hitting her like a powerful blow. Her breath whooshed out of her, and she instinctively looked down, hiding her face.

Surveillance Rule #1: Never be seen.

"Sorry. Just going to the bar for a drink." She glanced back over her shoulder at the man in the brown suit. He had stopped about ten feet behind her. One glance at Rex and he walked away. Exactly what she should be doing. But she couldn't give up. Not without a picture of Rex engaged in some morally or legally reprehensible behavior. A week of surveillance and the worst thing he had done so far was toss a gum wrapper on the street. He just *had* to be planning something bad tonight. The press hadn't nicknamed him Rex the Hex for nothing.

Intending to head back to the changing room and slip on a new disguise, she tried to sidestep around Rex, but he thrust a meaty finger under her chin and tilted her head back, forcing her to meet his gaze. She inhaled sharply as he loomed over her. Bulky and barrel-chested, he had to be well over six feet in height and he had the coldest eyes she had ever seen. There was nothing behind those eyes. Not a flicker of emotion. Only darkness.

Oh God. Oh God. Oh God. Not again. She knew that darkness. It lived in her nightmares, flitted through the shadows, crawled through her skin even on bright sunny days. Instinct told her to run, but her feet remained frozen to the floor.

"I'll buy you that drink." A statement, not a question. His cold, domineering tone reminded her of her father.

A shiver coursed up Lana's spine, and she shook her head to loosen her tongue. "I'm meeting someone."

His rough, gravelly voice deepened. "Right now, you're meeting me." His gaze crawled over her, unleashing a wave of cockroaches under her skin. By the time his eyes returned to her face, a cold, sticky sweat covered her body.

With all the faux bravado she could muster, she gave him a tight smile and took a step back. "And...the meeting is over. Nice to meet you. Goodbye."

His arm shot out, grabbing her shoulder, holding her in place. "Usually when I see a cop, I get an itch in my trigger finger. I look at you and I get an itch somewhere else. Ditch the boyfriend. One night with me and you'll forget he exists."

An itch? She suspected it might have to do more with his extramarital affairs and visits to the Seymour Street brothels than a desire to hump and pump with a curvy redhead in a dirty cop costume. Talk about putting a girl off.

Rex smiled, all nicotine-stained teeth and ashtray breath. "Yeah. I can see it in your eyes. You know what I'm talking about."

What did he see exactly? Fear? Disgust? Or her desperate need to find the number for the local STD clinic?

Lana gave him a vacant smile as she considered her options. *Option #1: Find a boyfriend.* Heart thumping, she looked around the bar for a pseudoboyfriend—someone big, strong and sufficiently threatening. No one measured up except...maybe...Master Tony? She raked her eyes over the tall, broad frame of the club's owner, but when he turned to greet someone at the door, she gave a little sigh. He had been less than pleased the last time she'd sneaked into the club. She doubted he would help her once he discovered she'd sneaked in again.

Option #2: Run. Excellent option. Lana wrenched herself from Rex's grasp and took a step toward the door.

Damn.

Three bikers, two wearing the Hades patch, and one so young he had to be a prospect, were making their way through the crowd toward Rex. Blocking her path.

Lana's pulse pounded in her ears. Rex was bad enough. But four bikers? It was almost like being back in the Wolverines' clubhouse with Levi all over again.

The tallest of the three had swept back his long, dark hair and tied it at nape of his neck in a ponytail. Dark eyes, olive skin and a broad, hard body to match the strong planes of his striking face. Yum...even though he was a biker.

"Ryder." Rex shook the hand of Mr. Deep, Dark and Delicious.

Ryder's gaze flicked to Lana. He tilted his head to the side, giving her first a considered look, and then a sympathetic smile. He turned back to Rex. "I thought we were here for a meeting, not to pick up fender fluff."

Lana grimaced at the backhanded compliment. She knew the slang. He thought she was pretty. Anything less and she would have been a "fender bunny" or even worse, a "mattress cover".

Lucky her. Well, at least he hadn't made fun of her hair. Usually men made some reference to the inferno on her head— Carrots, Ginger Snap, Big Red, Fire Bush, Rusty, Copper Top, Flame Brain, Matchstick Head or her current favorite, Red Zilla.

"You know what they say, 'red in the head, fire in the bed'." The second biker, a bruiser with crazy dreadlocks gave her a lascivious wink and an oh-so-enticing crotch grab.

"Good one, Bones." Rex thumped the thick-necked thug on the back. "I was thinking that myself."

Lana rolled her eyes. Oh ha-ha-ha. So funny. As if she hadn't heard that one before. Some day she'd meet a man who could insult her hair with some originality.

"Leave the girl alone. We've got a meeting to get underway." Ryder gave her a wink and stepped to the side, clearing her path to the door.

Rex gripped Lana's arm just as she took her first step to freedom. "You jealous, Ryder? Been a long time since you had a back warmer."

"Maybe he's fucking bent." The prospect, a blond Adonis who looked like he should be playing high school football instead of pledging to join a biker gang, gave Rex an obsequious smile and was rewarded with a slap to the head.

"You're an idiot, Kickstand," Rex growled. "You don't disrespect a full-patch brother when you don't even have the right to breathe without his permission."

Kickstand stumbled into Lana from the force of the blow, knocking her off balance and out of Rex's grasp. With incredible dexterity, Kickstand caught her before she fell.

"Sorry," Kickstand murmured as he helped her balance. "I

don't usually make a habit of knocking down pretty girls just to get their attention. Every time I'm around these guys I do something wrong."

She gave him a soft, reassuring smile, but her heart went out to him. He was trying so hard to fit in. She'd seen dozens of prospects like him during her time with Levi—young and desperate to be part of what they perceived to be the glamorous world of bikerdom. Very few were accepted and fewer still earned their patch. Kickstand would never make the cut. Too good-looking, too kind-hearted and too eager to please. What the hell was he doing with Hades?

While Rex, Bones and Ryder lamented the lack of good prospects in the biker world, Lana edged her way toward the door, only to be cut off again, this time by a late arrival.

Almost as tall as Rex and Ryder, the new biker was lean, lithe and powerful, with a narrow waist and long, hard thighs. His thick, dark hair just brushed his collar. His eyes were an unusual steel blue.

A familiar steel blue. Her heart stuttered in her chest.

James?

No, it couldn't be. She blinked her eyes. Once. Twice. Was it him? Two years had passed since she'd last seen Heartless Bastard. The man in front of her had the same physique, strong nose and chiseled jaw. But the James she knew had kept his hair military short and would have been appalled to sport a five o'clock shadow, much less three days' worth of stubble over his unyielding chin. James was a cop through and through. No way would he ever join Hades.

As if sensing her perusal, he frowned. "Take off the glasses." The velvet rasp of his deep baritone voice sent tiny quivers of need straight to her core.

Heart pounding, she took a step back and inadvertently hit Rex's chest. "Take them off, pet," Rex snapped. "Ice isn't a man who asks twice."

17

Ice. He had a road name, and from the mini salivating puppies on the front of his jacket, he was no prospect, like Kickstand, currying favor in the hopes of being allowed to join the club. He was a fully initiated member of Hades.

Swallowing hard, Lana removed her glasses and stared down at the fishnet stockings peeking out of her boots like a hundred crisscrossing lines of black gunpowder. One of the garters was still loose, leaving her even more exposed—as if that was possible—to the explosive heat of his gaze.

"Look at me," Ice demanded. His rich, husky voice rolled through her, stirring longings she had hidden away in the darkest recesses of her memory. Heat settled at the juncture of her thighs, her nipples tightened and her mouth went dry.

Disconcerted by her body's responses and unable to meet his gaze, she looked away.

Ice cupped her jaw and firmly turned her face toward him, pulling her away from Rex. Her gaze locked with eyes now as deep blue as the ocean. Commanding, captivating eyes. Framed by thick lashes. But it wasn't his eyes that finally sparked her recognition; it was the aura of pure power that hit her like the painful thud of her heart when she had realized he was never coming back.

He stroked his thumb over the apple of her cheek, the gesture at once comforting and familiar. A tangled web of emotions swept through her body like a firestorm. The world fell away.

James.

Heartless Bastard.

Lana swallowed hard and fought the warring urges to kiss him and slap him across the face.

For a split second, his breathing hitched and his eyes widened. He glanced over at Rex and back to her. His expression shifted from curious to considering, and she caught a gleam in his eyes. Calculating. Determined.

Barely Undercover

Did he recognize her? Two years ago she had been twenty pounds heavier, her pale complexion marked with freckles and her curly hair just brushing the top of her shoulders. Two years ago she had been stupid and naive, thinking she had found a man she could actually trust—someone who would never hurt her.

Now she knew better. And that kind of knowledge changed a girl. Made her immune to a Heartless Bastard's bone-melting cheek-stroking and irresistible charms.

She slapped his hand away and, boy, did it feel good.

"Roxie." His sharp tone snapped her out of her reverie, but not as much as his warm hand clasping her own. "What the fuck are you doing here, dressed like that? I almost didn't recognize you."

Lana's breath caught in her throat. Only two men knew her as Roxie: Levi and James. Once, in a quiet after-sex moment, she had told James she'd changed her name from Roxie to Lana when she'd moved to Vancouver, but she had never told him why. And since Levi couldn't possibly know where she was, much less radically alter his appearance, she was definitely, 100 percent, in the presence of Heartless Bastard.

Damn. She should have slapped him for real.

"JJJa..."

"Ice," he said quickly. "You forget my name already, babe? Just this morning you were screaming it so loud in bed I thought the neighbors would call the fucking cops."

Lana yanked her gaze to James, her numb brain scrambling desperately to play catch-up. Was he jerking her around, or was he trying to save her from Rex? She sifted quickly through her memories. Aside from walking out on her in the middle of the night and never contacting her again— definitely jerking-her-around behavior—he had always been a straight-talking, straight-shooting, down-to-earth kind of guy. She had always known where she stood with him. But now?

Now, she didn't trust him.

Dragging his attention away from a thoroughly chastised Kickstand, Rex frowned at James. "You know her?"

"Yeah, I know her." Disapproval and exasperation tinged James's voice. Still, there was something in the sincerity of his concerned gaze that made Lana fairly certain he was trying to help her escape.

"She said she was waiting for her boyfriend," Rex grumbled. "That was you?"

James sighed and gently clasped Lana's arm. "She was supposed to wait for me in the lobby until we were done with our meeting, not skank around the fucking bar dressed like she's needing attention. Weren't you listening this morning, babe?"

Lana exhaled a breath she hadn't realized she had been holding. Damn he was fast with the lies. Almost as fast as he'd been at sneaking away in the middle of the night. Still, if he was trying to help her, he'd definitely come up with a plausible story. She would have to put aside the urge to pummel him, at least long enough to escape Rex's clutches.

But how was she going to act like his girlfriend when she could barely stand the sight of him? Even worse, how was she going to act like a biker's old lady? Even when she had been a biker's old lady, she hadn't fit in. She had the fire but not the thick skin; the anger but not the attitude.

Unlike Angel. She closed her eyes for the briefest second and imagined herself as a tough, wiry biker chick, long platinum hair, high-heeled boots, leather jacket and a spandex, leopard-print dress. She imagined the confident rasp of Angel's voice, her don't-fuck-with-me attitude and her total fearlessness at the possibility of facing the wrath of an entire motorcycle club when she divorced their leader.

Lana opened her eyes and gave James a tight, hard, Angel-like smile.

"Sorry, *honey*." She dripped the last word. "I must have been caught up cooking your breakfast, oiling your leathers and servicing your motorcycle this morning."

"She your old lady?" Confusion clouded Rex's face.

"Yeah. She's my old lady." James released his grip and slid his arm around Lana's waist, pulling her into his chest. Her cheek pressed against the soft cotton of his Harley Davidson T-shirt pulled tight over a sheet of rock-hard muscle. She breathed in his familiar scent—sharp and clean, like soap—and the heavier musk of leather and grease. Desire licked its way up her spine.

"Can't seem to keep her out of trouble," James said, his hand firm and reassuring against her back. "Second time she's caused a problem in this club."

Lana closed her eyes. The deep rumble of James's voice took her back to the nights he had gently coaxed her deepest, most secret desires from her lips and made them real. She fought the urge to plaster her body against him and beg him to take her there again. Free her from the torment of her past.

As if sensing her need, he ran his hand up and down her back, a seemingly absent caress that set her blood on fire. "Looks like you'll have to stay with me until the meeting is over, babe. I can't have you causing more trouble in the club."

Stay? With James? And a group of bikers? In Master Tony's club? No damn way. Her take on his unspoken plan had been to get her out and away from Rex. Angel or no Angel, she wasn't sticking around. The situation had gotten entirely out of hand. She would have to get her pictures another day. And figure out what James was doing with Hades.

She wrenched herself out of James's arms. "Change of plans, *honey*. I've got a sudden urge to spit shine your spare boots. I'm going home."

"No, babe, you're not."

"Watch me." Lana spun around and walked away.

Chapter Two

He watched her.

He couldn't help but watch her.

For two years he had dreamed of seeing her again, and here she was.

And there she went.

Lana strode toward the door, perfect ass swaying, long, lean legs showcased by her barely there skirt and knee-high stiletto boots. His heart pounded against his rib cage and he wanted nothing more than to grab her and haul her back into his arms.

She had to be fucking kidding. Didn't she realize he was the only reason Rex hadn't laid a hand on her? A brother didn't touch another brother's old lady. That unspoken rule was a code of honor followed by every motorcycle club…everywhere.

No way would Rex believe his bullshit story if he let her walk away. No self-respecting biker would take that kind of crap from his old lady, especially in front of his biker brothers. And he couldn't afford to lose Rex's respect. After two years undercover, busting his balls to get into Rex's inner circle, the end was finally in sight. He had to stay strong, focused.

Fuck. Of all the women Rex had to pick, it had to be her.

Lana.

The biggest regret of his life.

It had been two years since he'd held her in his arms. Two years since he'd kissed her full, lush lips. And yet he remembered their last night together as if it were yesterday. And he remembered her fire. God, he'd loved her fire. It had awakened a passion he'd long thought dead—killed by a bullet meant for him.

He drew in a long, slow breath and watched her ass wiggle beneath the thin layer of Lycra. His cock twitched. Lana, in or out of clothing, set his blood to boiling. But that slicked-on naughty-police outfit was a whole new level of hell for his self-control.

Two years ago he'd fucked up. He should have ended it gently. Told her about the undercover assignment. Explained it could never work between them. Maybe even mentioned Christine. Walking out on Lana in the middle of the night had been the wrong thing to do.

But now he had a chance to make amends, even the score. Saving her from Rex would put his guilt to rest. Then he would be able to move on with his life without being tormented by the memory of her peaceful, trusting face, beautiful in the moonlight as he walked way.

Easier said than done. Especially when he had to ensure he didn't blow his cover. And that was a possibility if he let her leave the club. Clearly, he wouldn't be able to convince her to stay, so his only option was to get Tony to throw her out. And Tony would only do that if she broke the rules.

Time to fire her temper.

He dropped his voice low, commanding, and raised it loud enough for her to hear. "Babe. Stop right there."

She pulled up short, as if she had hit an invisible wall, and spun around to face him. A shiver ran through her and her pupils dilated. For a second, even her breathing stopped.

"What did you say?" Fury flared in her brilliant green eyes.

A thrill of anticipation shot through him like a bullet, hardening his cock in an instant. "Come here. Now." He did not dare tear his gaze away from her, but he could sense his biker brothers watching with avid interest.

Unable to resist the challenge, her jaw tightened and she

stomped toward him, stopping so close he could feel her breath, hot and sweet on his lips.

Her nostrils flared. "You did *not* just speak to me that way."

"I did. You came. Good girl." He pressed his lips together and repressed a smile. Lana had only two reactions to that particular tone of voice. Part of her attraction was never knowing which he would get.

"Fuck you." She slapped him. The crack of her hand on his cheek echoed through the bar. Heads turned. Rex frowned. Ryder chuckled. Kickstand sucked in a breath.

James reacted quickly, grabbing her wrists and pinning her hands behind her. He backed her up to a nearby pillar and caged her with his body. Her gaze dropped, copper eyelashes brushing over creamy cheeks. A sound escaped her lips, a cross between a growl and a whimper, and a tremor shook her body.

Arousal surged through him like a tidal wave, fierce and uncontrollable. *Stupid. Stupid. Stupid.* He should never have put them in this position. It took all his effort not to tear off her clothes and take her right there.

God, he'd missed her. A woman who would bend but not break. Yield but not submit. With Lana, his control was limited, and in this emotionally charged situation, it was a cable, taut and ready to snap.

He raised his voice loud enough for Rex to hear. "I'll allow that only once." Then he leaned over and whispered, "And only because I set you up."

"Let me go, Heartless Bastard."

James pressed his mouth to her ear and steeled himself against the instinct to wipe the lascivious smirk off Rex's face. "I'll spell it out for you because you don't seem to understand the gravity of the situation. Rex wants you. He wants you so bad he's willing to take risks with the law. The only thing standing in his way is me. He cannot touch a brother's old lady. If you run from me, he will hunt you down and he will take you whether you want it or not."

Her mouth opened and closed, and a shudder racked her body. Sensing her distress, he released her hands and wrapped his arms around her, holding her tight to stop her from doing something that would force his hand. Like slap him again. Unpredictable on a good day, Lana was almost uncontrollable when riled.

Big mistake. His body responded to the soft curves pressed against him. No doubt she could feel his arousal pressed tight against her soft belly, but she didn't pull away. Save for the rapid rise and fall of her chest, Lana was incomprehensibly, and uncharacteristically, still.

Taking advantage of her moment of confusion, he buried his nose in her hair and inhaled her familiar floral fragrance—wild flowers in the sun-drenched earth.

"You always overreact," she grumbled into his chest. "He doesn't know me. I ran into him by accident. We barely spoke. I find it hard to believe he would risk jail time just to get me in his bed."

James stroked a finger over her cheek. "I don't find it hard to believe at all."

"Are you undercover?" she whispered. "I mean...meeting me...helping me...isn't that a risk...wouldn't it be better to let me go and—"

"Everything okay here?" The deep voice startled them both. James whirled around, tucking Lana against his chest. The cavalry had arrived.

Master Tony, the owner of Carpe Noctem, frowned and raised an eyebrow. Taller and broader than Rex, but no less muscular, the dark-haired lawyer wore a leather vest and tight, black leather trousers. He studied the group and then dipped his chin—an almost-imperceptible nod of understanding. Trust Tony to pick up on the vibe without needing a word of explanation.

"I've got it under control." James flicked his gaze to Rex and then to Lana, giving Tony all the information he needed.

Tony shook his head in mock disapproval. "I see you've caught the same little ginger mouse twice. She clearly didn't learn her lesson last time."

Lana instinctively curled into James's body. He tightened his arms around her, warmed by a trust he knew he didn't deserve.

"I'm dealing with her." He feigned a scowl.

"Not very well if she felt the need to slap you. As you know, I have a zero tolerance policy for nonconsensual violence in my club—in any form." Tony gave Lana a tight smile. "I'm afraid you'll have to leave, little mouse."

James pushed her away and frowned. "You messed up, babe. Again. Get your ass home and I'll deal with you later."

Lana's eyes blazed, but she was hip to the game. "Fine," she growled through gritted teeth.

"Kickstand will walk you to your car." James nodded at the club's newest prospect, so named because on his first night he had forgotten to put down his kickstand and knocked over a row of motorcycles.

"I don't need a chaperone."

Hell. Did she think he was making a power play? Even when they'd been together, he would never have let her wander around the wrong side of Gastown at night.

"Babe, Kickstand will walk you to your car. I saw a gang on the prowl on Hastings Street when I drove in. It isn't safe."

Her eyes warmed with understanding and a tentative smile built on her lips. Sweet. Sexy. Soft. Lana behind the fire. He'd missed that side of her most of all.

And then it was gone.

She released an old lady sigh, and her eyes flicked to Kickstand. "Well? Let's go, golden boy."

Kickstand jerked away from Rex and licked his lips as he panted behind Lana's lush ass.

James waited until she was five feet away and then called out softly, "Babe."

"What now?" She whirled around, her face breathtakingly beautiful in her fury.

"See you soon." He knew he was pushing her, but damned if he could stop himself.

She pressed her lips together, her body trembling as if she was about to explode. "In your dreams," she spat out. Spinning on her heel, she disappeared into the crowd with Kickstand scampering after her.

"She must be a goddamned wildcat in bed," Rex muttered. "She needs to be fucking tamed. What a rush that would be."

Ryder shook his head and exhaled a low whistle. "Man, Ice. Why did you keep her hidden away?"

James shrugged. "My business."

"Now she's Hades's business." Rex's gaze fixed on the closing door. "Bring her to the barbeque on Saturday. You got an old lady; she's part of the club. Everyone should meet the fireball who melted Ice."

His phone rang and he sent Ryder to find a table while he took the call. James headed to the bar to round up some drinks. Tony followed hot on his heels.

"No more biker meetings in my club," Tony said when they reached the granite-topped counter. "Especially if you're planning on getting slapped again. Slapping, spanking and other forms of discipline are limited to the private room in the back. Surely there are other places you could have had your meeting—places with less chance of you being recognized? Don't they have a clubhouse?"

"I'll bet you know more about them than I do," James said dryly. "You seem to know everything about everybody."

Tony snorted. "I know I don't want them back in my club.

Rex already asked for a membership form, and I have a feeling he won't take kindly to being turned down."

"It won't happen again." James placed his order with the bartender and pointed him toward Ryder at a table in the corner. "Thanks for the help back there."

Tony reached over the counter and grabbed a bottle of whiskey and two glasses. "You going after her?"

"She hates me. I walked out on her two years ago to take the assignment. No warning. No explanation. I told myself I was protecting her. And me."

In short, he'd been an ass. But he'd known he couldn't sustain a relationship, and especially not one as intense as what they had together. He couldn't go through the pain of losing someone he cared about again. Better to end it sooner rather than later.

Tony chortled. "If I were her, I'd hate you too. Doesn't mean you can't go after her. Maybe apologize."

"The past is past." James took the glass of whiskey Tony offered. "I helped her out of a sticky situation tonight. Evened the score."

Time to move on. The reasons behind his decision to leave her hadn't changed. Now, more than ever, he knew his instincts had been right. Seeing her again, his blood fired up after their verbal altercation, his cheek burning from the imprint of her hand, his cock throbbing from the soft press of her body against him, he felt dangerously alive. But he knew too well her fire burned with an intensity he couldn't handle.

Tony poured himself a shot of whiskey. "There's a fine line between love and hate, but at the root of both is passion. If she'd been indifferent to you, then I would agree, there's no point. But I didn't see indifference. I saw passion. A hell of a lot of passion."

"You're beginning to sound more like a psychologist than a lawyer." James shot back the bitter liquid, savoring the smooth burn before it scorched its way down his throat.

"I wasn't always a lawyer."

Eyebrows raised, James spun his glass on the table. "I heard rumors that you'd had a colorful past. Not that being a psychologist qualifies as colorful..."

"I suppose it depends on what you do with the psychology degree," Tony murmured, cutting him off.

For a moment James considered pursuing the line of conversation, but the arrival of Trixie, the club receptionist, drew Tony's attention and James filed the information away for later. Although Tony was a good friend, he'd always been guarded about his past and if he had something he wanted to share, James would let him do it on his own time.

"So, are you giving me relationship advice as a psychologist or as a lawyer?"

"As a friend." Tony's gaze remained fixed on Trixie's curvy bounce as she walked a nervous young woman up to the bar.

Trixie glanced up and caught Tony and James watching her. Her cheeks flushed and she flashed them a warm smile. Generous, creamy breasts strained against the top of the tight, red corset dress encasing her voluptuous body. Her shiny red stilettos tapped in time to the bass pounding through the speakers. Although the multiple facial piercings and spiked platinum hair weren't James's taste, her warmth and bubbly personality had made her one of the most popular staff members in the club.

Tony turned away and Trixie's smile faded. There was an obvious attraction between her and Tony, but as far as James knew, Tony had never acted on it. For all the relationship advice he gave to his clients and friends, he couldn't see what was staring him in the face.

"Maybe you're right." Tony drummed his fingers on the table and sighed. "Women add unnecessary complications to life. Might be better not to reopen old wounds. Especially when you're undercover."

James nodded his agreement, pleased Tony had been on the list of people cleared to be informed of his undercover status. His request list had been small: His dad, Lana, Mark and Tony. He'd added Lana to the list on a whim despite thinking he would never see her again.

"I'm just waiting for this damn assignment to end, and I don't want to do anything to mess it up. It's been hard on my mind. I don't like the man I've had to become or the things I've had to do in the name of justice."

"What will you do when it's over?" Tony spun his glass on the table.

"I need a break. Try something different. Maybe I'll sail around the world."

"Alone?" Tony raised an eyebrow.

James shrugged. "Yeah. Alone."

Chapter Three

Lana huddled in the front seat of her rusty Jetta and trained her binoculars on the front entrance to Hades's clubhouse. Even without Angel's directions, the vacant airplane hangar just outside the King George Airpark would not have been difficult to find. She had spotted the huge painted Cerberus a mile away and if that wasn't a dead giveaway, motorcycles of all shapes and sizes filled the paved parking lot.

Sweat trickled down her back and beaded on her brow. The thick plaid shirt, baggy jeans and rumpled blonde wig Jackie had assured her would enable her to blend in with the other airplane watchers were too hot for a summer day. But she trusted Jackie. Her best friend, business partner and fellow private investigator specialized in disguises, boasting a collection that would make even CSIS (Canadian Security Intelligence Service) jealous.

Lana slid a hand under her wig and flapped it up and down, trying to cool herself off with a pathetic waft of warm summer air. She suspected it was the same wig she'd accidentally grabbed off Jackie's head in the self-defense course where they'd met.

The memory made her laugh. Acting on instinct, Jackie had punched her in the jaw and then, overcome with remorse, she'd collapsed on the floor, inconsolable. Her theatrics had made Lana smile for the first time since James had left. When she'd discovered Jackie was living on the streets she'd offered her a place to stay, as much for her spirited company as for helping out someone in need. With Lana's help and encouragement, Jackie had turned her life around. And in return she'd pulled Lana out of her James-induced depression and introduced her to the world of disguises.

Unfortunately, Jackie hadn't warned Lana that this particular disguise might lead to death by melting in the heat of the summer sun.

Sort of like last night at Carpe Noctem.

Memories stirred. For an instant, she was back in the club, her nose buried in James's shirt, breathing in his clean, sharp scent, safe and warm in the circle of his arms. And then she was two years in the past, lying on his chest, listening to the steady beat of his heart in the darkness, wondering if the deep tug on her soul was love. And then she was alone in her bed on a cold, gray rainy morning, contemplating what she'd done wrong.

No. She wasn't going back there. She was over him. Their meeting at Carpe Noctem had been a blip. It had to happen at least once. Vancouver was big, but not that big. With both of them in law enforcement, they were bound to end up following the same bad guy occasionally. She would move on, just like she had before.

A flash of movement in front of the clubhouse caught her attention. She focused her binoculars on the door. *Damn.* Ryder and Kickstand. No Rex. No James. Not that she wanted to see James. He would be a distraction in more ways than one.

Lana waggled the wig again to create a light breeze around her neck. A red curl escaped. She glanced up in the rearview mirror to tuck it back in and startled when a black leather jacket came into view. Seconds later, her door swung open, and a hand reached in and yanked her out of the car.

Surveillance Rule #37: When threatened, run.

Without even raising her head, Lana bolted. Heart pounding, lungs burning, she raced into the field. At least she thought she did. As fast as she moved, her assailant was faster. Before she could take a step his hand clamped down on her shoulder. He spun her around and pushed her against the car, trapping her with his body.

Her heart pounded against her ribs. She brought her hands up between them to push him away, and her fingers fanned out over a broad expanse of hard muscle.

Familiar.

"Stop, Lana. I don't want to hurt you." His voice was a cool caress over her heated skin. She'd heard that voice in her dreams. She'd heard that voice last night.

"Good. Then let me go." She lifted her head, only to meet James's furious glare.

"What are you doing here?"

"Airplane watching."

"Airplane watching? You?" The incredulous look on his face almost made her laugh. Almost. Self-preservation held her amusement at bay. She could sense anger simmering beneath his skin, barely contained. Although he had never hurt her before, he was different now. Rougher. Less controlled. More aggressive. Potty mouthed.

She still hadn't figured out if he had officially joined the gang or if he was undercover. But she couldn't take a chance that his anger might turn to violence. Her father was an angry man, but he had had nothing on Levi. And after a string of failed relationships she no longer trusted men. Hell, she didn't even trust her own judgment.

Folding her arms with feigned nonchalance, she leaned against her faithful Jetta and gave him a weak smile. "Sure. It's a...new hobby."

James snorted a laugh. "You can't sit still long enough to drink a coffee. Do you really think I would believe you're into airplane watching? Dressed like that?"

She widened her eyes and shrugged. "I was worried I might bump into someone I know and they might laugh at my new hobby. The thrash crowd isn't very forgiving of mundane pursuits."

His lips curled into a devastating smile. "I can always tell when you're lying. Your eyes widen and your lips twitch. Dead giveaway, at least to me."

Lana narrowed her eyes at the insult. "And you're in my way. The 4:53 p.m. Boeing 757 should be flying overhead any minute. It's a breathtaking sight."

Surveillance Rule #17: Always be prepared with a plausible cover story.

Eyebrows raised, grin splitting his face, James looked into the sky. "Maybe I'll stay and watch. I didn't think there were many 757s left in the air. They were discontinued in 2004."

"Seriously?" She realized her mistake at once and dropped her voice. "I mean, seriously, it *is* a real 747. There are still a few that are operational."

"I thought you said it was a 757."

Lana swallowed hard and stared at her flip-flops. *Damn.* Usually she lied with aplomb while undercover, but he was unnerving her with his handsome face, kick-ass leathers and cocky attitude.

"Slip of the tongue. I get so excited when the planes fly overhead, sometimes I can't think."

"I remember other things that excited you," he murmured.

Phwoar. Long-buried feelings stirred inside her. God, she'd missed their banter. And his sexy talk. And his body.

Bad ears. Don't listen.

She tugged her wig over the betraying auditory appendages lest he continue to beguile her with his forked tongue and panty-dampening words. But, oh, the things his tongue could do...

He checked his watch and leaned in close. Lana swallowed hard and tried to arch away, but with the vehicle behind her, she had nowhere to go.

"It's 4:58 p.m.," he said. "Looks like you missed your 757.

Sorry I distracted you. You should get along home."

"There are other planes to see."

He tugged the wig off her head and ran his fingers through the damp tendrils of her hair. Delicious cool air rushed over her scalp. Lana's eyes slitted closed. She had always loved the feel of his hands in her hair.

"Not here," he said softly. "No case is worth this risk, and I know you're on a case. You are leaving. Now."

Lana gritted her teeth against the onslaught of endorphins rushing through her veins. Of course he had seen through her ruse. Was he worried she would blow his cover—if he was undercover? As before, their sexual chemistry got in the way of everything else. Like communication. But right now she didn't want communication. She wanted him gone so she could get on with her surveillance.

"Do you see my feet moving? No. That's because I'm not leaving. Now skedaddle. Go back to your new biker life of drugs and murder and mayhem, and leave me in peace."

He cupped her jaw with his warm, broad hand and tilted her head back. The look he gave her—sensual, carnal, predatory—curled her toes.

"Not going anywhere, babe."

Heat flooded her veins and a strangled sound escaped her throat. She took a deep breath to regain her composure. "It's easy. Just turn around and walk away. You did it before."

James tightened his grip on her jaw and held her gaze. Strong emotions flickered through his eyes, deepening the steel blue almost to black. "I did it for you."

Lana's vision sheeted red. Heartless fucking bastard. She shoved against his chest as hard as she could, breaking his hold and forcing him back. "Oh. My. God. Could you be any more condescending? Are you seriously telling me you broke my heart for my own good?" Her voice rose, almost to a shriek. "Did it occur to you I might've had something to say about that?"

She clenched her fists to keep from slapping him. Again.

He looked at her aghast. "I didn't mean it like that."

"I liked it better when I didn't know," she snapped. "I imagined all sorts of scenarios: a serious illness in the family, an abduction by aliens, a mysterious overseas assignment to rescue hostages, or maybe you were imprisonment by rebels in a war-torn country. Something that would make me think you weren't the heartless bastard you really are."

The loud rumble of a motorcycle startled them both. Her head jerked up and her eyes widened at the sight of the immense, chromed-up custom Harley chopper inching its way across the field toward them.

James followed her gaze and hissed in a breath. "Fuck. It's Rex. He must have seen your vehicle on the surveillance camera. No one parks on Hades's turf without getting checked out. You're damned lucky I recognized your bucket of bolts and found you first. Strip off your clothes."

She sucked in a sharp breath. "What?"

"Strip them off. I can think of only one reason why we would be in the field outside the clubhouse at dusk, and you wouldn't be dressed like that. Unless you can think of something else, you'd better strip."

Lana's pulse raced. "Maybe we were just talking. Or watching airplanes...and I was cold."

His face tightened and she caught a hint of concern in his steady gaze. "He's already suspicious because I never mentioned you before. We need to do something that will leave him in no doubt you're mine."

A thrill of fear shot through her veins and she slid along the car and away from him. "No. I am not getting naked and having sex in front of Rex. Especially not with you. Not even to save my life."

The corners of James's lips curled into a wry smile. "We don't need to go that far. I might need to fight him. Can't do that with my dick hanging out of my pants."

"Nice language. Now you even talk like a biker."

"I am a biker."

Lana rolled her eyes. "You're a cop, James. It's written all over you. It's who you are. It's part of what I like...liked about you. At the club, I couldn't decide if you were really a biker or undercover, but seeing you again now, you don't have to tell me. I know. So don't insult my intelligence by pretending you've had a personality transplant and become the very kind of criminal you've spent a lifetime trying to put away."

James rubbed the back of his neck and then shifted his weight and sighed. "You're right. I'm undercover. And you being around the motorcycle club is a significant risk for you, me and my assignment. Once we deal with Rex, you'll have to drop your case."

Before she could refuse, he touched her chin gently until she looked up and gazed into his eyes, softer now, but no less determined.

"Easier said than done, I know," he murmured. "We'll deal with that issue later. Right now, you need an excuse to be here and I'm giving you one. You'll be safe if Rex understands he can't touch you."

Her heart squeezed. He knew her well, or at the very least he sensed there was something about this case that wouldn't let her just walk away. Was he purposely making it difficult for her to hate him?

Eyes still focused on Lana, James jerked his head back toward Rex. "Where is he?"

"He just parked his motorcycle under the trees. He won't have a clear view of us until he walks a semicircle."

His eyes raked over her flannel- and baggy-jeans-clad body. "Are you wearing anything under your disguise?"

She gave him a half smile. "Maybe I like to dress this way."

He chuckled. "You think I'm going to believe the woman

who paraded into Carpe Noctem wearing two strips of barely there, electric-fucking-blue Lycra now dresses like a character from *The Big Bang Theory*?"

Butterflies fluttered in her belly. He remembered what she'd worn the night they met. Did he also remember how she'd offered to take the outfit off to distract him from searching for her hidden camera? Or how he'd made her wear it one night after they'd started dating so he could take her on the kitchen table the way he'd wanted to take her in his office during her interrogation?

"I've got a sports bra and spandex shorts underneath," she rasped. "Thought I might hit the gym after plane watching, burn off the adrenaline." Anticipation and dread ratcheted through her and she trembled, knowing what would come next.

Without hesitation, James unbuttoned her plaid shirt. His warm hands caressed her skin as he slid the warm flannel over her shoulders and down her bare arms. He had always enjoyed undressing her, turning a mundane act into a sensual feast, and it seemed, from the hitch in his breath as his hands glided over her skin, that hadn't changed.

Her body flamed at his touch, responding as if the two-year break had never happened. "I...ah...can...better do that." Her words came out no louder than a whisper.

James paused, his fingers on the waistband of her jeans. "I'm faster."

His hand dipped inside her jeans and pressed gently against her now-almost-flat tummy to undo the button. Lana's breath caught in her throat and her senses shot to high alert as he tugged down her zipper, his fingers grazing lightly over her mound. His gentle caress was more arousing than if he had stripped off her clothes and touched her bare skin. She bit into her lip and tasted the sharp tang of blood. She should never have let him undress her.

He crouched in front of her and slid her jeans over her hips. An image flashed in her mind of James on his knees in

Barely Undercover

her bedroom as she stood naked before him. She had thought for once she was in charge, but when he grasped her thighs and brushed his lips over her clit, she had known her control of the situation was only illusory.

He looked up and caught her gaze. His eyes deepened to an azure blue and his lips parted. Swallowing hard, he dug his fingers into her thighs, as if to steady himself, and slid her jeans over her feet.

Lana braced herself against the cool metal of her trusty Jetta and fisted her hands against the urge to thread them through his now deliciously long hair. The softest moan escaped her lips.

James froze. "Lana..." He choked back his words and managed only one more, "Rex."

Need, raw and ragged, turned her insides liquid. Swept up in a maelstrom of emotion and desire, she uttered the three words she had wanted so desperately to say over the last two years, needing to reassure herself nothing had changed. "I hate you," she whispered.

"I know." His eyes glittered and the look he settled on her—hot and hungry—seared her to the core. He knew her words for the lie they were and she sensed he understood her need to say them.

Lana closed her eyes and took a deep breath, trying to ground herself in the moment—a deliciously dangerous moment. "Let's just get this over with," she blurted out. "And then we can move on with our lives...our cases."

James rose to his feet and lifted her, settling her bottom on the hood of her car. "Open for me."

Her cheeks flamed and she froze. When they had been together, he had been able to bring her close to the edge with his erotic commands. But now, although her body was on board, her heart was running scared.

When she didn't move, he slid his hands up her thighs and

eased her legs apart. Her breathing increased and her pulse sped up. Did he know the effect his touch still had on her? Of course he knew. Better than she knew herself.

James eased himself between her legs and pulled her tight against him, locking their hips together. Awareness flared through her. The press of his hands on her thighs. The heat of his body. The raw scent of leather and the clean, fresh aroma of his cologne. His presence swallowed up everything—Rex, the field, even her anxiety. Everything but him.

His eyes crinkled as he studied her face and then darkened with sensual promise. "Ready?"

She could only nod her head. His warm breath brushed over her cheek and whispered over her lips. Tears, unwanted and unexpected, prickled at the back of Lana's eyes. Pulling away, she tried to contain the emotions skittering through her. How many nights had she spent tossing and turning, dreaming about kissing him again? He was the first man she'd ever trusted since escaping from Levi, the first man she'd believed would never hurt her.

The first man to truly break her heart.

Chapter Four

"Shhh." James wiped a rogue tear away. "Crying won't make for a convincing show."

"I'm not crying," she snapped. "There was something in my eye." Lana took a deep breath and locked all her emotions away in an imaginary closet—a survival trick she'd learned at the age of sixteen after her life had come crashing down around her. She sniffed and forced a smile. "Maybe I should cry. He might lose interest if my face is all puffy and my eyes are red."

James gently kissed away yet a second rogue tear. "Wouldn't deter me."

"I don't know why. You could have just left me to fend for myself. I managed to escape your clutches at Carpe Noctem the first time we met and you were pretty damn fierce."

He slid his arms around her waist and snorted a laugh. "You didn't escape. I threw you out of the club."

"That was my escape plan."

"And all the swearing and threats were for effect?"

Lana looked up at him through her eyelashes and her lips quivered with a repressed smile. "That was to get your attention. You didn't seem to be the kind of man who would be attracted to a quiet, mild-mannered woman."

James cocked his head and gave her a quizzical look. "I was particularly harsh with you during that interrogation. Are you saying even after that...even after I confiscated your camera and kicked you out, you were trying to get my attention?"

"Not 'even'. *Because.*" Her cheeks flamed and she looked away.

James tightened his arms, drawing her close. "Do you know why I threw you out?" he murmured. "Because if I hadn't..."

A stick cracked behind them, cutting him off. "Show time," he whispered. He cupped her face in his hands and tilted her face up. Lana closed her eyes. She imagined she was with the man who had made her trust again, the man she had thought was her future. She imagined she was Buttercup in *The Princess Bride* and she had just discovered Westley wasn't dead after all.

His lips found hers and he teased her mouth open, sweeping his tongue inside. Lana fisted his shirt and pulled him close, kissing him back with a fierce, unexpected hunger. James groaned into her mouth and he deepened the kiss, his tongue tangling with hers, stroking, searching, exploring. Breathless, she opened to him, wrapping her legs around his hips, pulling him closer.

"Thought I might catch a cop out here," Rex growled. "Maybe another one of Angel's fucking investigators. I was damn sure we were being watched. Not often I'm wrong."

Lana jolted. In the back of her mind, she had known that Rex was coming and this show was for his benefit, but for a moment she had lost awareness of anything but James. She dropped her forehead to his shoulder to hide her puffy eyes, and his arm circled protectively around her.

"Told the old lady it was time she met the brothers, but we got distracted, if you know what I mean." James chuckled. Lana cringed. Although she knew it was a game, a part of her resented the harsh words and the cold, detached tone of his voice. At least he hadn't punctuated his words with a pelvic thrust.

Rex gave an annoyed grunt. Lana didn't need to look up to know he was studying her. She could feel his eyes drilling into her head, willing her to meet his gaze. She leaned her forehead against James's shoulder. She had seen enough of Rex last night, and until she got her photos, she would be forced to see more. James's shirt held more appeal than staring into Rex's soulless eyes.

Rex exhaled and his voice turned cold. "Send her home. I've called a meeting of the inner circle. She can meet everyone at the barbeque on Saturday."

Lana's head jerked up. "Barbeque?"

James shoved her head back down to his shoulder. "She can't make it. She's going out of town."

Lana's mind whirled. She couldn't think of a better way to get the pictures she needed. Rex on his home turf, beer in hand, his newest squeeze under his arm, Lana's camera snapping in the background. But she would have to go into the clubhouse. Her heart protested with a violent thud and her stomach clenched. No clubhouse. Not for her. But the pictures...Angel. Her mind spun in circles. What to do?

As if sensing her indecision, James pressed his lips to her ear and whispered, "You are not going anywhere near the clubhouse. No fucking way. And that's final."

The hair on the back of Lana's neck stood on end. "Don't tell me what to do," she growled. "We need to *discuss* it. Do you know that word? Discuss? Ever thought about using it?"

She looked up at Rex and forced her lips into a smile. "I *might* be able to change my plans. I'll discuss it with Ice. I would love to meet everyone. I've heard so much about you all."

A sound erupted from James's chest, a cross between a snarl and a choke, and the look he shot her was nothing short of...well, icy.

"We've heard nothing about you." Rex gave her a snake-oil salesman smile. "And I'd like to hear how you and Ice hooked up. You're not his usual type."

Lana's face fell. "What type is that?" The question came out before she could run it through her internal censor. As usual.

Rex's dark eyes glittered with all the warmth of an

43

Antarctic summer. "You come to the barbeque. I'll tell you all about Ice and you can tell me all about you." He licked his lips and Lana shuddered. Why did she suddenly feel as if she was prey?

"Wear something very short and very tight," Rex added in a firm voice.

"My old lady wears what *I* tell her to wear," James said, his voice low and even. He turned to face Rex, his body in front of Lana like a shield. "She does what *I* tell her to do. She goes where *I* tell her to go. I thought we sorted this out last night."

James played the old man pretty good, Lana thought. She hoped it wasn't because he'd had scores of old ladies. He was still breathtakingly gorgeous...and in those leathers... Her throat tightened at the thought of James with other women. If he did have a past littered with old ladies, she didn't want to know.

"If she's your old lady—and I'm not convinced she is—she's Hades." The undertone of warning in Rex's voice sent a shiver down Lana's spine.

"Last I checked," he continued, "I was in charge of Hades."

James folded his arms and leaned against the vehicle, forcing Lana to part her legs around his hips as if he was about to give her a piggyback ride. Although his posture seemed casual, his position protected both Lana and his back.

"I think we're done here," James said in a completely different voice, so deep and powerful it resonated down her spine.

Undaunted, Rex's lip curled and he stood his ground. "I believe Roxie and I were having a conversation. Seems to me she wants to come to the barbeque and you're standin' in her way."

"The conversation is over," James snapped. "She's going home and she's gonna stay there. She won't be showing up on Saturday, and she won't be showing up at Hades. Ever."

Lana frowned and sucked in a sharp breath, drawing Rex's attention. He studied her face and smirked. "She might have something to say about it. Look at her. She's chomping at the bit to tear into you. I don't think you have what it takes to deal with a fireball like her."

"You want me to prove myself, I will. Here and now." James's hands curled into fists and he took a step forward.

Rex folded his arms. "Got better things to do than scratch your itch, Ice. Back down."

To Lana's shock, James loosened his fists and leaned back against the vehicle. Rex gave him a curt nod, turned and walked away.

"Saturday, Roxie." Rex looked back over his shoulder and gave her a wink.

For the longest time, she and James didn't move, didn't speak.

"You backed down," she whispered, unbelieving. The James she knew never backed down. Never gave up without a fight.

"Had to. Don't want him to think I'm a threat or he'll slit my throat while I sleep, and two years of undercover work will go down the drain."

The loud rumble of Rex's engine cracked the stillness and she watched it disappear across the field. James turned to face her, his eyes glittering with an intense light, wild and untamed. She could feel his anger, taste his power, and it took all her self-control not to throw herself on him in a frenzy of animal lust.

Her breath hitched. Unnerved, she slid off the vehicle and tried to sidle past a thoughtful James, but he grabbed her shoulders and pulled her close.

"I'm not done with you yet."

Maybe not, but she was done with him. She had to be—for her own sanity. Never had she felt such an internal disconnect. The James she'd known was still there—protective, possessive, sweetly caring and utterly confident. So at odds with the man who'd walked away. How could she still want him after he'd hurt her so much?

Her rational mind cut through the fuzz of lust and the question she'd asked herself a thousand times fell from her lips. "Why?" she gritted out. "Why did you leave me?"

He drew in a ragged breath. "At the time I thought it was the right thing to do. I got a call about an undercover assignment—this assignment. Too dangerous to have any ties. I didn't want you to get hurt."

"And you couldn't have told me that? I would have understood if you couldn't share the details."

James shrugged and she studied him closely, marking the shift in his eyes from blue to gray, solid to insubstantial.

"That wasn't all of it," she said on a hunch, "was it?"

"No."

She bit her lip to stop any possibility of tears. He didn't deserve her tears. He didn't deserve to know how she really felt. "Are you going to tell me the rest?"

He hesitated, twisted his lips as if considering, and then finally shook his head.

Her heart shriveled, her breath leaving her in a rush. "I deserve more than that."

"You do," he said softly. "But I can't give it to you."

She seethed inside, angry at him, angry at her own weakness, angry she wanted him so desperately she ached inside. Turning her back on him, she scooped up her clothes and yanked open the door to her car. "Guess I'll see you on Saturday."

"Not happening."

Oh yes it is.

She slid into the safety of her vehicle and turned the key in the ignition. The Jetta wheezed and died. She tried again. Her betraying car refused to allow her the dignity of a clean escape.

"I told you to get rid of that piece of junk two years ago," he growled. "It's not roadworthy and in your line of work you need a reliable vehicle. What if it had been Rex and not me who caught you out here?"

She bristled at the harsh words he threw at her beloved Jetta. "He would never have recognized me and I could have talked my way out of it. You know that. I went along with your little show because I had nothing better to do with my time. But in the end, I didn't need you. Just like I didn't need you two years ago. Just like I don't need you now."

Shocked by her own harsh words, she slammed her lips together. She had never in her life been purposely mean. Not even to her father who had all but ignored her in favor of her two older brothers after her mother died. But then she had never been as badly hurt. The pain Levi had inflicted had been skin deep—superficial wounds that had disappeared within days, sometimes weeks. But James had bruised her heart, and seeing him again only opened up a wound she had long thought healed.

James tightened his jaw. "We need to—"

The Jetta finally sputtered to life, cutting him off. She hit the gas, speeding across the grass like there was no tomorrow.

But there was a Saturday. And Hades was in it.

James waited until Lana was safely away before walking across the field to the small clearing where he'd parked his motorcycle, a custom Harley Rocker. Life hadn't prepared him for moments like this. Duty had always been the dominant force driving him forward. From a family background steeped in law enforcement, James had adhered to tradition and entered the police force, rising through the ranks from the beat to drug enforcement, then to homicide and finally undercover. A clear path. But now duty warred with desire and a soul-deep longing he'd spent the last two years trying to deny.

Lana's scent still lingered on his clothes, her warmth on his skin. But it was her fire that drew him, aroused him. Beneath the flames smoldered a passion he had been—was still— helpless to resist.

He drove the short distance to the airplane hangar and parked alongside the motorcycles of Rex's closest advisors. He could only hope—with Rex's entire inner circle present—the discussion would turn to the club's latest drug-smuggling scheme. The Royal Canadian Mounted Police Drug Enforcement Unit (DEU) had assured James his wiretap recordings had given them enough evidence to justify a raid on the club. They just needed an opportunity and some hard evidence.

He stopped at the keypad and punched in the code, then checked his wire. Although Rex had no compunction about announcing the club's presence to the world with the garish patch artwork over the door, he was almost obsessive about security. The clubhouse was impenetrable, thanks to a state-of-the-art security system. If he ever found out James had been recording his conversations over the last two years, he would kill James on the spot. And if he found out Lana was sniffing around Hades...

James shook his head. Her disguise had been damned good. If he hadn't recognized her Jetta, even he might not have known her in that blonde wig, her beautiful body hidden under those bulky clothes. He knew from past experience, Lana could talk her way out of almost anything, except with him. Rex would likely have bought her story.

But now he had a bigger problem. If Lana was investigating Hades, he had to stop her. Not only could she compromise his cover, she would likely get herself killed. Problem was, stopping Lana when she was set on a course of action was next to impossible.

The door swung open and he walked inside. The twenty-thousand-square-foot space had been completely renovated and now housed an office, workout area, showers and bathrooms, kitchen, full bar, two lounges, media room, pool table and a suite of bedrooms on the second floor where he, Ryder and most of the single club members lived.

Dawg and Punch were sprawled on the couches in Rex's office. Bones and Diesel had dragged in a few chairs. Ryder leaned against a wall, his arms folded. Rex, as always, reclined in his oversized leather chair, feet propped up on his desk. All of them were dressed in leathers and black T-shirts, the unofficial Hades uniform.

"She gone?"

"Sent her home." James took a seat beside Dawg. The high-ranking member of Rex's inner circle had released his long, wavy brown hair from its usual hair tie, and it brushed over his shoulders as he turned and nodded a greeting. With his long, thin face and slender frame, he now, more than ever, resembled his namesake, the chocolate lab curled at his feet.

"Heard you'd found yourself a bitch." Dawg barked a laugh. "Never thought I'd see the day. She must have one sweet pussy to take your attention away from the club. I was beginning to think we were all you had in your pathetic life."

"Just you, Dawg. You're all I fucking need." He feigned the usual banter, even going so far as to blow Dawg a kiss, but his mind was on Lana. He couldn't let her anywhere near the barbeque. It had been hard enough to pull off the old-lady act in the field in front of Rex. How could he keep it up for an entire afternoon? All the old emotions had come surging to the fore, and for a moment she'd been his again and he'd forgotten they'd ever been apart.

"Don't worry." Rex smirked. "You'll get to meet her on Saturday. She's coming to the barbeque. Ice is afraid of letting her near us, but I have a feeling once that little fireball gets an idea into her head, she doesn't let go easily."

A wave of possessive jealousy surged through James,

followed by an even fiercer urge to keep her safe. Although there was no future for them, he could damn well ensure she had a future without Rex. Whether she liked it or not.

Rex folded his arms behind his head and stared up at the ceiling. "I've always liked the wild ones," he mused.

James's brows drew together. Although Rex's infidelity was no secret in the club, he had always kept things discreet, usually taking the women straight to his office and then sending them home. He never talked about them. Never touched them in public. But even if he had, the brothers wouldn't talk. What happened in the clubhouse stayed in the clubhouse. So what had changed? Had he and Angel split? What about their daughter?

"Won't be anytime soon," James spat out.

Rex's eyes darted to his, picking up the undertone of a threat. For a long moment, they stared at each other. James forced himself to drop his eyes first. He'd worked hard to gain Rex's trust. He didn't want to lose it so close to the end of the assignment. And over a girl.

His pulse quickened. *Not just a girl. Lana.*

Rex grunted his satisfaction at James's tacit acknowledgment of his top-dog status, and nodded as if something had been settled in his mind. "Got a job for you tonight. We got a tip the police are going to raid the mobile home of Punch's mom and her husband out on the Fraser Highway. We just relocated all the club's firearms and explosives out there. Need you to collect them. Take Ryder with you."

"Ryder?" Short, portly and balding prematurely, Punch pushed himself to his feet. "It's my mom. I should go with Ice."

"Your mom or her husband probably ratted us out," Rex growled. "I want to keep you out of it. Ryder won't dip his dick in the drug trade, but he's got no problem with weapons. He and Ice will get the job done." He nodded at James. "You'll need a hockey bag and a place to store the weapons. I don't want them on Hades's turf."

Damn. The weapons cache in the clubhouse would have been enough to trigger the raid, but Rex knew the law and was always careful to keep the clubhouse clean.

James's stomach churned. No doubt the DEU had just heard about the arsenal over his wire. If they decided to confiscate the weapons—which they had done once before on the basis they couldn't condone leaving illegal weapons in the hands of known criminals—he would be put in a difficult position. That time, James had been able to explain away the loss of a few guns, but the entire arsenal? When Rex called for their return, what would he say?

"You sure you want to send Ice?" Bones said. "Last time you put him in charge of weapons he let them get fucking pinched."

James drummed his fingers on the arm of the couch, feigning irritation, although on the inside every muscle was locked tight. Bones had been watching him too closely over the last few months. Every job, every pickup, every errand Rex asked him to do, Bones had an excuse to be nearby. Meeting his handlers was becoming a challenge. If the DEU didn't raid soon, Bones could become a serious threat to his cover.

"It happens," Rex said dismissively. "If I didn't trust Ice, he wouldn't be in my inner circle. Are you questioning my judgment?"

Bones raised his hands and backed off. "Of course not. I'm sure he'll tuck them safely away."

Rex and Bones shared a glance and then Rex moved on to the next order of business. He ordered Diesel and Punch to go out trunking to raise some extra cash. Short and stocky, barrel-chested and foul-mouthed, Diesel and Punch could have been twins save for the fact Diesel had a woman's face tattooed on the back of his bald head and Punch sported dreads that would make even a Jamaican jealous.

James breathed an inward sigh of relief at not being sent out with them. Trunking involved snatching off the street underworld characters with known wealth, locking them in the trunk of the vehicle and driving around until someone paid their ransom…or they died. He had done it a few times and once had almost called for backup when the drug dealer's family initially refused to pay.

"Got another deal going down in a couple of weeks." Rex leaned back and dropped his feet off the desk. "We got serious kilos coming in by helicopter. I'll give you the details later."

James's heart pounded. This was it. The break he had been waiting for. The DEU would be able to take down the inner circle and probably a large contingent of full-patch members. With the wiretap evidence he had collected over the last two years, they should have enough to shut down Hades for good.

It would all be over.

Until then, he just had to keep Lana away. And he had to stay focused. Keep his thoughts on the assignment and not on the beautiful woman with liquid green eyes, kick-ass curves and sass to match.

Simple.

Chapter Five

"Chip?"

Jackie held out the chip bowl and Lana shook her head. Jackie knew better than to bring fattening junk food to Lana's apartment, especially when Lana was emotionally distraught. She was the one who had pulled Lana out of her James-induced doldrums by suggesting they start working out and go into business together. The work involved in merging their PI practices had given Lana the kick she needed to get out of bed and into Jackie's morning strategy sessions at the local gym.

"I lost over twenty pounds pining for Heartless Bastard over the last two years," she said. "I'm not about to gain it back now that he's seen the new, svelte me. I want him to suffer. I want him to regret the day he walked out my door."

"Chip?"

Lana grabbed the bowl. "Did you bring any dip?"

Jackie shook her head. "I was trying to be sensitive to your new healthy-eating regime when I picked up the snacks on my way over here. Chips, yes. Dip, no. Soda, diet. Oreos, mini."

"Very thoughtful." Not that Jackie ever had to worry about what she ate. Utterly gorgeous, tall and tan, Jackie could have held her own on any runway or movie screen. Her hair was a sleek, smooth black curtain that had never seen a tangle. Irritatingly and perpetually slim, she had all the right curves in all the right places and a metabolism that meant her svelte figure could not be destroyed by multiple packages of Oreos or weekly chip binges. Lana did not begrudge Jackie her beauty because her striking blue eyes hid a kindred wild child and thrash enthusiast, and more secrets than Lana had curls.

Lana delicately nibbled her chip. Only one. She would eat only one chip and give the bowl back to Jackie. "Now, if only I could find a boyfriend who cared as much."

A curious expression crossed Jackie's face—part longing, part regret—but it disappeared so quickly Lana wondered if she had imagined it.

"From what you told me on the phone earlier, sounds like you found not one, but two, at the sex club the other night," Jackie said.

"I don't consider evil, scary biker dudes who threaten to kidnap me and take me back to the clubhouse to do God knows what, to be particularly thoughtful."

Stretching out on Lana's worn velvet couch, Jackie sighed. "I think you should call Angel, give her back the deposit and move on. Rex saw you. If he is after you, then not only are you compromised, you also have a professional conflict."

Lana finished her chip and then ate another, and another, and another. *Damn addictive chips.* She shoved the empty bowl in Jackie's direction. "I can't leave Angel in the lurch. She wants out of the biker world and she wants to protect her daughter. Rex threatened to fight her every step of the way if she ever tried to divorce him, so she needs to get her evidence together before she files her divorce papers. I just need one picture of him doing something wrong—infidelity, drugs—anything that makes him look like a bad father and a bad husband. Problem is, I've been following him for a week and he's been squeaky clean."

Jackie refilled the bowl from the bag of chips on her lap and handed it back to Lana. "Well, if you won't drop the case, you need to get closer, maybe even into the clubhouse."

"As a matter of fact, I have an invitation." Lana shoved a chip in her mouth and savored the crisp saltiness on her tongue. "From the high king himself."

"So what's the problem?"

Lana sighed. "I might have acted a bit rashly."

"You?" Jackie widened her eyes and grabbed at her heart. "Rash? I can't believe it."

"Sarcasm is the weapon of the weak." Lana glared, but Jackie just laughed her off.

"So is self-delusion."

Lana's shoulders sagged. "Heartless Bastard does it to me every time. He makes my blood boil faster than anyone I've ever met. I really don't want to go to the clubhouse. But Rex invited me to the barbeque and almost immediately Heartless Bastard said no. Then Heartless Bastard called me this morning—he still has my number, although his showed up as unlisted—to warn me away. That just got my back up. I mean, it's the perfect way for me to get the evidence I need, and he didn't even open it up for discussion."

Jackie rolled her eyes. "Uh-oh."

"Can you imagine?" Lana shook her finger at her friend and lowered her voice to a deep, menacing James-like growl. "'You are not going anywhere near that clubhouse', he says to me. 'No fucking way.' He swears a lot now that he's a biker. I mean *a lot*. He said 'fuck' more times in our two meetings than I heard him say in the six months we were together. And his hair is deliciously long. And he wears hot biker clothes. And he has a mouth-watering bike."

A grin spread across Jackie's face. "You'd think after going out with you for almost six months he would know he was pretty much waving a red flag in front of a bull by telling you how it is."

"Actually, we never talked that much when we were dating. He was always busy, and I was busy, and when we got together we usually had wild sex and then went to sleep, and then one of us would have to leave to go to work in the morning."

"Sounds rough. Where can I get some of that?" Jackie's eyes dimmed for a heartbeat, and then she looked away.

Lana immediately regretted bringing up James. Although Jackie always had men panting after her and took a fair number to her bed, she couldn't sustain a relationship. Something had happened to her during her years on the streets that made her run whenever she thought things were getting too serious. Lana had tried to drag it out of her, but Jackie had always kept that vault firmly closed, hiding it, like her other secrets, behind her infectious exuberance and outgoing personality.

Lana handed over the chip bowl and rolled her eyes as Jackie nibbled on a crumb. "We don't have to talk about him. I mean, you must be sick—"

"So you told him you were going?" Jackie cut her off with an admonishing eyebrow, and then licked her lips as if she'd just eaten a family pack of chips instead of a fingernail-size morsel.

Lana shrugged. "Of course I did...for Angel's sake."

Jackie snorted. "Sure. For Angel's sake. Even if I did buy that line, what's the problem? Go to the barbeque. Get the pictures. Stare at Heartless Bastard's leather-clad ass. Case closed. Move on."

"I don't think I can do it." Lana's voice dropped to a hoarse rasp. "I haven't been in a biker clubhouse since I escaped from Levi. After I cooled off this morning, I almost had a panic attack. What if someone recognizes me? What if I freeze up? What if my heart explodes from terror?"

Jackie sat up and squeezed her hand. "I can't even imagine what you went through. Bad enough that Levi abused you, but to let the other bikers beat you..." She choked on her words. "I don't know if a person can ever really recover from that. But I do know you haven't really dealt with it. If you had, you wouldn't still be jumping at every shadow, wondering if one day he'll come for you. And you wouldn't mistrust every man who shows an interest in you."

Lana cringed. Jackie was right. She still shuddered when

she heard a certain timbre of voice, and froze when she heard the roar of a motorcycle. She had dated since James, but the minute her dates expressed an interest beyond a casual fling, she broke it off. James had been the only person who had ever made her feel safe.

Grabbing a whole chip, Jackie continued. "I never told you this, but after we hooked up and you pulled me off the street and I pulled your sorry depressed ass out of the ice cream tub, I went back to the area in East Van where I used to hang out. I walked down the streets. I talked to the people I used to know. I sat in the place where I used to beg. I found the people who used to harass me and I showed them the new me. I faced it down."

"Jackie..." Lana's voice broke.

Jackie swallowed and shook her head, cutting Lana off. "After that day, I wasn't worried I would wake up one morning and find myself there. I could see I'd changed. Maybe going into the clubhouse will do the same for you. Think of it as...therapy."

Lana snorted her derision. "I was outside the clubhouse with James wrapped around me and his tongue halfway down my throat. Can't get much closer to a biker than that. Do I look healed to you?" She stuffed a handful of chips in her mouth then washed them down with diet soda and an Oreo chaser.

Jackie's eyebrows shot up to her hairline. "First time you've used his name since I've known you. I was beginning to think maybe his momma had christened him Heartless Bastard."

"Slap me next time I slip up. I don't want to start thinking of him as anything but the heartbreaker he is."

A heavy thud on the door rattled the windows. Lana shot out of her seat and shared a wide-eyed glance with Jackie.

"Were you expecting anyone?" Jackie twisted her long black braid around her finger, her trademark stress move.

Lana shook her head. "Except for an enraged Heartless

Bastard, no one. Go look through the peephole. If it is him, I don't want him to know I'm here."

Jackie walked across the room and peered through the tiny security window. "It's a biker. He's facing the other way. Dang nasty patch. Three evil-looking dogs."

Heart pounding, Lana ran to the window, almost overwhelmed with the need to escape. She opened the catch and pushed against the glass. "Describe him."

"Tall. Broad shoulders. Longish hair. Kinda like a rock star. Very sweet tight ass," Jackie whispered. "Oh. He's turned around. Sweet mother of hotness. He's got the rough, grizzled thing going, but he's one hell of a looker. Blue, blue eyes. One of them is staring right at me."

"Lana. Open up." The rough edge to James's voice sent a shiver down Lana's spine.

"It's him," Lana rasped. "Heartless Bastard. Get over here and help me with the window. If he comes in, he'll find a way to stop me from going to the barbeque, but once I'm there he'll just have to roll with it." She tugged on the window. "Damn. It's stuck."

Jackie looked back over her shoulder and gave Lana an exasperated toss of her hair. "Just be quiet and I'll tell him you're not here."

"Who is it?" Jackie yelled.

"I need to speak to Lana."

Jackie giggled. Lana shot her a glare. "Don't laugh. You're not supposed to know who he is. A strange biker is at the door. Do you laugh or threaten to call the police?"

"I can't help it," she snorted. "It's like a bad movie. Your ex is at the door and you're trying to escape through the window. Who does that? Come on. Pull up those big girl panties and tell him where to go."

"Just tell him I'm not here."

Jackie took a deep breath. "She says she's not here."

Barely Undercover

"Jackie!"

"Sorry. I can't think straight," Jackie whispered. "I'm running on a junk food high after that chip." She turned back to the door and yelled, "I mean she doesn't live here anymore. She moved after some two-bit loser ripped out her heart."

"That's good. That's exactly how I felt." Lana pounded her fist on the window, but it wouldn't budge. "Tell him I also felt betrayed."

Shaking her head, Jackie called out, "It was the worst kind of betrayal. She never recovered. Last anyone heard she was living on the streets."

"Too much." Lana made a chopping motion with her hand to silence her friend.

"Lana, open the fucking door."

"Bad language. Just like you said." Jackie gave her a wicked grin. "He's a feisty one, and in that badass jacket... You sure you don't want him to come in?"

Lana frowned. "How many weekends did you sit here with me, eating ice cream and watching B-rated sci-fi movies? You know what he did to me. How could you even suggest I let him in? And how will I face down my fears if he stops me from going to the clubhouse?"

Jackie gave her an apologetic shrug. "I only met you after you guys split up. I never got to meet him. But after hearing what happened in the field and seeing your cheeks all flushed, I'm thinking you should let him in to talk. He looks anxious, not angry. I don't think he came here to hurt you. Maybe he's worried you'll go to the clubhouse alone. Do you think he'll go away?"

Lana gave a bitter laugh. "Ironically, except for walking out on me, he's not the going-away, giving-up type. But he's not coming in. I don't want to see him."

"You should." Jackie's face softened. "If only to get it all out, once and for all. Then you can move on, whether to the

59

barbeque or another guy. At the very least, all the things you wanted to say won't be burning a hole in your gut."

"Babe. Last time. Open the fucking door or I'll break it down."

Jackie's eyes widened. "He's like the big, bad wolf. Would he really break down the door? I thought he was a cop. Aren't they all about restraint and obeying the law?"

Lana sighed. "Not when it comes to me. For some reason, I make him overreact. And he is a man of his word. So the answer to your question is yes, if he's pushed enough, he will break down the door."

"I'd like to see that," Jackie mused.

"Well, I wouldn't." Lana's hands found her hips. "I don't have the money to pay for—"

Crash. The door flew open, smashing against the cupboard before it dropped to the floor. James stormed into the apartment, his leathers creaking as he strode over the splintered wood. Jackie raced to the kitchen and then peeked around the corner and whistled her appreciation.

Lana tried to hold his gaze, but her eyes wouldn't stay fixed on his face. She drank in the smooth planes and ridges under his snug black T-shirt as he stalked across the floor. Her eyes skimmed past the belt just resting on his lean hips and then down over his long, powerful legs rippling with muscles beneath his black denims. Well over six feet tall and powerfully built, his physical presence had always been intimidating, but with the leather biker jacket hanging off his shoulders, he was sex personified.

She dragged her eyes away and looked at the pile of lumber on the floor. "You broke it," she said lightly, as if they were discussing a china vase and not a heavy, three-inch-thick safety door with a *Guaranteed Impenetrable* sticker on the back.

James's eyes focused on her like laser beams. "I wanted to come in."

His answer was oddly comforting. Two years later and he was still incontrovertibly direct.

"Most people would take the closed door as a refusal and not an invitation."

He kicked aside a few splinters. "I took it as a challenge." Everything below Lana's waist tightened. "Like when you saw Rex with me in the club?"

James stopped in front of her, so close she could feel the heat radiate off his body. "That was a disaster waiting to happen. You're lucky I arrived when I did."

"Lucky," she whispered, although she didn't know why. The part of her that wanted him gone didn't think she was lucky at all. Life would have been easier if she'd never seen him again.

He studied her for a long moment, then looked away, hands clenched, jaw twitching. "I'm glad to see you listened to me for once. I was worried you'd already be on your way to the clubhouse."

"I'm still planning to go. Jackie came over to help me decide what would be short and tight enough to wear to a biker barbeque."

His gaze slid over to Jackie. She batted her long movie-star eyelashes from her vantage point at the kitchen door. He gave her a dazzling smile, all crinkled eyes and boyish charm. Then his gaze returned to Lana and his smile faded.

She shrugged at the question in his eyes. "I would introduce you, but I don't know what name you go by, and since you're leaving anyway, it doesn't matter."

"Ice." He nodded at Jackie.

"Jackie." She cracked a grin. "So you're the hot undercover cop. I've heard a lot about you. Mostly bad things. I'm afraid as Lana's best friend I have a duty to hate you vicariously for breaking her heart, which is a shame because you're kind of cute, and the whole kicking down the door thing..." She fanned herself and finished with a light giggle.

Lana glared at her friend and fumed. Jackie never giggled. She laughed, cackled and chuckled, but she never, ever giggled. Cutesy was just not Jackie's style. Clearly, she had just lost her only ally to James's panty-melting smile.

"Jackie!"

Jackie had the good grace to blush. "Sorry. I'll just hustle over to the window and make myself busy looking out on the street."

"You don't have to worry about her," Lana said to James. "Despite her recent demonstration of disloyalty, she would never betray you. She's a PI too, and we work together. She understands about confidentiality, although she lacks discretion when it comes to my personal life."

"Maybe I should wait in your bedroom," Jackie mused. "I can find you something short and tight to wear to the barbeque." She gave James a wink. Lana had a sudden urge to smack her over the head with the bag of Oreos.

James turned his attention back to Lana. "What's going on, babe? I've told you twice now it's too dangerous to keep pretending you're my old lady. You've always been headstrong but never suicidal."

"I have a job to do," she snapped. "It may not be as important as yours. I'm not saving the world or putting hoards of bad guys in jail, but it's important to me and my client."

"Angel."

Lana sucked in a sharp breath. How the hell did he know? She had been very careful not to mention Angel's name. In the PI business, confidentiality was paramount.

"I can't disclose my client's identity. You know that."

James folded his arms and huffed out a breath. "I know it's Angel. You were in Carpe Noctem before everyone except Rex. I might have believed it was a coincidence until I saw you outside the clubhouse. Neither the police nor anyone in the underworld would hire a PI. He and Angel are having problems. She's the type to go behind his back. It's gotta be her."

"I can't..."

Before she could finish, James cut her off. "I need to understand what's going on, babe. You've got yourself in some serious trouble. You know I won't break your confidence; same way I know you won't break mine. And I'm the one with the most to lose. If Rex finds out about me, I'm done and I'm not just talking about the assignment."

Lana shot a quick glance at Jackie, still at the window, and received a curt nod of assent. She didn't want to divulge a client's details without Jackie's agreement.

"Okay. You're right. It's Angel." She filled him in on the details, leaving out the week of surveillance she'd already completed.

James raked his hand through his hair. "I know Angel. Maybe she spun out a sob story to you, but she's as tough and ruthless and hard-nosed as they come. And she's no saint, I can guarantee you that. You think Rex is bad; Angel is worse."

Stiffening her spine, Lana leveled her gaze at the man she once thought was her entire world. "I don't care who she is or what she's done. I saw a woman who wanted out of a bad life and a mother who wanted to protect her daughter. She needed my help and had the money to pay. She's my client and I'll do my best for her. The same way I'll do my best for all of them."

For a long moment he said nothing. Then he shook his head. "You've always had a soft heart. Too soft. You don't see people for who they really are."

Like him. She had never been so wrong about anyone in her life.

"You're right about that." She knew from the way he flinched, he understood her meaning.

James perched on the edge of her sofa and sighed. "I know this case means a lot to you. But for two years I've been..."

"Hooah." Jackie's breathless gasp cut him off. "There's a

parade of man candy down on the street. It's like every fantasy I've ever had, all rolled up in four badass leather-and-steel packages of biker heaven. They come with you, Ice?" She looked over her shoulder at James, and he and Lana joined her at the window.

"Fuck." James thumped his fist on the windowsill. "Those are Rex's boys. He had Kickstand follow you home from the club so he would know where you lived. He's clearly still not buying our story."

"Or maybe he is." Lana's voice wavered. "And he doesn't care."

"Lookit them standing there, all tough and manly in their leathers, leaning against their crotch rockets." Jackie's voice was thick with lust. "Where did you say that barbeque was? I'm suddenly in the mood for some flame-broiled beef."

Lana's blood chilled. She had done this to herself.

Surveillance Rule # 12: Be discreet.

"I don't understand." Her brow creased in a frown. "Why are they here?"

James grimaced. "Because if I don't bring you, Rex will consider you fair game. He'll think I can't control my old lady, or that you weren't my old lady at all. He'll tell his boys to escort you to the barbeque as his guest, whether you want to go or not. I didn't realize until now that his invitation wasn't really an invitation. It was a test. And it was directed at me."

Lana bit her lip. "Didn't you say being your old lady would protect me from his advances? Isn't it actually safer for me to act as your old lady than stay away?"

He fell silent, toying with her curls as he studied her face.

Finally, he said, "I don't know if I can keep up an act around you when I'm already acting a part. It's stressful enough and then worrying about you..." He took a deep breath. "I'm worried I'll blow my cover. A lot of time, money and effort have gone into this operation. We'll save a lot of lives by taking down

Hades. I know you want to help Angel, but I can't take the risk. Too much is riding on this assignment."

Lana wiggled the toe of her shoe into the carpet as she begrudgingly admitted he was right. She couldn't interfere with his assignment, and she didn't want to put his life at risk. She hated him, but not that much. A little ingenuity and she would find another way to get Rex off her back and get Angel's pictures. Such a shame. It was the only break she'd had in the case. A perfect opportunity.

Suddenly, she had an idea.

"What if it's just once? We go late to the barbeque to minimize the time we're there. You introduce me to everyone as your old lady. Rex won't be able to touch me because he'll have to answer to the entire club if he does. And best of all, you save face. Your old lady did as she was told. You don't put your cover at risk and you don't lose Rex's respect. I'll mingle so you don't have to worry about keeping up an act. And from what Angel told me, I'm almost guaranteed to get some kind of picture of Rex being the biker of badness she says he is. Then we leave and go our separate ways."

"That's my girl." Jackie punched the air. "I like it. Nice and neat and all tied up with a big red bow."

Maybe. But why wasn't James smiling?

James sucked in his lips and stared at the ceiling. Then he shook his head and paced the room, back and forth, window to wall, until he was once again in front of her. Finally he sighed and leveled his gaze with hers. "Once." His voice was heavy with resignation. "This is the one and only time I will allow you near Hades or Rex. If you don't get your pictures today, you give up the case. Deal?"

Lana twisted her lips to the side. He was asking a lot, but then, so was she. "I guess that'll have to be okay."

"Looks like I'm no longer needed to solve your relationship problems, so I'll be off." Jackie grabbed her bag and headed for the door, giving James a finger-wiggle goodbye. "And I'm thinking James might have more fun helping with the wardrobe selection."

Lana followed her out into the hallway and Jackie paused at the top of the stairs.

"Fifty bucks says you sleep with him before next Saturday."

Lana snorted a laugh. "Easiest fifty bucks I'll ever make."

Chapter Six

Fucking hell.

James stared at the ruins of Lana's door. So much for calm and detached. The thought she might not talk to him—or worse, that she might go to the clubhouse without him—had driven all rational thought from his brain. Instinct had taken over—a primal need to protect. And he couldn't do that with a damn door in the way.

He pulled out his phone and called in a few favors from some local carpenters and locksmiths. His friends didn't disappoint. The door would be fixed by the time they were back from the barbeque. He still couldn't believe he was going along with her plan.

The creak of wood alerted him to Lana's return. She stepped gingerly over the splinters and shook her head.

"The door was supposed to be unbreakable. Did you wing it or were you taught how to break down unbreakable doors at the police academy?"

Relieved her humor had returned, he shrugged. "There's no magic involved. First you need to make sure the door opens away from you. Then you kick near the handle, weight in your heel, dominant foot. Doors are weakest where they contact the frame. If you try running at it with your shoulder like they do in the movies, you'll break your shoulder and nothing else."

"Good to know. I would practice, but I have no front door."

"I've called some friends," he assured her. "It'll be fixed by the time we're back."

"So we're going?" A faint smile curled her lips. So beautiful. The risk inherent in taking her to the club was almost worth it to see her smile again.

"Yeah, I guess we're going." He stuffed his hands in his pockets and gave her a begrudging sigh. "But there's one more condition. You promise to stay the hell away from Rex. You don't go near him. If you need to get a picture, you do it with me beside you."

"Promise." Her smile broadened. "I like it when you agree with me. You should do it more often."

"Still with the sass," he rasped.

"Only for you. The rest of the world gets to see my soft, sensitive side."

A lump the size of his fist clogged his throat. Once, he'd had both—her sass and her sweetness—and he'd thrown them away.

She held his gaze for only a few seconds before her bottom lip quivered and she turned her head. The tiny glimpse of her vulnerability inflamed his desire. God, he wanted her. He wanted to strip off her clothes and run his hands over her lush curves. He wanted to feel the softness of her skin against his chest and the heaviness of her breasts in his palms. He wanted to hear her laugh, and moan, and whisper his name in the still of the night. He wanted her to sass him like there was no tomorrow, and kiss him like it was the day before he'd walked away from the best thing in his life.

He gritted his teeth against the ache of wanting what he couldn't have, but he couldn't stop himself from cupping her soft cheek in his palm.

She breathed out a quiet "oh" and stepped back, her face wary. "I guess I should…get…ready."

Her words tumbled out, tripping over each other, as she backed away. So unlike the Lana he remembered. She had always been cool and confident. He had never seen her unnerved.

Lana bumped into a chair and froze.

Something moved inside him, triggered by her desperate retreat. Frustration that she no longer trusted him? Wounded pride? Fear he might never heal the rift between them? Anger at her rejection? He didn't know, and right now he didn't care. He needed to touch her, reassure her and let her know he only wanted to keep her safe.

He closed the distance between them in three easy strides. Although his mind told him to stop, his body kept going, reaching for her, drawing her in, not slowing down until he held her in his arms. And then he just hung on, wishing he could have made a different decision two years ago.

Lana's breath hitched, and trepidation carved lines into her face. With a gentle stroke, he swept his hand along her jaw, cradling her face and tilting it back, until their gazes met, locked. Without thinking, he dipped his head and brushed his mouth over her soft, lush lips.

She pulled away.

"Please...James." Her voice broke and dropped to a pained whisper. "Don't."

He froze and silently cursed himself for giving in to his base desires. He'd made his decision two years ago. His circumstances—the past—hadn't changed. It didn't work then and it wouldn't work now. He was just making things worse.

For both of them.

Lana drew James's hand away from her cheek. He offered no resistance, as startled by her words as she was. When had she ever turned him down? But he was moving too fast and presuming too much. Although she appreciated his concession, she still didn't trust him. Not by a long shot. Not with her heart.

Still, she didn't miss his sharp intake of breath, or the way his shoulders tightened when she stepped away.

"We'd better get going." His voice was cool now, guarded. "The sooner we let everyone know you're mine, the sooner we can get you out of danger."

Mine. Her breath caught in her throat and longing squeezed her heart. Her father hadn't wanted a daughter, particularly one he hadn't planned, and after her mother had died, he'd wanted her even less. Rejection and a desperate need to be loved had sent her into Levi's arms. But he wasn't the savior and protector she'd thought he would be. She had been his possession but she had never had his heart. And he had never had hers.

Oh God. What was she doing? Reality crashed down on her fleeting moment of happiness. Could she really face a biker clubhouse again?

She sank down onto the couch and scrubbed her face with her hands. But nothing could banish the memories—so many hands, so many voices. Struggling, screaming…and the pain. So much pain. Her body chilled and a violent tremor shook her body.

James knelt in front of her and rested his hand lightly on her head. "What's wrong? Do you not want to go? I won't hold you to it. In fact I would be relieved if you don't go. I can deal with the fallout and Rex."

Lost in the past, she barely registered his words, and when she tried to answer, her throat tightened and she couldn't speak, much less meet his gaze.

"You're afraid." His calm, even voice held no trace of judgment or scorn, just puzzled curiosity.

He brought her hand to his face and pressed his mouth to the sensitive underside of her wrist. Warmth flowed through her veins, beating back the chill of old memories. He'd never seen her afraid because she'd never been afraid around him. James had always made her feel safe. But she'd been too ashamed to tell him about her past when they'd been together. She was too ashamed now.

"You don't have to worry, babe." He threaded his fingers

through hers and gave her hand a reassuring squeeze. "If this is what you really want to do, I won't leave you alone. Not for a minute. You'll be safe with me."

Safe. Lana swallowed past the lump in her throat. She hadn't felt truly safe since the night he'd left. But, of course, he would feel obligated to keep her safe. His unerring sense of duty had been one of the things that had attracted her to him. Like her, he wanted to put things right. But, unlike her, James had a clear path to follow. She'd always envied James the strength and purpose he got from the simple act of doing his duty. So unlike Levi and his flagrant disrespect for the law.

"One visit will be enough to face down the problem," he said. "No one will touch you after that."

Face down the problem. Just like Jackie had said. Walking into a motorcycle club after all these years would take her one step closer to dealing with her past. She could get her pictures, close the case, get rid of the tattoo that marked her as Wolverine property using the most expensive and effective technique available, and never see James or the bikers again. She just needed a little courage.

"I do want to go," she said. "But yeah, I'm afraid. Hades doesn't have a reputation for being all warm and fuzzy."

"Trust me." The confidence and conviction in his voice wrapped around her like a warm, thick blanket. She studied the firm set of his jaw and his steady blue eyes, dark now like an ocean storm. Something sparked inside her. Maybe hope. Maybe desire. Maybe both. At this point, she had more to gain than to lose by trusting him. He couldn't hurt her any worse than he already had.

"I don't trust you." Her voice shook despite her best efforts to keep it steady. "But I do think you'll keep me safe and that's enough for me to deal with...get through the door. You are a cop, after all. Protecting people is your job."

"Let's get you changed then." His gruff voice betrayed strong emotion, but whatever he was feeling he kept hidden.

With a resigned sigh, Lana made her way to the bedroom. James followed behind her and settled himself on the bed.

She lifted an eyebrow. "You planning to have a nap?"

James winked and lay back on her pillows. "Thought I'd watch."

Playful again. How could he so blithely bounce on her bed after she'd just rejected his kiss and told him she didn't trust him? What happened to Mr. Sullen and Serious? How could he turn it on and off so quickly?

"You're suddenly in a cheery mood," she grumbled.

"You're going to be taking off your clothes. Nothing cheers a man up more than a naked woman." He crossed his arms behind his head and his T-shirt rose to expose the ripples of his six-pack covered in the faintest shadow of soft, dusky hair. She followed the trail to his belt and then tore her eyes away.

Don't go there.

An image crept into her mind. James, naked, stretched out just like that on her bed, watching her strip to Danzig's "She Rides", his eyes burning into her until she thought she might combust. When she had finished her routine, she crawled over his body intending to settle herself exactly where she wanted to be. But before she reached her destination, he flipped her over and pinned her hands to the bed. It was the first time he had restrained her. It was the hottest sex she'd ever had. And it had just gotten better and better.

But this was life, not sex. Although her body craved him with a soul-deep ache, she had work to do and a heart to protect. Her cheeks flushed and she looked away.

"Babe," he said softly, "what are you thinking? You keep looking at me like that and I'll get ideas that'll make us late."

Liquid lust shot through her veins but she reined it in. "I'm thinking about how I'm going to change in the bathroom, so there's nothing for you to see except me pulling clothes out of the closet."

"There's a hell of a lot for me to see." His voice dropped to a rough growl.

Lana closed her eyes and tried to calm the dancing butterflies in her stomach. "James Hunter, are you looking at my ass?"

"You've still got the finest ass I've ever seen."

She snatched a dress off a hanger and spun around, her lips quivering with a repressed smile. "You're still cocky as hell." She stomped into the bathroom and closed the door.

"And you're still sexy as fuck," he yelled.

"Don't use that biker mouth on me." *Damn.* Did she just say that? Maybe he wouldn't catch the unintended innuendo. His mouth had taken her to places she'd never realized existed.

She splashed cold water on her face and took a few deep breaths. If she didn't get a grip, she would never be able to spend an entire afternoon with him without trying to rip off his clothes.

"Babe, I know your dark side. You like it when I swear."

Fire spread through her limbs. He didn't just know her dark side; he had teased it out of her and fed it with his own corresponding needs.

"I'm older now. More mature." She tugged on a high-collar, no-skin-revealing, stretch, leopard-print minidress. A muss of the hair. A heavy hand with the makeup. Fug boots. All ready for a biker barbeque. She hoped they were into thrash.

James ripped open the bathroom door and Lana threw herself back against the wall, heart racing and eyes wide.

"You're only twenty-six," he announced. "And age has nothing to do with what turns you on."

Lana straightened herself and sidled past him. "You always were good at math. Not so good with doors." She made it halfway across the bedroom before he grasped her arm and spun her around.

His eyes roved over her body and stopped at the floor. "Lose the boots."

"The boots stay. They're part of the outfit."

"You're my old lady. You need to look the part."

Lana's heart slammed against her ribs. She hadn't expected a confrontation over something as trivial as her attire. Putting their lives in danger...*that* she could understand. But boots? She loved her Zombie Stompers. Comfy. Flat soles. Easy to run. Although a tad warm for summer, they made her feel safe. And, right now, she needed safe.

She gave an exasperated sigh. "I've done very short. I've done very tight. Rex said nothing about footwear and I need to know I can run if I have to. The only way these boots are coming off is if you pull them off. Try to remember. We're pretending. I'm not really your girlfriend."

"You were."

"You didn't want me," she said, her voice small and tight. And that in a nutshell was the source of her heartache. No one had ever wanted her. Not her father, after her mother died. Not the relatives he begged to take her in. Not the kids in high school who had teased her mercilessly about her hair. Not Levi who had put on a show good enough to lure her to Seattle. Not even James.

James closed his eyes and rested his forehead against hers. "Babe, I never stopped wanting you."

A knot formed in her stomach. The man who'd broken her heart had no business being tender and sweet. Caught in a whirlwind of emotion, torn between fear and fire, she suddenly, desperately and inexplicably wanted him to rip the boots off her feet.

As if he could read her thoughts, he murmured, "I pull off your boots. You flip out. We kill what little there is left between us."

Lana let out a soft sigh of disappointment. "Hard to kill

something that's already dead."

He cupped her jaw with his hand and stroked a thumb over the apple of her cheek. "You still feel something for me, Lana." His voice dropped to a sensual whisper. "What we had isn't dead. I hear it in the hitch of your breath. I see it in the flush of your cheeks. I can taste your desire on my lips. And if I stripped you bare, and licked my way down your body, I would find you wet and ready for me."

Her lips parted in a silent gasp and for an endless second she forgot to breathe. He was right. She was slick with need. He knew her body better than she did. But where did he get off talking to her that way? Crossing that line? Seeking an assurance he wasn't prepared to give first? Did he think she would jump into bed with him for a bit of fun, only to watch him walk away again? Did he think forgiveness came cheap, with a side of fries?

She eased out of his grasp and grabbed her backpack, prefilled with surveillance equipment, disguises, snacks and her iPod—all the necessities for a stakeout.

"Leaving."

James's mouth opened, but before he could say anything, two men in coveralls appeared in the doorway. While they discussed the door replacement with James, Lana reached into her closet for a jacket and caught sight of her new black leather boots covered in a lattice of laces. The heel was high enough to make them dressy, but not so high as to prevent her from running in a bad situation. "Classy chic," Jackie had called them. Definitely better with the dress. She kicked off her fug boots and pulled the buttery soft leather over her feet, dismissing the not-so-fleeting thought that the boots would make James happy.

After receiving assurances from the carpenters that her apartment would be locked tight when they finished the job, she followed James into the hallway. His gaze dropped to her boots and then snapped up to her face. His eyes softened.

"Babe—"

"Don't."

He didn't. At least not in words. He brushed his lips gently over hers, so soft and sweet this time she couldn't bear to pull away.

Chapter Seven

She changed her boots.

James grinned and cranked the throttle on his Harley Davidson Rocker. One of the benefits of the undercover assignment had been the opportunity to choose his own wheels and when he'd seen the sporty, vivid-black Rocker in the Harley Davidson showroom, he knew he'd found his bike. The hardcore chopper—low, long, sleek and chromed out—lacked the huge ape-hanger handlebars most of the other bikers favored, but suited his need for speed over style. For the first time, he was glad he had splurged on the hidden passenger cushion. Choppers were not known for a comfortable pillion ride.

Lana's arms tightened around his waist as he took a wide corner and then blasted along the Vancouver-Blaine Highway toward the clubhouse, leaving Rex's minions in the dust. He could not have imagined a more perfect day—fuel in the tank, sun in the sky, an endless stretch of road and Lana's soft, sweet body pressed tight against his back, encased in the riding leathers he had brought for her protection just in case he failed to convince her to stay behind. Ride free, but ride safe.

For a moment he wished they could just drive until they ran out of road. Go back in time. What would have happened if he hadn't walked out? He had nothing to show for the last two years. The assignment wasn't over. The bad guys weren't in jail. He had compromised his identity and his integrity. And he was tired. Dead tired. He needed a break. His career had been one case, one file, one assignment after the other and for every criminal he put away, two more took his place.

He turned onto the King George Highway and zigzagged

through dirt trails until he came to the clubhouse. Claw, one of the new prospects, slid open the chain-link gate and James maneuvered the bike into a parking space and eased to a stop.

As they walked to the entrance, Lana's steps slowed. Her hands clenched and unclenched. Her jaw tightened and she kept her gaze firmly fixed on the ground. He made one last attempt to discern the reason for her anxiety, but she remained uncharacteristically quiet.

He keyed the security code into the lock and pressed his thumb against the print sensor. The door swung open and he stepped to the side to let Lana through.

She didn't move. Instead, she blanched and sucked in a sharp breath. Shadows swirled through her eyes, darkening them almost to black. A drop of blood welled up on her lip as her teeth sank through the tender flesh.

James frowned. "What's wrong?"

She squeezed her eyes shut, drew in a few deep breaths and straightened her spine. "Nothing."

"Doesn't look like nothing to me." His pulse raced and his muscles tensed, his body instinctively responding to the unseen threat.

"I'm good," she said in a hoarse whisper. "No problem. I can do this."

Warning bells clanged in his mind, but the minute his motorcycle had hit Hades's turf the surveillance cameras would have picked them up. There was no turning back now.

He clasped her hand and stepped through the door. She clung to him like she was drowning and her tight grip sent his body into full alert.

"Babe..."

"Let's go." She gave him a tight smile. "We don't want to be late."

The barbeque was in full swing when they reached the outdoor patio. Bikers and their babes lounged, danced, drank and ate to the dirty guitars of Pat Savage's "Born to Ride". Punch flipped burgers on the grill. Dawg cracked open beers at the bar. Kickstand sucked shooters from Tally's cleavage. Tally caught his eye and winked. The curvy, stacked brunette had become a permanent fixture in the clubhouse since she had hooked up with Dawg and with Angel rarely around, she was now the top old lady.

Heads turned when he walked into the melee, Lana plastered to his side. Her unease tugged at something deep inside him, and he put his arm around her and gave her a reassuring squeeze. "I'm here, babe. Not going anywhere."

"Yo, Ice! We've all been waiting to meet the old lady." Dawg tossed him a beer and gave Lana a questioning look.

She rolled her eyes. "Got anything stronger?"

A grin split Dawg's face and he pulled out a bottle of whiskey. "I like her already, Ice. She's got balls."

"Just what every man wants." Portia's snippy voice cut through the chatter.

"Who's that?" Lana looked over at the tall, leggy blonde with interest.

"Hades's mama. She...she's there for the guys if they need...have needs."

Lana cracked a smile, the first one since they'd left her apartment. "I see there's still some of the old you in there. Most bikers wouldn't have put it quite so delicately."

James gave her a puzzled frown. How did she know what bikers would say?

They joined Dawg at the bar and the brothers trickled over to meet her. Although James had been concerned about maintaining the appearance of being a couple, they slid easily into the friendly banter they'd had when they first started going out. After an hour he'd almost forgotten it was just a ruse.

Almost. He continued to keep a watch out for Rex, and over by the clubhouse, Ryder did the same. He gave Ryder a nod and got a smirk in return.

Ryder was one of the few club members who rode clean, refusing to participate in any of Hades's drug-related activities. A crack shot and a first-rate fighter, he'd always had James's back and James returned the favor. When the club went down, he would pull every string to make sure Ryder wouldn't be going to jail with them.

Cheers and shouts drew James's attention to a group clustered around the picnic tables. Bones held up Kickstand's club jacket and Punch sat astride Kickstand's motorcycle with a can of spray paint in his hand. Kickstand had spent every penny of his savings to buy the Harley Sportster when he was accepted as a prospect and his agitation was clear on his face.

"Didn't guard your stuff so now you gotta choose," Bones yelled over the cheers of the crowd. Prospect hazing was one of the club's favorite activities and Kickstand was as green as they got.

"He doesn't understand it's a test," Lana murmured, half to herself. "Someone needs to tell him there's nothing worse than losing his colors. If he loses the jacket, he won't need the motorcycle."

"How do you know that?"

Lana startled and looked away. "Probably something I saw on television." She gave him a sideways glance. "Aren't you going to help him?"

"Not my place," James said. "If he doesn't know the rules, he shouldn't be in the club."

"He's a good guy." Lana tried to shove him off his seat and James raised a cool eyebrow.

"They don't need good guys. They need tough guys. And if you want to get me off this seat, babe, you'll have to try harder than that."

Lana pressed her lips together and her eyes glittered. "Are you sure you want to challenge me? It'll be pretty damn embarrassing for you when I knock your sorry ass off that stool and onto the ground."

James thumped his beer bottle on the bar counter and folded his arms. Even if she did get him off the stool, seeing her sparkle instead of her fear would be worth every second of the ribbing he would suffer from the brothers. "Go for it, babe. I guarantee you won't get me off the stool and I won't even need to use my hands."

"I am *so* going to enjoy this," Lana growled as she stepped back to assess the stool.

"One minute warning," Bones yelled at Kickstand. "Make your decision."

Lana glanced up again and her mouth tightened. "Your humiliation will have to wait. I can't let them take his colors." She reached over the bar and grabbed a beer.

"Give the guy a break," she yelled at Bones. "A man can't make an important decision without a beer in his hand." She pushed her way through the crowd and handed Kickstand the bottle. A few minutes later she was back at James's side.

Kickstand stared at the bottle. Then he took a swig of his beer. Color returned to his cheeks. He perched himself on the edge of the picnic table and leaned a casual elbow on his thigh. Then he looked over at Lana and winked.

"What did you say to him?" James murmured.

A smile ghosted Lana's lips. "Nothing."

Tally started the countdown, but before she reached ten seconds, Kickstand eased himself off the table, held up a hand and snapped his fingers at Bones with all the bravado of a full-patch brother.

"Colors."

The bikers roared their approval. Bones tossed him the jacket. Punch gave Kickstand a salute and threw the spray paint in the trash can. Kickstand staggered back in relief and downed the rest of his beer. Then he turned and grinned at

Lana.

"Like I said before, you have a soft heart, Lana Parker." James leaned over on his stool to whisper in her ear. "How did you know he would get the hint?"

She tilted her head to the side and shrugged as her hand slid down the stool behind James's back. Did she think he hadn't noticed?

"We were talking about beer the other night when he walked me to my car. He said he'd never seen a more colorful label than on the Lost Coast Downtown Brown he'd had at Hades. He also said being part of the club meant everything to him."

"Looks like you've got yourself a puppy now." James jerked his chin toward a wide-eyed Kickstand hovering just out of earshot. "That's the problem with feeding strays."

"And this is the problem with making bets with me." She yanked the stool out from under him with a vicious jerk. James jumped easily to his feet and laughed, his mirth increasing as a grin spread across her face.

"Come on, babe. I saw that one coming a mile away."

Without thinking, he hauled her into his arms and kissed her, a long, deep, laughing kiss that tugged at his soul. His laughter died away as desire flamed through him.

Lana trembled in his arms and he released her lips, exhaling his disappointment as a tiny frown creased her brow. Then her hands smoothed slowly over his chest and she smiled.

"When did you suddenly become Mr. Spontaneity?"

"Since a beautiful redhead thought she'd knock me off my stool and conceded her defeat with a dazzling smile."

Her laughter ignited something deep inside him. He swept his arms around her, pulling her fully against his body, capturing her mouth with his. Two years of regret fueled his fire, and he claimed her in a deep, hungry kiss. Her soft body molded to his, her hands tangling through his hair. She tasted of whiskey and she smelled of sunshine, and he didn't give a damn that they'd become the next show.

"Can I get you a beer, Roxie? You need a burger?" Kickstand shifted from foot to foot, desperate to please and blissfully unaware of how close his interruption had brought him to death.

James tore his mouth from Lana and gazed down at her as she gasped in a breath.

Christ. Her lips were swollen from his kisses, her cheeks flushed and her eyes half-closed with passion. His cock pressed painfully against his fly, and it took all his effort to tear his gaze away.

"Fuck, Kickstand. Don't you have somewhere...?"

Lana cut him off. "Thanks, Kickstand," she said, breathlessly. "I'm good. I'll let you know if I need something."

"I'll tell you what you need." Tally came up behind Lana and slid an arm around her waist, drawing her away. "You need to come and meet the other old ladies. After that little display of tongue gymnastics, we want to know all about you and Ice."

James made a move to follow them and Tally glared. "Girls only."

"I'll be okay." Lana brushed her soft lips over his cheek and gave him a half smile. "For some reason, I'm not afraid anymore."

Squaring his shoulders against the pulse of want still raging through his body, he leaned in and whispered, "I promised to stay with you. I don't go back on my word, even if it means spending an hour listening to hen talk."

Lana snorted a laugh and her eyes sparkled. "Hen talk. Nice. Very chauvinistic and fitting with your new persona. I'll add that to the list of misdeeds for which I'll be knocking you off your stool later."

James pressed his lips together until she was out of sight and then allowed himself the luxury of laughter.

"Kickstand." James motioned the starstruck prospect over to the bar with a sharp jerk of his hand.

"Sir?" Kickstand almost flew across the patio to get to James's side.

"Keep an eye on Roxie for me. But don't let her know you're there. She doesn't know the clubhouse. I don't want her getting lost."

A grin split Kickstand's face. "Yes, sir."

James grabbed two bottles of beer and joined Ryder under a tree within view of the main door.

"You can relax." Ryder took one of the bottles from James. "I'm looking out for her like she's my own and now you've got Kickstand licking at her heels. Rex won't get near her."

"Don't know what's up with Rex," James said. "He knows he'll lose respect if he messes around with my old lady. It'll kill his leadership as fast as a bullet to the heart."

Ryder took a swig of his beer. "Bullet to the heart doesn't always kill. Seen a guy survive it once, but it wasn't pretty."

James gave him a sideways glance. Ryder had often hinted about a dark and troubled past, but he'd never talked about it and James respected his need for privacy.

Gravel crunched under heavy boots, and Bones and Diesel joined them in the shade.

"How did the weapons move go?" Bones stared at James unblinking and then flicked his gaze to Ryder.

"I couldn't believe the arsenal in that old guy's trailer," Ryder said. "Punch's dad has got to be at least eighty but cool as ice. He unloaded machine guns, grenades and automatic weapons from the storage compartment under the bunk beds his grandkids sleep on when they come to visit and threw in a teddy bear for free."

James gave a thin laugh. "Hell yeah. I thought we were going to pick up a couple of pistols, not three hockey bags worth of weapons. And those grenades…when he tossed one to us I thought it was all over. I told..."

Bones cut him off. "Where did you hide the weapons?"

James's blood chilled. As he had expected, the DEU had confiscated the weapons as soon as Ryder drove away, leaving him with three hockey bags full of dick-all and a ticket to an early grave.

"Friend of mine," he lied. "He's a trucker. Lives alone. Has no problem keeping stuff for a fee."

Part two of his plan was to stall when Rex asked for the weapons by saying his friend was out on a job and not due back for however long he expected it to take to think up a new excuse or get the hell out of town.

"Convenient." Bones's eyes narrowed and they locked gazes for what seemed to be an eternity. Finally, Diesel asked Bones a question, drawing Bones's attention away.

Sweat trickled down James's back. He knew Bones was suspicious, but he hadn't anticipated him coming this close to an outright confrontation. If he wasn't careful, he might wind up being the one with a bullet in his heart.

"Anyone seen Rex?" James asked. "He hasn't been around this afternoon. Not like him to miss out on a party."

Diesel frowned. "He was getting his chopper serviced this morning. Maybe he got held up."

"I thought I saw him in his office." Bones tossed his beer bottle in the trash. "And he wasn't alone."

Rex was inside. And so was Lana. Anxiety ratcheted through James and he shot Ryder a worried glance.

"I'm going to get another case of beer from the kitchen," James stepped away from the group. "Looks like Dawg is running low."

"Think I'll join you." Ryder clapped a hand on his shoulder and lowered his voice to a hushed murmur. "Can't let you go hunting for trouble alone, and I had something to ask you before we were interrupted."

They crossed the patio to the clubhouse. James pushed open the door and paused to let his eyes adjust to the low light.

"I'm leaving in a couple of weeks." Ryder kept his voice so low James could barely hear him. "I'm taking ten guys and starting a new club. We're going to run it clean. No drugs. No gun running. No serious illegal activity except for some vigilantism, the odd beating—but only guys who deserve it—and we might misappropriate goods, but only from those who stole first. There's no one I would rather have riding beside me than you."

Nausea roiled in James's gut. *Damn.* He'd known this was coming, but he hadn't expected it to happen so soon. Ryder had butted heads with Rex so many times no one would be surprised to see him go, but taking ten brothers with him turned his defection into a rebellion. And James couldn't afford to be in the middle.

"I'm honored. Let me think about it. Kinda preoccupied right now."

Ryder nodded. "Take all the time you need, but I'm gonna keep riding you until you say yes."

"That why they call you Ryder?"

The door slammed closed behind them and they walked through the workout area toward the lounge.

"My name is a whole different story," Ryder said with a grin. "The day you ride up to my new clubhouse is the day you get to hear it."

As they crossed the lounge, Tally and the girls headed toward them. No Lana. A chill wound its way up James's spine. He called Tally over and she left the group to join him.

"You seen Roxie?"

Tally shrugged. "She skipped out to the restroom when we started doing each other's nails. Didn't come back. I thought she was with you."

"What about Kickstand?"

Tally shook her head. "Haven't seen him either."

James's heart pounded against his rib cage. He should never have let her go in alone. He had made her a promise—to keep her safe—and he had spent the last half hour drinking beer and shooting the breeze while she was alone inside with Rex. Dammit. He just couldn't do right by her.

"We'll find her," Ryder said, his face tight. "She might have got lost."

"She might have got caught."

"If she did, make sure you leave a piece of him for me."

Chapter Eight

Crap.

Crap. Crap. Double crap.

A shiver of fear slithered up Lana's spine as she watched Rex strip off Portia's clothes. Why hadn't she just stayed in the doorway to get the pictures? Why had she felt it necessary to creep into Rex's office? Her new lipstick camera had a zoom. Jackie could have blown up the pictures. She could have taken a few snaps of them lip-locked together and gone back to the party.

But no. Stupid Lana had to try for a better shot. Clumsy Lana had tripped. Terrified Lana had dived into the storage locker reeking of Rex's unwashed gym clothes. And now, Peeping Lana had a front-row seat to a show she did not want to see.

A fully clothed Rex lifted a naked Portia and settled her on his desk. He barked a few words and she parted her legs and leaned back on her hands. Lana's stomach clenched. Voyeurism was so not her thing.

Well, since she was here, she might as well make use of her time. She pulled out her lipstick camera and slid it through the crack in the door. She took a few shots of Rex fondling Portia's breasts and sighed. Breast fondling was good but her 15 percent bonus hinged on Rex's full nudity. She silently urged Rex to get on with it, not that she wanted to see him naked, but why waste time?

Sweat trickled down her back. Did the locker have its own heater? Even her palms were slick. She twisted in the locker and repositioned herself to get a better angle and a breath of fresh air. The camera slipped from her sweaty fingers and crashed to the floor. Lana squeezed her eyes shut and willed the ground to swallow her up.

Boots thudded across the concrete floor, and the locker door banged open, sending a rush of cool air over her heated cheeks. Seconds later, a hand clamped around Lana's arm and yanked her out of the locker. She fell forward, landing at Rex's feet.

"Wildcat." The pure-carnal delight in Rex's voice turned her knees to jelly.

Lana's pulse raced and her mouth went dry. "I...got lost on my way to the restroom, and was just leaving when I saw you coming, and I panicked and hid. I'm sorry. Really sorry. I'll just be on my way." Her words tumbled over each other in a garbled rush of sound. She scrambled backward, crab-walking at top speed across the floor. Not fast enough. Rex grabbed a fistful of her hair and hauled her to her feet.

"I knew you were wild," he hissed in her ear. "And I know why you're here. Ice isn't enough for you. You want a real man."

She pressed her lips together, willing herself to be silent while all manner of sarcastic retorts tumbled over her tongue.

He jerked his chin at Portia. "You. Out."

Portia shot Lana a dirty look and tugged on her clothes in less than a minute: a bra, a white spandex dress and a pair of four-inch white stilettos. Lana made a mental note to wear less so she could dress faster in the morning.

"Wait." Lana tried to free her hair from Rex's grip and succeeded only in having him twist it more firmly around his hand. "I didn't mean to interrupt. I'll leave you two alone."

Portia rolled her eyes and gave Lana a derisory sniff before she sashayed out of the office, slamming the door behind her.

"Don't fucking play games," Rex growled. "You came to me."

"I told you. I got lost and panicked. Let me go or I'll...scream."

Rex laughed. "I've wanted to hear you scream since I first laid eyes on you. Go on. Scream. No one will hear you over the music. Or maybe you're waiting for Rex to make you scream..."

"Ice will come looking for me." Her voice rose to a thin whine.

Rex dragged her closer and yanked her head back. "No doubt. And when he finds you jumped ship, he'll cut you loose."

Lana's throat tightened. "You don't know him very well. My guess is that he'll go crazy."

Rex leaned closer and pressed his lips against her ear. "I hope so. It will give me an excuse to put him in his place. He's been getting a bit of an attitude."

Lana closed her eyes and took a few deep, calming breaths. She wasn't helpless. She had taken self-defense classes as part of her private investigator training. Motivated by a desire never to experience the type of powerlessness she had suffered with Levi, she'd practiced until she could do the moves in her sleep.

She crouched down, shifting her center of balance, and laced her fingers over her head, trapping Rex's hand. A quick spin and Rex lost his grip.

Success!

Her freedom was short-lived. Before she could make a run for the door, Rex grabbed her and slammed her into the locker with a bone-jarring crunch.

She struggled against him, but his massive thigh pinned her legs, and his hands easily held her arms down by her sides. Her attempts at head-butting him were rewarded with laughter and the faint whiff of stale beer and cigarettes.

Racking her brain for a self-defense move to escape being crushed against a locker by a mammoth, she was suddenly barraged with unwanted memories. Another room. Another clubhouse. Her hands pinned. Unable to move. And pain. So much pain.

Her heart thundered in her chest. Her pulse pounded in

her ears. Lost in her memories and a barrage of emotion, Lana screamed.

Crash. The door splintered off its hinges and skittered across the floor.

James stormed into the office with Ryder on his heels. Taking advantage of Rex's momentary distraction, Lana wriggled free. James grabbed her and shoved her into Ryder's arms.

"Take her," he barked at Ryder.

Lana turned and caught movement at the door. Bikers jostled in the hallway for a view. Of course. No biker worth his salt could resist a good fight, and she could smell a good fight coming the way her grandpa could smell a storm.

Rex folded his arms, his mouth tightening into a thin line. "She came to me."

"Doesn't matter if she did. Doesn't matter if she didn't." James's voice was low and dripping with fury. "She's mine until I say she's not. You don't touch what's mine, and in particular, you don't touch her."

Rex glanced over at Lana. "Tell him you want to be here."

Lana frowned. Was he delusional? Had she given any indication she was interested in him at all, besides following him down the alley into Carpe Noctem and hiding in his gym locker?

"I'm with Ice."

Rex's eyes narrowed. "You don't have to be afraid of him."

He *was* delusional. "I'm with Ice," she said in a loud, slow voice, emphasizing each word.

James and Rex locked gazes. No one moved. Tension hung thick in the air.

"You gonna fight me over a piece of tail?" Rex unfolded his arms and cracked his knuckles one by one. How lame.

"Last thing I want to do."

"Last thing you want to do is the last thing you're gonna do." With a roar, Rex charged. James met him with a punch to the gut, sending Rex reeling backward. Ryder pulled Lana into a corner, and a few bikers pushed their way into the room, giving James and Rex even less space to maneuver.

Fast, furious, dirty fighting ensued. James moved with economical grace, his moves purposeful and consistently powerful. But Rex absorbed each blow, meeting him punch for punch. Hades's leader had to be able to defend his position, and he clearly had the skill and strength to put down most of the bikers she'd seen in the clubhouse.

But damn, James could fight. His pecs rippled beneath his shirt with every punch. Biceps twitching, quads tensing, tendons pulsing, he was a vision of an enraged, red-hot alpha male.

Despite the fact he and Rex were doing some serious damage to each other, Lana's mouth watered and lust, raw and ragged, swept through her bones. Badass biker Ice was even more of a turn-on than dangerous, crusty cop James.

The bikers cheered every time Rex landed a blow, but he tired quickly. His punches became slower. His leg sweeps were always a second too late. For a heartbeat, Lana thought James would win. And then, inexplicably, James dropped his guard.

Taking advantage of James's exposure, Rex lunged in with a punch that sent James clear across the room. He bounced off a shelf and fell to the floor. Ryder called the fight for Rex and dispersed the crowd. He released Lana and they raced across the room to James.

"You kicked up a shitstorm, darlin'," Ryder murmured as they knelt down beside a groaning James.

"Didn't mean to." She brushed her finger along James's jaw, prickly with a five o'clock shadow. Her jaw tightened as she took in his closed eyes and the gray pallor of his skin.

"Are you okay? Should I call an ambulance?"

"Just need a minute," he rasped.

"You're not looking so good." Tears prickled the back of her eyes. "I really think you need to go to a hospital."

"Shhh, babe. I'm okay." He squeezed her hand and she wiped a rogue tear off her cheek.

Ryder patted her on the back. "He has a hard head. Takes more than a little bump against a shelf to do any serious damage to him. Hell, he once got his head slammed in a car door when he was chasing down some druggie who tried to steal the chrome from Rex's bike. Didn't slow him down. Neither did the two-by-four the druggie's friends beat him with. I actually felt for the druggie when Ice caught him. I think he's still on crutches."

Lana shot Ryder a sideways glance. "Ah...thanks for that. I guess I'll just leave him then and go have a beer until he gets up off the floor. Or maybe I should hit him with a two-by-four first, just for kicks."

"I'll go get one." Chuckling, Ryder left them and went to check on Rex.

James snorted a laugh and Lana frowned. "You better damn well be unconscious after I shed a tear for you. Those tears are hard to come by."

He opened his eyes and a smile tugged at the corners of his mouth. "I was wondering what it would take to get your attention."

"You had my attention outside. You're a difficult man to ignore, especially when you're engaged in a public demonstration of French-kissing and naughty behavior."

But was it real naughty behavior or was it just for show? The question burned in her brain, but this wasn't the time to ask. Still, the memory of that kiss sent her heart racing again. How could a kiss like that just be for show? He felt something for her, just as he had accused her of feeling something for him.

"I like naughty behavior," he murmured, bringing her back

from their moment of passion on the patio.

"And I like James not beat up." She paused and gave him a sultry grin. "Although watching you go all alpha crazy on Rex...knowing you are all sorts of badass dangerous..."

"You like dangerous." He shifted his weight and groaned. Then his eyes shuttered closed.

Lana's heart stuttered in her chest and she looked around frantically for someone to help.

"Ice." She shook his shoulders and her voice wavered. "Ice..." She leaned over and pressed her lips to his ear. "Yes, I like dangerous and you'd better open those damn eyes and give me some."

Chapter Nine

Lana paced James's room on the second floor of the clubhouse. Ryder had whisked her away from Rex's office, telling her Ice was fine but he needed time to cool off. She hadn't made it easy on him, but in the end he was bigger, stronger and willing to drag her by her hair if she didn't listen.

Just as well. She needed the time to deal with the guilt clawing at her belly. She shouldn't have let herself get caught sneaking around Rex's office. She understood biker culture, the hierarchy, the challenges, the constant jostling for position of top dog. She should have known if she was caught it would end like this.

She looked around, but the room gave no clue as to the personality of its occupant. No pictures, mementos, books or magazines. Just the basics—bed, dresser, night table and bathroom. A small window overlooked the courtyard where the barbeque was still in progress.

Her investigative instincts and an overwhelming curiosity drove her to peek into the dresser drawers where she found jeans, T-shirts and underwear, all neatly folded. The last drawer held socks, folded in pairs, and belts coiled around Harley Davidson buckles. She carefully sifted through the contents and pulled out two pictures.

The first was a picture of her. James had taken it the day before he left. They were on the little ferry boat connecting Granville Island to downtown. She traced her finger over the beaming Lana, her hair in wild disarray from a sudden gust of wind. So happy. She didn't remember how it felt to be that happy.

The second picture was of a tall, slim woman with long brown hair. Her almond-shaped eyes were warm and deep. So beautiful. Her perfect oval of a face glowed. Was she from James's past or present?

Lana's heart skipped a beat. Of course he'd had other lovers. He had briefly alluded to fleeting relationships when they'd first hooked up. And, no doubt, after he left her he would have had more. He was a highly attractive, incredibly fit, enigmatic alpha male. During their brief time together, she'd often wondered what he was doing with her. He needed someone calm, sedate, slim and toned like he was. Not a curvy girl weighed down with baggage and a mass of wild curls to match her temper.

She replaced the pictures and sank down on the bed. He'd never mentioned a serious past girlfriend when they were together, so the woman in the picture was probably his current squeeze. She shouldn't be surprised. James never backtracked on his decisions.

A loud thud sent Lana scrambling to her feet. James stalked into the room and slammed the door behind him. Still pumped after his fight, muscles twitching under the thin cotton of his T-shirt like he wanted to have another go at Rex, he was breathtakingly gorgeous and sexy as hell. The cuts and bruises on his face only added to his appeal. A quiver of desire chased across her skin.

"Are you...?" Anxiety pounded through her veins.

Jaw clenched tight, blue eyes cold and hard, James held up a hand, cutting her off. Lana shivered at the raw violence in his taut face. But the question he asked wasn't the one she was expecting.

"Did he...touch you?"

Relieved at being spared his anger at going near Rex alone, Lana shuddered, considering for the first time what could have happened. "Just a little shake and slam against the locker. Some hair pulling..."

Like magic, his eyes softened. "When I heard you scream, I thought the worst. If he had..." He choked on his words. "I don't know if I could've held back. It was hard enough to throw the fight after I saw his hands on you."

She should be appalled at his words, frightened even. Instead, the thought of James out of control stirred her most carnal desires, turning her brain to mush, igniting the adrenaline still pumping through her veins after the fight.

God, she wanted him.

No. Don't do this. Her mind railed even as her body quivered with need. It had taken her almost two years to get over him. And after Jackie forced her back on the dating circuit, she'd run at the first hint of anything more than casual affection.

And yet, here she was, desire rising through her body like the tide, heedless of the warning of her battered heart.

Chest heaving, he lifted his hot, heavy gaze to hers and she trembled at the sensual promise in his eyes. Her mind flashed back to steamy nights, his seductive voice rumbling in her ear, his lips hot on her skin, his hands conducting her body in a symphony of pleasure.

No. He didn't want her. He had walked out the door without even a goodbye. She tore her gaze away, but before she could move, he had her in his arms.

Curling his fingers around her neck, he crushed her to his body and captured her lips in a passionate kiss, plundering her mouth without restraint. Their first kiss without an audience was a savage kiss. Brutal. Wild. Unrestrained. A kiss that sent her temperature soaring and her blood pounding through her veins.

Dangerous.

"God...Lana. Want you. Need you." James drove her back into the wall, pinning her with his body. Engulfed in hot, hard, sweaty male, Lana tilted her head to the side, exposing her neck to his heated lips. Her hands tightened on his biceps, her fingernails scraping his skin, as he licked and sucked down to the sensitive spot between her neck and her shoulder blade. Without hesitating, he drew the skin between his teeth and bit. Lana cried out and moisture flooded her sex.

"You still like that," he rasped, his voice a husky growl.

"Hell yes." Not only that, she wanted more. More kissing. More biting. More raging alpha male. His passion on the patio had taken her breath away. But now that they were alone she wanted all of him, damn her aching heart.

"Don't stop." Lana ground her hips against his erection, rock-hard against her belly. The small movement inflamed him. He threaded his fingers through her hair, yanked her head back and growled. The raw, feral, dominating sound undid her. Her head spun. Her nipples hardened. Her insides turned liquid and her sex pulsed with need. She gave herself over to unbridled lust with a whimper.

"Lana." He said her name reverently, triumphantly, and then he bent his head and covered her mouth in a hard kiss that left her in no doubt she was going to get what she wanted.

She slid her hand over his taut abs and past his belt to trace the rigid line of his cock trapped beneath his jeans

James hissed in a breath and tore his mouth away, pressing Lana hard against the wall. "Babe, I won't be able to stop and I won't be gentle."

She pressed harder, feeling his erection thicken under her palm. "I don't want you to stop. And I don't want gentle. I want badass biker Ice going badass with me."

"Christ," he muttered half to himself. "How the hell did I walk away?"

He drew in a ragged breath then jerked her dress up over her hips. "Damn dress doesn't leave much to the imagination. You had all of Hades panting after you."

"Right now, the only man I want to hear panting after me is you."

Barely Undercover

He gave her a wicked grin and held her hand to his chest as it rose and fell in a quick rhythm. "Been panting since I saw you in that dress."

"I've been panting since you kicked in the door and pounded on Rex."

He cupped her sex, and then shoved her panties aside, sliding his finger along her slick folds. "Watching me fight made you this wet?" He spread her moisture up and around her clit in slow, torturous, delicious circles. Lana tilted her hips, trying to get his fingers where she wanted them.

"I told you. I like dangerous." She nuzzled his neck and nipped gently, a move she remembered he liked.

The deep rumble of his groan vibrated against her chest. "Babe, I won't be able to hold on."

"Then don't."

His gaze snapped to hers and with one sharp movement, he tore her panties away. "I'm gonna fuck you, Lana," he whispered in her ear. "Hard and fast and against the wall until you scream my name." His soft voice, so at odds with the dirty words he knew she liked to hear, undid the last threads of her control. She slid her fingers under his belt buckle and jerked him toward her.

"Now. Don't make me wait."

A thud on the door pulled her out of the moment and she froze, her fingers caught tight between his belt and the taut ridges of his abdomen.

"Ice. You gotta get out here," Ryder shouted, his voice low and urgent. "Fight's brewing downstairs. Some of the brothers think you let Rex win. Rex's boys aren't too happy. After drinking all day, no one is thinking straight. Rex took off with the rest of the inner circle about half an hour ago, so that leaves you and me to sort it out."

Noooooooo. Lana whimpered softly and pulled James closer.

James closed his eyes and drew in a deep breath. And then

another. He gently tugged her hand away and released her. "Gotta go, babe. Last thing I want, but I've got work to do." He straightened his clothes and turned away.

How could he just let everything…drop? How could he walk away as if they had been doing nothing more than chatting about the weather? A shudder ran through Lana's body as her arousal plummeted. What the hell had she been thinking? She'd been seconds away from getting her heart broken yet again, and for what? A moment of unbridled lust.

She swallowed hard. "I'll…get going. Leave you to business."

"You're not going anywhere," he growled. "You came on my bike. You leave on my bike. For now, you stay in my room until I get everything sorted."

Lana's eyes narrowed at his cold, abrupt tone and her stomach clenched. This had definitely been a mistake and he clearly thought the same. *Stupid, stupid, stupid.* Why had she even thought of trusting him again? When would she ever learn? No one wanted her. She was flawed. Fundamentally damaged. Better off alone.

"I'm not a prisoner. If I want to leave, I'll leave."

"Babe, there is nowhere to go from here. Taxis won't come to Hades. We are miles from the nearest bus stop. No one will give you a lift without my say-so."

"What about Kickstand?"

He spun around and a pained expression crossed his face, but it was so fleeting she could have imagined it. "You want to leave that bad?"

She tightened her lips into a thin line and nodded. "Yeah, I want to leave. This was…a mistake. I just got caught up playing your old lady."

He stilled and exhaled a long, slow breath. For several moments he studied her and then his face tightened. "Probably right. I'll tell Kickstand to take you."

Her heart sank to the floor. But what had she expected? Protests? Declarations? Begging? Not James.

She followed him out of the room and down the narrow stairway to the main floor. James took Ryder and Kickstand aside for a hushed conversation. As Lana waited, her stomach a queasy knot of confusion, Portia sauntered over to her with a cold smile on her face.

"You sure keep busy." Her thin nasal tone set Lana's already frayed nerves on edge. "First you're after Rex, then Ice. You gonna fuck Ryder too? Who's next on your list? Bones? Diesel? Kickstand? You angling to be the next mama? Because I'm warning you, there is only one mama in this club and that's me."

Drowning in a sea of self-hatred and self-pity, Lana almost forgot she had to keep up the act as Ice's old lady. Still, having no desire to be the woman who slaked the sexual needs of any club member without discrimination, she was able to answer honestly, "Um. No. I'm a one-man kinda woman."

"Didn't seem like that to me when you were hiding in Rex's locker. Every woman here wants a piece of Rexy, but he's mine."

The hair on the back of Lana's neck stood on end. She glanced back over her shoulder and spotted James and Ryder heading their way. Time to change the topic of conversation.

"I like your...uh...dress." She flashed Portia a desperate smile. "I can't wear white. It washes me right out, but it highlights your tan."

Portia's eyes narrowed and she pulled out Lana's lipstick camera just as James and Ryder joined them. "Might look better if I added a little color."

Damn. Had she opened it? Did she know? Heart thundering, Lana shrugged her shoulders. "You might not want to use it. I have...a...cold. Bad cold. You wouldn't want to get sick. I'll bet Rex likes his girls...healthy."

James snorted a laugh. Ryder gave her a curious glance.

Portia's lips curled into a positively evil smile and she placed the lipstick camera between her fingers and started to pull.

"Give me that." James reached for the gold tube and Portia let it drop. Lana's hand flew to her mouth as her most expensive piece of surveillance equipment hit the floor with a crack. James quickly snatched it up. He stared at the camera and then shot Lana a glance that made her wince.

Gripping her forearm, he dragged her away from Ryder and Portia and into a quiet hallway. "This yours?" He pulled open the camera and Lana nodded.

"Same piece of equipment I confiscated from you the first time we met?"

Heart pounding, Lana shrugged. "Actually, you never gave that one back. This one is new."

James's jaw tightened and he backed her up to the wall. This time it wasn't arousal that made her pulse race, but fear.

"You promised you wouldn't go near him without me."

"I didn't have time," she said, striving for a calm she didn't feel. "I saw him meet Portia at the door. I overheard him saying he was taking her to his office. I didn't have time to find you. I just had time to…take up a covert surveillance position before they got there. Unfortunately, I was discovered."

James inspected the camera and then slapped it into her waiting palm. "Did you get your pictures?"

Lana looked at the battered and dented gold tube in her hand. "I got some pictures but I don't know if they survived the two falls."

"You better hope they did," he snapped. "You're done here. Your case is closed. You are leaving now with Kickstand and you are never to come near the clubhouse or Rex again. Have I made myself clear?"

Lana narrowed her eyes. She wasn't some kid who'd been caught with her hand in the cookie jar. She was a professional. She had a job to do. Although she'd agreed to make only one visit to the club, she hadn't agreed to stay away from Rex. Damned if she would let James interfere with her case.

"Goodbye, Ice." She turned on her heel and stalked away, nodding to Kickstand as she rounded the corner.

"I didn't hear a yes," James yelled.

Lana looked back over her shoulder and indulged in one last, lingering glance. "That's because I didn't say it."

Chapter Ten

"Where is the infamous Rex?" Jackie adjusted the braids on her blonde wig and tugged down the ruffled bust of her German milkmaid costume as she followed Lana into Vancouver's Schnitzel Club, lavishly decorated for the summer Oktoberfest celebration.

"I hope to God he's on his way out the door," Lana moaned. "This is the most humiliating disguise I've ever worn. I feel for German milkmaids." The dirndl-style minidress with its blue apron and explosive red skirt just barely covered her ass, and the ridiculous white cap was already askew. Her breasts were thrust out and up by the tight, black-laced bodice and highlighted by the pleats of her overly puffy peasant top.

Jackie twirled one of Lana's blonde braids. "I'm the milkmaid. You're the frisky *fräulein*. And I think those thigh-high stockings with the giant black bows at the top are the cutest things ever."

"Just wait until I start tap-dancing on stage." Lana snorted. "These shoes seem to have a mind of their own." She stopped to adjust the strap on her shiny Mary Janes and the choker around her neck tightened, cutting off her air. Her hand flew to her throat and she ripped it off. She hadn't been able to wear anything around her neck since leaving Levi. The choker had been a mistake.

Maybe this was a mistake too. Watching Rex from the safety of her car was one thing, as was her trip to Hades with James at her back, but walking into a packed hall, knowing she had no protection from the rowdy group of bikers in the far corner, added a whole new level of meaning to the word *fear*.

Jackie gave her arm a sympathetic squeeze. "We don't have to do this," she whispered. "You can go back to your normal surveillance routine. Eventually, you'll catch him."

"I'm okay." Lana handed her the choker. "And I don't want to pass up a great opportunity. He's sure to get frisky surrounded by babes and beer steins. Hades already has a fan club." She pointed to the group of dirndl-clad women hanging around Hades's table.

"Is James here?" Jackie asked. "The last thing you need is for him to see you and drag you out by the braids."

Lana made a more careful inspection of Hades's tables. She counted at least twenty bikers, including Kickstand and a few familiar faces from the barbeque, but no James. She shook her head. "Kickstand said he's on guard duty at the clubhouse tonight so we don't have to worry about him. Rex is the big, scary one at the end. The guy beside him is his right-hand man, Dawg. The others close to him are Diesel, Punch, Ryder and Bones. The baby-faced guy with the golden hair is Kickstand. He's the one who told me the Hades crew was coming here tonight."

Jackie licked her lips. "So cute. I could eat him all up like a *schweinshaxe*. This might be my best wingman assignment ever. A table full of hot biker dudes, endless steins of beer, giant sausages, pretzels, sauerkraut and God-awful oom-pah-pah accordion music. What more could a girl want?"

"We are *not* getting drunk." Lana shot her friend a warning glance. "And you can't fraternize with the enemy. We're here to just observe and snap a few pictures of Rex with his hands, or his dick, up a milkmaid's dirndl. And if they do recognize me, I might have to act...different. I still have to pretend to be Ice's old lady or I'll have Rex's paws all over me."

Jackie laughed. "Different. Gotcha."

They plunked themselves down at a table with a good view of the Hades crowd. Jackie flagged down a waitress and ordered two one-liter steins of nonalcoholic beer and a plate of mini suckling-pig sandwiches. "Remind me to thank that Portia woman for breaking your camera," Jackie said, her gaze roving over the packed hall. "I'm already having a good time."

They took turns following Rex whenever he left the table. Lana remarked on his unusually small bladder on her third trip back from the restrooms and Jackie pointed out the correlation between the size of a man's bladder and the size of...other things. When Rex left the table for a fourth time, Lana groaned. "You want to take this one?"

Jackie shook her head. "I was just at the bar watching him drink shooters from some poor girl's cleavage. Plus my new friend Hans promised to teach me the words to the famous Oktoberfest song. Maybe I'll get lucky tonight." She pointed to a tall, skinny blond in green *lederhosen*. Lana snorted a laugh as she slid out of her chair.

"You're scraping the bottom of the barrel. There is nothing remotely attractive about a man in short pants and suspenders." She skirted through the tables, slapping away the stray hands that seemed to take her short skirt as an invitation to cop a feel, and turned down the corridor to the restrooms. Just as she took up her position against the wall, she caught a glimpse of Rex heading through the exit door leading to the parking lot.

Lana's heart pounded and she pulled out her new minicam. Easing open the door, she peeked around the corner and spotted Rex engaged in a heated discussion with Bones and a familiar-looking man in a dark suit. No milkmaids or frisky *fräuleins* in sight.

Disappointing.

She was about to go back inside when she heard Bones mutter, "It's Ice."

Curious, she dashed over to a blue Ford Focus and crouched behind the vehicle to eavesdrop.

"You sure your source hasn't made a mistake?" Rex

growled. "How could a rat get into Hades? I vetted every prospect personally. I know everything about every full-patch brother. There's no fucking way one of them is a rat, unless he was turned."

"The source is good," the man snapped. "He works in the DEU. If you want a name or a picture of your rat, it will cost you extra."

"Don't pay him," Bones growled. "I'm telling you I know who it is. That fucking Ice is always sneaking around, disappearing for hours at a time, losing weapons. Who hooks up with an old lady—especially a hot tamale like Roxie—and keeps her a fucking secret?"

Hot tamale? And she thought she'd heard all the redhead jokes.

Lana peeked over the hood of the car just as the man in the suit stepped into the light. She recognized him instantly. Rex had met him before. Once at the pizza shop. Another time in an alley downtown. She'd thought it strange someone in a suit would be having clandestine meetings with Rex, but now she knew why. She snapped a few quick photos, hoping there was enough light for her cheap replacement surveillance camera. When she heard the crunch of gravel, she ducked down and pressed herself against the vehicle's wheel.

"I think you're wrong about Ice," Rex said to Bones as they walked past Lana. "But I think we should set a trap wide enough to catch our rat, whether he's in the inner circle, full patch or a prospect."

"What do you have in mind?" Bones pulled open the door and polka music blasted into the parking lot.

"We'll have an opportunity at Kirkland Island two or three weeks from now. I've set up..."

Lana strained to hear but a loud accordion riff cut off Rex's words and then the door slammed shut behind him.

Damn.

Lana pushed herself to her feet. She had no way of contacting James. On their way out of her apartment, he'd told her his phone had been bugged by the DEU so he used it only for Hades business. Undercover procedures meant he couldn't have a personal phone.

She drummed her fingers on the hood of the vehicle. *Option #1: Tip off the DEU.* She could head down to the local DEU office in the morning and give them an anonymous tip that James's cover was about to be blown. *Bad option.* If there was a leak in the DEU, she might put James at risk. *Option #2: Airplane watching.* She could go airplane watching outside the clubhouse and hope James would see her vehicle and storm out to yell at her. *Another bad option.* What if it was Rex who found her this time? *Option #3: Naughty behavior.* She could disobey James's orders and go to the clubhouse.

Again.

Her stomach clenched, but an illicit visit to the clubhouse seemed to offer the highest chance of success. No one would be surprised to see her, except maybe James. And he wouldn't really be surprised. Infuriated, maybe. Enraged, possibly. Apoplectic, likely.

Lana sighed. No doubt he would shout and stomp around, but in the end he was all bark and no bite. Although, when he found out she was trying to help him, maybe some biting would be involved—the hickey-leaving kind. Maybe he would want to finish what they'd started the night of the barbeque...

She shook her head. What the hell was wrong with her? If he hadn't thought it was a mistake, he wouldn't have given her the cold shoulder after Ryder knocked on the door. And if she hadn't agreed, she would never have walked away.

Still, she couldn't let him fall prey to Rex's trap. She would have to plan her visit to the clubhouse carefully. And since she had two weeks, she didn't have to rush. Maybe tomorrow...

Decision made, she headed back to the table and spotted Jackie playing beer pong with Hans and his almost-identical *lederhosen*-clad friend.

"We bought you another stein," Jackie said as Lana slid into the bench beside her. "An alcoholic one. I was getting the feeling you were done with the surveillance tonight. Oh, and I got you a *weisswurst* sausage." She glanced around and lowered her voice. "The boys here are a little lacking in the meat department, if you know what I mean. The sausage is a poor substitute but the best I could do."

Lana hefted her stein and clinked glasses with Jackie. "Here's to finding the perfect sausage."

"Does that mean we're officially off restroom duty?"

"Unless we see Rex grabbing a milkmaid and sneaking her outside, I'm done for tonight," Lana said. "I need to have a little fun."

Three hours and two steins later, Jackie and Lana jumped on their table with Hans and Jens, and joined the rowdy, table-stomping crowd in a sing-along version of "Take Me Home, Country Roads".

When they reached the third verse, a hand clamped around her ankle and she caught the flash of Cerberus's red eyes just before a massive body lifted her off the tabletop and set her firmly on the floor. Eyes wide with alarm, Jackie jumped down after her.

A firm hand on the back and a march through the crowd later, she was up against the wall with a furious Ryder staring down at her.

"What the fuck are you doing?"

She glanced over at Jackie, but her friend was entranced with the lean, hard body and breathtaking good looks of the Adonis in front of them.

"Well, we were singing until you rudely dragged me off the table."

"That kind of...behavior is not allowed," he spluttered.

"Well, then you'd better make an announcement because right now everyone in the hall is on the tables," Jackie batted her eyelashes and a sultry smile graced her perfect lips. "Or, if you were planning on a group punishment, you could start with me." She twisted her hip and patted her left bottom cheek. "This cheek first."

Ryder sucked in a sharp breath and his eyes widened as he was hit with the full effect of Jackie, the seductive milkmaid, and the creamy expanse of her uncovered cheek. His mouth opened and closed. No sound came out.

"I think you've shocked him," Lana said. "That or you've turned him on so much he can't speak."

Jackie's lips quivered and her cheeks flushed. Lana tried to suppress a smile at the state of her usually imperturbable friend. But then Ryder, with his chiseled jaw and broad shoulders, certainly wasn't hard on the eyes. No way would he ever prance around in *lederhosen.*

Ryder dragged his gaze back to Lana. "Does Ice know you're here?"

Lana's pulse kicked up a notch and she tried to force her alcohol-fuzzed brain into a kick-ass old-lady mind-set. *Old lady. Old lady. Old lady.* "Of course not," she snapped. "I don't report to him. I don't tell him where I'm going to be every minute of the day. I don't ask his permission when I go out."

Hmmm. As natural as breathing. Maybe she was meant to be a biker's old lady after all.

Ryder folded his arms and leveled his gaze. "You do."

"I don't. So just chill. Jackie and I are just here having a good time, same as everyone else. It *is* summer Oktoberfest, after all."

Ryder shook his head. "You're Ice's old lady. 'You're his' means you don't stand on tables wearing..." he looked her up and down and swallowed hard, "...that...sexy little outfit.

Especially not when the brothers are here and Ice isn't around to keep them in line. They'll be thinking...things...they shouldn't be thinking. You belong to Ice and only Ice should be thinking those things."

Jackie snorted. "I think he's saying Ice is gonna be pissed he missed out on a fun evening. I don't speak bikerese so it's just a guess."

Lana tightened her lips and glared at Ryder. Yet another biker with attitude. Yet another man who thought he could boss her around. She could hardly wait to be done with this case and get back to sitting in her car, eating celery sticks and watching men cheat on their wives. He made it too damn easy to put on the old-lady attitude—or, maybe, she'd already been wearing it.

"I don't give a damn what anyone is thinking. I'll wear what I want to wear. I'll sing if I want to sing. And I'll stand where I want to stand." Her hands found her hips and she gave Ryder her fiercest scowl. "I would have attracted more attention if I had stayed in my seat since *everybody* in the hall is on the tables. Now clear off and let us get back to drinking and having fun." She poked him in the chest for good measure, despite the fact he could probably crush her with one mighty blow of his fist. The old ladies she had known always poked their men.

Ryder startled and stepped back. A chuckle escaped Lana's lips. God, if she'd had this attitude when she'd been with Levi, no one would have messed with her.

"I have no fucking idea how he controls you," Ryder growled, batting her hand away.

"He doesn't. I'm uncontrollable." She cocked her head and frowned. "What's it to you anyway?"

"You're Ice's girl. Means I protect you like you were mine. And if you were mine, I'd be taking you back to the club. A table full of drunken bikers, two pretty girls in...those outfits... It's a recipe for disaster, rules or no rules about touching old ladies."

Back to the club? She would have refused point-blank, save for the fact it would give her a chance to warn James about Rex.

She effected an exasperated sigh. "Fine. Take me back to the club. I suspect you would do it even if I said no."

Ryder's eyes twinkled. "I was thinking I'd have to throw you over my shoulder, maybe tie you to my bike. Good to hear you'll come along easily."

A small sound left Jackie's lips, a cross between a moan and a whimper. Ryder's head jerked in her direction and his gaze raked over her body, finally coming to rest on her flushed cheeks. His eyes softened and his voice dropped to a husky rumble.

"We can't leave you on your lonesome. I'll ask Kickstand and a few of the boys I trust to keep you company until I'm back. That is...if you're sticking around."

Jackie's cheeks brightened and she gave him her coy, endearing, come-hither smile. "I still have a stein of beer and a plate of *sauerbraten* to finish, so I'm not going anywhere." She gave Lana a wink then headed back to her table where Hans and his companion were comparing lederhosen length.

Best wingman assignment ever, Jackie mouthed over her shoulder. She gave Lana two thumbs-up to let her know she would be okay on her own.

"How did you know it was me?" Lana toyed with her blonde braids as she and Ryder walked to the door.

"A man sees you, Roxie, you're burned into his brain. No matter what you're wearing."

Lana's face flamed. Although hanging around the bikers still made her uneasy, they were damn good for the self-esteem. Well, these bikers anyway.

Was she burned into James's brain? He was burned into hers. And despite his postfight brush-off, masochist that she was, she couldn't wait to see him again. Especially wearing her milkmaid outfit. He had a bit of a kink for role-play.

But if they were done, they were done. At least he would be safe and she would have enjoyed the ride. Her heart would just have to heal all over again.

Chapter Eleven

"She was where?" James's shout rang through the empty Hades clubhouse.

Startled at the high decibel level of his outburst, Lana instinctively searched around the lounge for a place to hide. She should have gone with Ryder to find him. Maybe a little smile would have softened the blow.

"Wearing what?" His voice rose and Lana's heart pounded. Not good. Not good at all. She spotted a small closet and threw open the door. Too small. Especially with all the petticoats under her skirt.

"On the table? Jesus Christ." His growl became a yell and Lana fought the urge to dive behind the couch.

"Roxie! Where the fuck are you?"

Trembling, despite the calming effects of excess alcohol consumption, Lana gritted her teeth, clasped her hands in front of her, and stepped into the middle of the lounge, meeting James's fierce scowl with a cheerful smile.

"*Guten Abend.*" It wasn't really a good evening, but it was always prudent for frisky *fräuleins* to be polite when faced with an enraged biker and his erstwhile companion.

James's eyes bored into her like laser beams, raking over her body from her crisp but slightly askew linen cap to her shiny Mary Janes and back up again, hovering over her demicorset-enhanced bosom. His eyes darkened and his body stilled. Anger or arousal? She couldn't tell, but she wasn't afraid to play with fire. She racked her brain for the few German phrases Hans had taught her.

"*Ich kippe für die große Wurst warten.*" She licked her lips and panted rapid breaths to keep her laughter at bay. She was telling the truth. Truly, she couldn't wait for the big sausage.

His lips quivered but he didn't even crack a smile. Maybe he didn't understand German. Hell, how many people understood German? It would have to be her private little joke.

"Das wirst du noch bereuen," James growled.

Lana sucked in a sharp breath and her eyes widened. What the hell had he said? Who the hell cared? Despite the harsh-sounding words, the sensual promise in his voice sent fire licking through her body. With a flash of unexpected insight, given her partially fuzzed brain, she suddenly realized the danger of being scantily clad, heavily intoxicated and speaking German with a furious and very hot James.

"He said you're going to be sorry." Ryder chuckled. "And that's my cue to get back to my pretty little milkmaid."

"You understand German too?" Her blood chilled when Ryder winked. Joke was on her.

"Thanks for bringing her. I owe you," James said as Ryder made his way to the entrance.

Ryder laughed. "Ja sind Sie richtig!"

She and James studied each other in silence until the door slammed shut. Lana shifted her weight from foot to foot, trying to ease the pinch from her too tight shoes. "What did he say?"

"He said 'you're right'."

"So...how is it you both speak German?"

James shrugged. "My grandfather was from Germany. My family kept up the language and traditions. I didn't know Ryder spoke German until now."

"It's his fault I'm here," she lied quickly. "I had every intention of following your commands. No stepping foot in the clubhouse. No going near Rex. But as luck would have it, Jackie and I decided to go to summer Oktoberfest on the exact same day as Hades. Can you believe it?"

His scowl returned. So cute. "No."

Lana forced her mouth into a frown. "You never were very trusting."

"You never could lie to me," he said dryly.

"I tried not to look at Rex," Lana continued. "And I told Ryder I'd been forbidden to come to the clubhouse on pain of death. He insisted. He said you would want to see me. You're lucky to have such a good friend."

He folded his arms and his deep voice chilled. "You're lucky I wasn't there."

"I was thinking that myself." She lifted her gaze and froze. His mouth was a straight, thin line. Jaw tight. Eyes cold and hard. Maybe she had pushed him too far. Maybe he truly was done with her. Maybe he had someone upstairs…

Suddenly, she lost her nerve. "Actually, I had something to tell you and then I thought I'd head home. Get some sleep. Prepare for my day tomorrow that doesn't involve this case, Rex or Hades."

"Upstairs."

Lana's knees trembled. "Pardon me?"

"Now." His body was tense, his face taut, the pulse at the base of his neck throbbing. A man about to lose control.

She drew in a ragged breath. If it was over, he would be sending her outside, not upstairs. His bedroom was upstairs. And his bed. And there was a door they could close. Hope flared in her chest. She prayed he had a drawerful of condoms because she hadn't come prepared.

"Lana." The authoritative look on his face and his unyielding tone made everything inside her turn liquid.

"James?" She shivered uncontrollably as a thrill of fear coursed through her body, unleashing an endorphin rush like nothing she had ever experienced before.

"Last time. Upstairs."

"Or what?" she breathed, eyes wide with anticipation. His merciless smile almost made her come right then. "Do you really want to test me?"

Yes!

No. Her rational mind reminded her they were alone in the clubhouse and he seemed to be a tad annoyed. And this wasn't the James she knew. This was Ice. Rough, unpredictable and unrestrained.

With a sigh, she held her hands in the air. "Fine. I surrender. I'll go upstairs."

He grunted his approval. "Walk slowly. I want to watch your ass under that skirt."

And just like that her tension disappeared. Her lips curled into a smile. No man could resist a woman in a dirndl skirt, and James apparently even less than most.

"Nice." She stomped up the stairs, feigning annoyance, her Mary Janes announcing her presence with each clanging step.

"It certainly is. Especially from here."

She looked back over her shoulder and spotted James at the bottom of the stairwell.

"How juvenile." She snorted her derision. "I thought only teenage boys hid under the stairwell to peek up girls' skirts."

He gave her a salacious look and took the stairs two at a time to join her at the top. "Where do you think I learned my skills? I knew one day I would want to look up a milkmaid's skirt, so I made sure I had lots of practice."

"I'm not a milkmaid," she huffed. "I'm a frisky *fräulein*."

James pushed open the door to his room and ushered her inside with a firm hand against her back. "Well, frisky *fräulein*, you disobeyed my order to stay away from Rex and the clubhouse." He slammed the door closed and slid the bolt with a loud thunk. "You're going to need all that friskiness to pay the price for your disobedience, and I promise it's going to be high."

Breathless with anticipation, Lana forced herself to focus on the real reason she had come and backed up against the wall, out of his reach. "Before any prices are paid by frisky *fräuleins*, I have something important to tell you. There's a mole in the DEU. He's reporting to some guy who has met with Rex a few times. The guy told Rex there's a rat in Hades. He offered to give a name for a price but Bones said it was you. Rex isn't sure. He's setting up a trap to catch the rat himself. He said it was on an island…Kirkland, I think."

Other than a slight widening of the eyes, James appeared remarkably unperturbed. "I knew there had to be a mole. Every time I called in about a possible raid opportunity something went wrong. And Bones hasn't made any effort to hide his suspicions about me. I've been waiting for them to set some kind of trap."

Lana deflated. "I guess I didn't need to risk your wrath after all."

"You came to warn me." His eyes warmed and he closed the distance between them. "Don't think I don't appreciate it. It goes some way toward mitigating your otherwise unacceptable behavior."

He leaned his forearm against the wall, blocking her view of anything except him. She closed her eyes and breathed in his scent, raw and masculine, leather and grease, with an ocean-breeze chaser.

"That's a shame," she whispered. "I was hoping we might put this frisky *fräulein* outfit to good use." She bit her lip and whispered, *"Willst du mit mir schlafen gehen?"*

Her request for sex didn't meet with the expected response. James scowled and an angry rumble rolled through his chest.

"Did someone at Oktoberfest say that to you?"

Lana's cheeks burned and she bit her lip. "Mmmm-hmmm. Some guy outside the restroom. My friend Hans translated it for me."

"You will never wear that outfit again, except in front of me. Is that clear?" He traced her lips with his thumb, then gently parted them. Lana's insides quivered and she trembled.

"Crystal." Warmed by his smile, Lana leaned up and tentatively brushed her lips over his. "You didn't give me an answer."

"That's because I don't have to." In one swift, sudden motion he lifted her arms, pinning them over her head with one hand. His body pressed against hers, trapping her against the wall, his answer evident in the hard ridge of his erection pressed tight against her stomach.

Lana shivered uncontrollably. James had been the only lover to understand this side of her, to see her need to yield but not submit. The first time he'd fully restrained her had been the first time she had really let go. It had been the first time she'd ever trusted anyone enough to give up control. It had been the last night they'd been together.

A shudder racked her body. Too much. Too far. Too fast. They no longer shared that level of trust. Not even close.

"James..." Her words caught in her throat.

Somehow, he understood. Dropping her wrists, he leaned in and kissed her softly on the lips. "It's okay."

"It's not okay." She bit her lip and drew in a ragged breath, remembering as she did the picture in his dresser drawer. "And it's not just that. I can't do this. You have someone. It's not...right."

Chest heaving, James pulled back and frowned. "I'm not seeing anyone."

Her face flushed. "The girl. In the picture. In your drawer. I was looking around." She grimaced and her cheeks reddened.

His mouth tightened and pain reflected in his eyes. But only for an instant. "She died ten years ago."

Oh God. That's what she got for snooping. Her heart swelled, ached. "I'm so sorry. I didn't mean to bring it up."

"We'll just add it to your list of misdeeds," he said softly, his lips curving in a smile. He stroked the bloom of her cheek with his thumb. "Such a gentle heart for such a frisky *fräulein.*"

Before she could take a breath, he had her face between his palms, his lips on her lips, claiming her gently, driving away her every thought but the desperate need to have him inside her.

She melted into him, welcoming the hardness of his body and the long, demanding caress of his tongue. How many hours had she tossed and turned, remembering their wild nights together, his firm hands stroking their way over her curves, his tongue easing the ache between her thighs?

"You are impossible to resist at the best of times..." he murmured against her lips, his voice raw and husky with need, "...but in this outfit..."

She arched into him, offering herself to the soothing stroke of his hands. He cupped her breast, squeezing gently as he circled his thumb around her nipple through her clothing, drawing it to a tight, hard peak. Desire licked through her body and she burned for the moment he would be inside her.

She hooked her leg around his calf and pulled herself tight against him, rubbing the curve of her sex over the erection straining beneath his jeans, her core tightening at the exquisite sensation.

"No." He gently detached her and stepped back, leaving her confused and breathless, aching.

"There is a price for disobeying the rules." He reclined on the bed and folded his arms behind his head. "Strip."

Still reeling from his sudden withdrawal, Lana just stared.

"Babe, you're racking up the penalties like there's no tomorrow. I said *strip.*"

"Excuse me?"

"Everyone at Oktoberfest got a show. Hades got a show. Now it's my turn. You can start with the cap and work your way down." His eyes glittered fever-bright. "Once you're naked, I'll decide what to do with you."

"You'll decide?" Nervous excitement ratcheted through her.

He waved her toward the foot of the bed. "I'll decide."

She stared pointedly at the bulge in his jeans. "Seems to me part of you has already decided."

He gave her a warning look that sent quivers of need straight to her core. "Seems to me there's something you want and you know what you have to do to get it."

Of all the...

Her hands found her hips. "You think I can't just walk away?"

"Babe, I don't think you want to walk away. And neither do I."

Chapter Twelve

A thrill of fear shot through Lana's veins.

"How about we just have sex? I'm up for that. And apparently so are you. Right here. Right now. No foreplay needed. I don't even need a call tomorrow. No strings attached. Just a good old roll in the hay, or against the wall, or even on the bed. Your choice."

He gave her a measured look. "What are you afraid of? I know what's under that sassy little dress," he rumbled. "Seen it all before. Want to see it again. But slow and sexy like."

Her heart thudded in her chest and her stomach clenched. "I'm not afraid. It's just...too..."

Intimate.

How could she tell him that? Sex, she could do. Raw, physical, need-slaking sex. But the last time she'd stripped for him, her heart had been full to bursting. She had wanted to make him as happy as he made her—do something to give him as much pleasure as he gave her.

She sighed. "I can't."

He studied her for a long moment and then a glint of mischief lit his eyes. "I'll make you a deal. If you strip for me, I'll strip for you."

She snorted her amusement. James? Decorated homicide cop. Badass biker. Dancing around the room? Stripping for her? She couldn't even picture it in her mind. "Sure you will."

"You have my word. As fast or as slow as you want." His intense, steady gaze gave her pause.

"Seriously?"

His eyes crinkled when he smiled. "Seriously."

"Okay." She couldn't pass up the opportunity, no matter how much her heart protested.

"You want music?"

Lana swallowed, nodded. "Music is good. It's easier if I have something to focus on other than your lascivious grin. I like..."

James chuckled, cutting her off. "I know what you like." He flipped through his iPod and placed it in his iPod dock on his bedside table.

"You've changed," she said as she waited for the music to start. "You've become rougher. Also unrestrained, unpredictable, uncontrolled and, strangely, more relaxed."

"Seems to me you like rough and unrestrained." The deep, sensual timbre of his voice made her bones melt.

"Maybe we should just forget the deal and..."

James's eyes softened. "Babe, I fucking ache with wanting you. But it's been a long time and I want to enjoy your body. So strip for me. Nice and easy. Then we'll see where we go from there."

Her body thrummed with desire. When they had been together, she'd wondered if he could actually bring her to orgasm with just his words and the seductive tone of his voice. Now, she was pretty sure he could.

The first notes of Danzig's "She Rides" tugged her lips into a smile and for the first time since stepping into the clubhouse she felt some of her tension slide away.

"You remembered."

His eyes glittered. "I remember everything about you."

Twenty minutes and several repeats of "She Rides" later, Lana posed at the foot of the bed, breathless, wearing nothing but her stockings. "Last thing," she murmured. "Play it again, James." She couldn't believe how easy it had been. Maybe it was the alcohol still in her system, or maybe it was the music, or maybe his obvious enthusiasm and encouraging words had broken through her reserve.

"Leave them on."

She looked up slowly, gazing over the muscular chest, his corded neck, his jaw dark and prickly with a five o'clock shadow, and his firm lips curved into a smile.

"Please don't tell me you have a fetish for milkmaid stockings with big black bows."

"Too fucking sexy to take off." He pointed at the wall behind her. "Over there. Hands against the wall. Legs apart."

Caught in his gaze, her heart pounded. "You gonna frisk me, Officer Hunter?"

James pushed himself off the bed. "I'm gonna do something to you, babe, and it's not frisking. Now run."

Lana ran. Heart racing, she took the required position. A drop of liquid arousal dripped slowly down her thigh and she lowered her hand to brush it away.

"Don't move."

He gathered her hair into a ponytail and dropped it over her shoulder. One hand slid around her body to cup her breast and he rolled her nipple gently between his thumb and forefinger, sending zings of pleasure through her veins. His other hand feathered down her neck and along her spine. By the time he reached the cleft in her buttocks, violent trembles shook her body. She drew her thighs together, seeking even the slightest sensation to ease her aching clit.

"Mine to touch," he breathed in her ear. He gently kicked her legs apart and she whimpered her pleasure.

His hands glided over her skin, skimming over her shoulders, curving around her breasts, in and out of her waist, and over her hips. He slid his fingers into the elastic of her stockings and followed them around her thighs, his fingers cool against her heated skin.

"Won't last long if I have to look at you in those fuck-me

stockings."

Her breath caught in her throat and everything below her waist tightened. "Fuck-me stockings?"

"Every man's wet dream. Ryder must have had a fit when he saw you dancing on the table."

Lana turned around, dropping her hands. "They don't look very sexy to me."

"You're not a guy. And on you, with those legs... Christ. I can't believe the Hades crew wasn't all over you."

Lana smiled and ruffled her hand through his hair. "I like it when you talk dirty."

"Hands on the wall," he barked. Lana spun around and he covered her with his body, pressing himself against her as he positioned her hands. His thigh pressed between her legs and she angled herself to rub her throbbing clit against his jeans.

He fisted her hair and tugged her head back against his shoulder. "What did I say?"

"Yours to touch," she whispered as moisture flooded her pussy. "Please...James...touch."

"Not yet."

She grunted her displeasure. "I thought you were supposed to strip for me."

He pressed his lips to the sensitive skin of her neck, his hands cupping her breasts, fingers pinching her nipples, his thigh pressed tight against the curve of her sex. "You want me to stop and strip, babe?"

Lana's head fell back and she groaned. "No. Yes. I want your clothes off. Now."

"Turn around then." He backed away and she spun in a slow circle to face him. Her skin heated under his quiet perusal, her sex tightening as his gaze fell to the red curls at the juncture of her thighs, and then back to her face.

"God, you're beautiful," he rasped.

"And you're still dressed."

He gave her a wicked grin. "How do you want it?"

His words sent a tremor of excitement through her and suddenly she couldn't wait. She wanted him with a desperate ache that seared her to the core.

"Hard. Fast. Now."

He rumbled a laugh and tugged off his T-shirt, baring his lean, muscular body for her viewing pleasure. His fingers found their way over slim hips to the waistband of his jeans. With a quick yank, he unfastened the buttons and peeled them open. Lana's heart skipped a beat. Oh God. Now that he was a biker, he was going commando. No wonder he'd switched to a button-fly.

Slowly, he slid the jeans down long muscular thighs before letting them drop and kicking them to the side.

Lana's mouth went dry as she studied his perfect body. He was more defined than she remembered, his muscles smoother and less corded. But his shoulders and chest were just as broad, his hips just as narrow, and his powerful thighs still lean and tight. And his cock...

She licked her lips and gazed down at his erection, thick and ready, jutting from its nest of soft, dark curls. She couldn't tear her eyes away. So much bigger than she remembered.

"I think I got the better end of our deal," he murmured.

Her body tightened. "I'm not sure I agree."

Satisfaction creased his face and his firm mouth closed over hers, taking possession so quickly she was caught off guard. He licked along the seam of her lips and then thrust his tongue into her mouth as he cupped her sex, brushing his palm gently over her curls.

Her throat tightened. Her every breath seared her lungs as he slid his fingers through her folds.

"You're so wet for me." He held up his fingers so she could see them glistening with her need.

On impulse, Lana grasped his hand and leaned forward, drawing his fingers into her mouth, tasting her salty sweetness on her tongue. James groaned, his body tensing as she slid her lips up and down his fingers.

"Babe..."

Ignoring the warning tone in his voice, she sucked harder, licking his fingers, swirling her tongue over the tips until a moan broke from him.

"Christ." He wrenched his fingers away and slammed her hands against the wall. Pleasure crashed through her like a tidal wave, silencing the warning that had made her stop him only a short time ago.

"I've gotta have you now, babe," he rasped. "Hard and fast like you want and you are not going to move." The commanding voice, the knowledge he could keep her pinned to the wall, melted her inside.

Cupping her ass, he lifted her until she could wrap her legs around his waist, and then he anchored her against the wall and captured one nipple in his mouth.

As he sucked and laved her nipple into a tight, hard peak, the room heated past bearing and sweat trickled down her back. He teased one nipple, and then the other, until her breasts swelled to the point of pain and her body arched against the wall. Her sex throbbed in time to the beating of her heart and a violent tremor of need shook her body.

What happened to hard and fast?

"You have beautiful breasts," he murmured. "I could play with them all night."

Lana frowned. Not what she wanted to hear. "James..."

He arched an eyebrow and then slid his hand between them, trailing his fingers through her folds, drawing a gasp from her that made him chuckle.

"That close?"

She stifled a whimper as his fingers teased her entrance,

never venturing where she wanted them to go. She rocked her hips against him and he slowly pressed one finger up inside her. White-hot lightening streaked through her body and her sex clenched tight around him.

None of her lovers had made her respond like this. Nor had they ever taken such care to pleasure her. She wanted to cry that the one man who knew her body so well didn't know her heart.

James grunted with satisfaction and slid his finger out, then added a second and pushed in deeper until she mewled with pleasure.

"That's it, babe. I need you ready for me because I'm not going to last long."

"If you keep doing that, neither will I," she moaned.

"Good." His thumb slid up and around her clit, teasing but never touching, until her muscles burned with tension and her body was strung taut like a wire.

His mouth returned to torture her nipples as his thumb rubbed up one side of her clit and then down the other. Her clit seemed to engorge, the need for release almost painful. She wiggled against the erection pressed firmly against the side of her thigh, trying to ease him inside of her.

"Don't move." He slapped her bottom and the sharp sting shot straight to her clit.

Desire screamed through her body. Her head fell back against the wall and she groaned. "You never did that before."

"You didn't need it before."

Her sex clenched. How could such innocent words be so damned arousing? And why was his slap more pleasure than pain?

He released her to grab a condom from his dresser. The crinkle of the wrapper brought her back to reality long enough to tell him she was still on the pill.

He shook his head as he sheathed himself. "I'm not a saint,

babe. Better to be safe."

A shiver ran down Lana's spine and her arousal dropped with the speed of a skydiver in freefall. *Nice.* While she had been pining away, he was out fucking anything that moved. She stiffened, but before she could push him away, the head of his cock pressed against her swollen entrance, making her sex pulse and her clit throb.

Suddenly she didn't care. Saint or no saint, she wanted him, needed him to slake her lust, just once, and then he would be out of her system and she could walk away.

"Are you ready for me?" he rasped, lifting her again, his hands tight on her ass. He didn't wait for her answer. Instead, he brushed the head of his cock over her clit, shooting her right to the edge in a heartbeat. Her legs tightened around him and her fingers dug into his shoulders.

"Oh God. Don't tease," she breathed. "I can't wait anymore."

James eased his thick shaft between her folds, filling her, stretching her, but slowly, too slowly. She moaned and levered herself down, taking him inch by hard, thick inch, until he was completely inside her.

"That's it," he rasped. "Take all of me." He pulled back and eased inside her again, the slide of his hot, heavy cock almost exquisitely painful against her swollen tissue.

He slid out again and, without warning, he gripped her hips and hammered into her, finally making good on his promise. When she keened against his shoulder, he slid his hand between them and brushed his finger over her clit. Lana gasped. Too much sensation. Her body coiled tighter and tighter. James thrust harder and deeper. Finally, everything inside her exploded outward in wave after wave of excruciating pleasure.

James pumped up and down as her orgasm rippled through her. His hands tightened around her waist, his body stiffened, and then he came with a low, guttural groan, his cock pulsing in time to the last waves of her climax.

As they came down from the ride, he wrapped his arms around her and closed his eyes, resting his forehead against hers. For a long moment neither of them moved, breathing as one, their hearts drumming together. Finally, he kissed her gently and pulled out, then carried her to bed before going to the bathroom to dispose of the condom.

Lana lay back and stared at the ceiling, sated, dazed and discontent. Confused. She felt the bed dip as James climbed up beside her, and immediately pushed herself up, desperate for a moment alone to calm the maelstrom of thoughts and emotions swirling through her head.

"I'm just going to wash up." She was halfway to the washroom before she remembered he'd used a condom.

I'm not a saint. His words taunted her. He had no regrets about leaving her. He'd probably just hopped out of her bed and into another.

She slammed the bathroom door and leaned against the sink, staring into the mirror as regret chased the last remnants of arousal from her body.

What had she done?

It had taken so long to get over him, so many tears to mend her shattered heart. And now, here she was, back with the one man who had hurt her the most. Her earlier uncaring bravado now seemed foolish to the extreme. She couldn't separate the emotional from the physical. She couldn't just have sex and walk away. She'd done that with Levi and it had almost killed her. If she let James in and he hurt her again, she would never recover.

She scrubbed her hand over her face. It had to end now...before she got hurt again. They'd had their fun. Now she had a job to do, and so did he.

The door opened, as she knew it would. Part of his

attraction had been his sixth sense about her emotional disquiet, even if she wasn't in the room.

She watched him in the mirror as he stood behind her, his eyes searching, his brow furrowed. He'd put on his jeans, but his chest was bare and sported four painful-looking red scrapes from her fingernails.

Eyes still on hers, James trailed his hand along her spine, stopping at the mark in the center of her lower back. Although it looked like an ordinary tattoo, it was anything but. Lucky for her he didn't know what it really was.

"James...please. You know I don't like to be touched there."

He knelt down behind her and pressed a kiss to the stylized interlocking black *S* and *W*. Lana's stomach heaved and bile rose in her throat. She turned away, pressing the disgusting mark against the sink. Once she got her pictures to Angel and collected her fee, she would be rid of it forever.

Rising to his feet, James stroked a finger along her cheek. "What's wrong?"

Unable to wade through her confusion, incapable of vocalizing her disquiet, she sucked in her lips and looked away.

He cupped her jaw and turned her face. "Babe? Talk to me."

"I have to get going," she said hoarsely. She covered his hand with her own and drew it away from her cheek. "I have to work in the morning. This was...fun, but now it's over."

"Not to me."

"No?" she asked bitterly. "With all the women you've fucked since you left me, I'm surprised. I thought I'd just be another notch on your *unsaintly* belt and you'd be impatient to move on."

His hand froze in midair. "Is that what this is about? You're upset I slept with other women?"

She pressed her lips together and exhaled loudly. "Of course not. Why would I care? We were...are done. I'm sure you'll have someone new in your bed tomorrow."

"Lana..." He choked off his words when she pushed past him, but not before she saw the hurt in his eyes.

Well, he wasn't the only one hurting.

She grabbed her clothing off the floor. As she searched around for her bra, James leaned against the dresser and scraped his hand through his hair. "Where did this come from? One minute we're having a good time; the next, you're running out the door."

Her lips thinned. "It was a good time. With you, it's always a good time. But I think we both know it has to be the only time. You don't need complications in your life and neither do I."

She slipped on her bra and panties, and unscrunched her blouse. The door rattled and she froze, her heart skipping a beat.

"Ice. Need to see you. Now."

Lana sucked in a sharp breath at the sound of Rex's gruff voice. "They never leave you alone, do they? Am I not supposed to be here?"

"You're supposed to be anywhere I am," he growled. "But stay inside, just to be safe."

James slipped on a shirt and opened the door. But before he could step outside, Rex pushed his way in.

Lana gasped and spun around to face the wall. Only then did she remember her tattoo.

Damn.

She spun back and covered herself with her shirt. It had only been a few seconds. Not long enough for him to see or even process what it was, if he even knew the mark at all.

Rex's eyes widened and he gave her a curious stare.

Damn. Damn. Damn. Lana's heart pounded and sweat beaded on her brow. He had seen it. Recognized it. Darkness sheeted her vision. She was doomed.

Her stomach became a boiling, seething quagmire. She would have to leave—her business, her apartment, Jackie, her friends.

And James.

New name, new town, new life. All over again.

James walked Lana and Kickstand out to the parking lot. One of a prospect's duties was to act as the designated driver for all club outings, which meant poor Kickstand, as the newest prospect, rarely got to drink on social occasions.

It also meant James didn't have to take Lana home. He could hide behind the excuse that Rex needed to see him right away and take the time to get his head straight. An hour's ride across the city with her soft, sweet body pressed up against him would put him right back where he started when he'd walked into the lounge and seen her in that outfit. If Ryder hadn't been there, they would never have made it up the stairs.

He could see himself falling for her all over again. Their sexual chemistry was undeniable. And after their heated encounter, he was headed straight back into the maelstrom of passionate intensity that had characterized their relationship.

Her sudden retreat had been the slap he needed. After all, nothing had changed. He couldn't handle their relationship before, why would he be able to handle it now? Especially when the risk to her life was as great as the risk Christine had faced. And look how that had turned out.

So why had he been so quick to deny it had been a mistake?

"I'm sorry about the barbeque," Kickstand said in a low voice only James could hear. "I was waiting outside the restroom for Lana when Rex came out of his office and told me to grab a couple of beers while he went to get Portia. When I came back, I couldn't find Lana and he told me to stand guard at his door."

"Just make sure she gets home safe tonight."

He gave Lana a perfunctory kiss on the cheek. "Nothing has changed," he whispered in her ear. "I don't want to see you at the clubhouse or anywhere near Rex. I can't maintain my cover if I have to look out for you. Going to Oktoberfest was flat out dangerous. If Ryder hadn't been there, Rex wouldn't have left you alone."

She tightened her jaw and pulled on her helmet. Her eyes darkened, hardened, and he caught a flicker of pain. Something he'd said? Or hadn't said?

"Don't worry," she said softly. "You won't see me again."

Not what he wanted to hear, in more ways than one.

Chapter Thirteen

"Don't panic."

Lana yanked an armload of *I Heart Thrash* T-shirts from her drawer and dumped them into her suitcase on the bed beside her worried best friend.

"I'm not panicked." Lana opened another drawer and tossed random socks onto the bed. "I'm leaving. I have to get out of town. Fast."

"Lana, honey. This is me." Jackie slammed the suitcase closed, leaving Lana with an armload of jewel-colored thongs and nowhere to put them. "You can tell me anything. I won't tell anyone and maybe I can help."

Tears prickled the backs of Lana's eyes. "I've been through this before. No one can help me."

"What about James?"

"No." Lana bit her lip, fighting back a wave of emotion. "This is all his fault. If he hadn't...seduced me..." Cutting herself off, she tossed the panties on the floor and collapsed on the bed.

Jackie snorted a soft laugh and ran a soothing hand down her back. "I'm supposed to be the drama queen. It takes two for a seduction and, knowing your history together, I have a feeling you were a full and enthusiastic participant."

Lana shrugged, keeping her face pressed into the cool silk comforter. "I may not have been as discouraging as I could have been," she mumbled into the bed. "The minute I'm near him I lose the ability to think rationally. And when he touches me, that's pretty much the end of the line for my self-control."

Stretching out beside her, Jackie propped her head on her elbow. "If you had pushed him away, then I would have serious concerns about your mental health. That man is hot with a capital H-O-T. Not just hot. He's hot for you."

Lana drew in a ragged breath and rolled off the bed. What should she pack next? Jeans or hoodies? What would the thrash scene be like in a smaller city? Could she fit in, in her fug boots?

"I thought so too until he told me he's not a saint. So unsaintly, in fact, we had to use a condom to protect me from the myriad diseases he may have picked up from the dozens, maybe even hundreds, of women he's slept with since he left me."

"So he's safe." Jackie shrugged. "You can't hold it against him. And he's a guy. He can have sex with no emotional attachment. Maybe he just needed to blow off some steam."

"You're defending him," Lana grumbled. She flipped open the suitcase and retrieved her panties from the floor, tossing them one by one onto the bed. "I can't believe you're defending him. Over me. Your best friend. Well, you'll be disappointed to know I realized right away our mind-blowing sexual encounter was a mistake and I told him as much. I can't have sex with James without emotional attachment. I can't even have coffee with James without emotional attachment. I almost had a breakdown in his bathroom after it was over."

"You should have called me."

Lana rolled her eyes. "That would have gone down well. Me, naked in the bathroom, having a relationship discussion with you while he stomps around outside, loses it and kicks in the door."

Jackie gave her a wry smile. "The whole door-kicking thing is all kinds of hot."

"You're defending him again," Lana snapped. "Not that it matters. I have no interest in getting hurt again and I have him out of my system now. I'll be able to ride that orgasm for a couple of months at least."

Jackie grinned. "I might have been jealous if I hadn't had some damn good sex with Ryder last night. I think I might be too wild for him though."

Lana squeezed the suitcase shut and fastened the latch. After heaving it to the floor, she joined Jackie on the bed, head propped on her elbow in a mirror image of Jackie's posture.

"Ryder's a biker, a full-patch member. He's involved in all sorts of crazy, illegal, dangerous activities. How can you be too wild for him?"

"He's not like other bikers, and I've known a few," Jackie said, her smile fading at some remembered pain. Not for the first time, Lana wished Jackie would confide in her, share the trauma that threaded its way through every aspect of her life. She suspected Jackie's fun-loving, irreverent nature hid something dark and serious. Something she couldn't even face herself. Maybe her penchant for disguises was another way for her to hide.

"There's something different about him," Jackie said quietly. "He's got heart."

"Sounds awful." Lana rolled her eyes. "Damn good sex, hot biker dude, and he has heart. Definitely don't sleep with him again. Too bad you didn't ask advice from your best friend."

A frown creased Jackie's brow. "Soon to be ex-best friend if you run away. Who will I thrash with? Who will I get thrown out of bars with? Who else would appreciate my disguise emporium? What about our business? Tell me what happened. You never know, I might be able to help."

Emotionally exhausted and desperate to confide in someone, Lana capitulated with a sigh. "The tattoo on my back. It isn't just a tattoo. It's a...mark." Memories blanked her mind. Her hands fisted and a tear slid down her cheek.

"Lana, look at me." Jackie gently turned Lana's face toward

hers. "It's okay. Let me see it. It's been a long time since I saw it last. Maybe it's not as identifiable as you think. I've always just thought of it as a tattoo."

Lana rolled over and lifted her shirt and Jackie traced the mark lightly with her fingertips.

"What does it mean?"

"I can't tell you. Not because I don't trust you, but because it would be dangerous for you to know."

Jackie brushed Lana's hair back over her shoulder. "Why does it mean you have to run away? Does it link you to Levi?"

Lana nodded. "Rex saw it when he burst into the room. At least, I'm pretty sure he saw it. I did turn around pretty fast. But he gave me a look, like he knew what it meant. He just has to make one phone call, and I would disappear forever."

Jackie tilted her head and gave Lana a curious look. "Sounds very ominous. But how can you be sure he saw it or even knew what it was? Maybe he saw it and thought 'hey cool tat' or 'nice tramp stamp' or 'I want one of those'. Maybe he wanted to know who designed it so he can get one too. Maybe he has a tattoo fetish. Maybe he didn't see it, but he thought you were all kinds of hot standing in James's room, half-naked and all sexed up. You can't throw your entire life away on a guess."

Lana hesitated, hope blossoming in her chest. Jackie could be right. She had turned quickly. It had been an emotional moment. Could she have misread the look in Rex's eyes? Nothing had happened to her so far.

She sighed and collapsed on the bed. "God, I hope you're right. This is the happiest I've ever been. I love my work, Vancouver, my friends…you."

"I would have followed you," Jackie said, kissing away the rogue tear on Lana's cheek. "Since I have no family, you're all I've got, and I don't give up best friends so easily."

A hissed intake of breath from the doorway sent Lana

rolling off the bed and into a crouch on the floor. Heart thumping, she reached for her hidden baseball bat and lifted her eyes.

"James." She sagged against the dresser, even as she drank in his hard, muscular body encased in black leather and the black, kick-ass sunglasses hiding his eyes. Dark and dangerous. As usual. "What are you doing here?"

"I came to watch." James pushed up his sunglasses. "Continue as you were. Just pretend I'm not here."

"Did it ever occur to you to knock?" she growled.

"Not when I have a key." He held up a shiny gold key and Lana's blood boiled. She pushed herself up and popped the catch on the suitcase, then tossed a few clothes back into her drawers. Anything to keep her hands busy and not doing something violent and destructive like assaulting a police officer.

"You asked the locksmith to give you a key?"

He shrugged. "How else would I get in?"

Jackie flipped to her back and eased herself up on the pillow. "You two just crack me up. Don't mind me. I'm just going to lie here and watch the fur fly."

Lana glared at James. "I didn't offer you a key. I didn't invite you in. This is a private party so I think you'd better leave."

"Not if the party involves more of what was going down on the bed."

Jackie barked a laugh. "Sorry to disappoint, J—I'm gonna call you J because you just don't look like a James to me—but I don't share my sugar."

"Neither do I," he growled.

"I do believe he's threatening me." Jackie looked over at Lana who was tossing panties back into her drawer. "Your boyfriend is threatening me."

"He's not my boyfriend."

James caught a pair of green lace panties midtoss. "I remember these," he said, musing. "I thought I tore them off you."

Heart pounding, pulse racing, body tense, Lana snatched the panties from his hand. What the hell was he doing here? Hadn't she made it clear last night was the one and only night? Did he not get the message?

"I believe I uninvited you from my apartment," she said, her voice cold. "I don't see your feet moving."

Silence. She followed his concerned gaze to her suitcase.

"Are you going away?" He tapped the suitcase with his finger, and his voice rose from low to midrange. "Are you leaving because of me?"

"Don't flatter yourself." She sighed. "I have things to do and places to be. A life that doesn't involve you. If you recall, you made it very clear you didn't want to see me around the clubhouse again, which I took to mean around you."

"You're the one who said it was a mistake." James paced across the room. Although her bedroom wasn't small, he managed to take up almost all the space.

"And you're the one who didn't disagree," Lana snapped. "So now that we have that sorted, you can be on your way."

"Not until I find out if you're packing or unpacking. And if you're packing, where are you going?" He frowned and looked over at the bed. "Jackie?"

Jackie shrugged. "I have half a story and I'm sworn to secrecy. I can say she thought someone might be after her and I recommended she contact a certain police officer we know. However, I have since convinced her she might be delusional."

"Jackie." Lana gave her friend a warning glare.

All traces of humor disappeared from James's face. "Who's after you?"

Lana ignored him and continued to slam panties back into her drawer. Why was he here? They were done. He had made that abundantly clear by his silence after sending Rex out of his room. He had watched her dress, led her outside, warned her away and pecked her on the cheek. No discussion. No talking. No trying to convince her she was wrong. If that wasn't a brush-off, she didn't know what was.

"Lana, I want an answer. Now." The tone of his voice—forceful, commanding—touched the last of her raw nerves. She rounded on him, drawing in a deep breath as she prepared to berate him for daring to speak to her like that.

And then he kissed her. His firm mouth closed over hers, taking her so deeply, so swiftly, she melted into his arms.

Sweet. Gentle. Tender... Concerned.

Angry tears welled in her eyes. "I hate it when you do that."

Damn.

James tightened his arms around Lana's waist and plunged his tongue into her hot, wet mouth. Her body softened and her hands snaked around his neck, pulling him close. If Jackie hadn't been there he wouldn't have stopped with just a kiss.

Christ. This was exactly what he hadn't wanted. He had come to tell her she was right. They had made a mistake and the best solution was to stay apart. But because she was still on Rex's radar—Rex had made that clear in their meeting last night—James had come up with a plan to protect her. A way to keep her away from Rex and Hades.

Away from him.

A quick morning call and it had all been sorted. She would stay with Tony in his West Vancouver mansion until Rex was arrested in the raid James had been promised would happen soon.

But then he'd seen the suitcase.

The thought of her gone had fuzzed his brain. It didn't matter if it was for a weekend or a holiday, or even for business. His brain had registered Lana and gone, and his great plan had flown out the window. The potential threat Jackie had alluded to brought it all home. He couldn't walk away. He couldn't leave her. Not even in Tony's care. Not now.

Maybe not ever.

His phone buzzed in his pocket and he gently pulled away from her soft, sweet body and checked the caller ID. Ryder. He excused himself and headed for the kitchen to take the call.

They exchanged greetings and Ryder's voice tightened. "Rex wants the weapons for the brothers who'll be guarding an unexpected shipment coming in at the end of the week. Thought I'd give you a heads-up and we would arrange to meet to collect them."

Damn. He had appealed the confiscation multiple times, but in the end the DEU had decreed the danger to innocents was a bigger risk than the danger to James's life. Bitterness from that conversation still coated his tongue. He'd always been prepared to give his life in the line of duty, but he'd never expected to be a deliberate sacrificial lamb.

"I left them with a trucker buddy and he's out of town until next week. He didn't leave me with a key to his place. What does Rex need?" The prepared lie rolled off his tongue, unconvincing even to him.

"A couple of semis and a few pistols. He'll be fucking pissed if you don't bring them."

James scrubbed his hand through his hair. "I need a day to figure out how to get in touch with my friend."

Silence.

"Ryder?"

"Leave it with me. I'll get Rex what he needs."

James froze. No way could he let Ryder get dragged into this. "Appreciate it. But it's my mess. I'll handle it."

Ryder snorted his disagreement. "The way I see it, you saved my ass at least four times over the last two years: the police shootout in East Van, the botched drop on Vancouver Island, the night we went trunking and picked up the wrong guy, and the time Bones faked that evidence to try and prove I was a rat. I'm not even counting the times you covered for me when I had to go away or when I knocked heads with Rex. Consider it handled."

The phone went dead.

Damn. James pounded his fist on the wall. Except for Mark, who was almost like a brother to him, he'd never had a friend like Ryder: straight-up, loyal and damn good in a fight. Somehow he had to warn Ryder or get him out of the clubhouse before the raid. After being screwed around by the DEU one time too many, he no longer trusted them to heed the request in his report and let Ryder walk free.

He returned to the bedroom. Jackie and Lana were tossing clothes into her drawers with reckless abandon. He drew Lana to the side and stroked a finger along her soft cheek.

"Who's after you, babe?"

She shrugged and her lips twitched. "No one. Jackie convinced me I was just seeing ghosts."

Frowning, he studied her face, taking note of the shift of her eyes up and to the left. Finally, she dropped her gaze. Her long auburn lashes fanned out over smooth, creamy cheeks and her lips, pink, plump and glistening, tightened into a thin line.

"I can tolerate almost anything except lying." Especially from someone he cared about. Christine had lied and the wound was still with him. Maybe if she had been honest that day, she would still be alive.

"Given what you do for a living, that makes you a bit of a hypocrite." Lana's soft, sultry tone took the bite out of her words.

"That's different." He brushed his finger lightly over the

smattering of freckles across her nose.

"Don't touch my freckles." Big green eyes frowned at him through her tangled thicket of curls.

James brushed her hair away and pressed a gentle kiss to the tip of her nose. "I like your freckles."

"Well, I don't. So paws and lips off."

He dusted featherlight kisses over the remaining freckles on her cheeks, smiling when her eyes slitted closed and her cheeks flushed pink. His Lana was a sucker for a gentle caress.

"Hellllloooo," Jackie yelled. "Best friend across the room. Don't forget about me."

Lana's eyes flew open and she spun around. "You want him to kiss your freckles too?"

"He can kiss any part of me he wants." Jackie slid off the bed and walked toward them, swaying her hips and licking her lips.

James stiffened. He couldn't tell if they were playing him, but there was only one woman he wanted to kiss.

Jackie's eyes flicked to him and they shared a glance. He'd never looked at her closely before, but as he studied her face he saw a maturity that belied her age and her seemingly irreverent nature. For the briefest second, her mask slipped and he saw secrets hiding in the depths of her eyes, a lifetime of experiences a girl her age shouldn't have, and a world of pain. No wonder she and Lana were so close. Lana was a giver, a healer. And Jackie desperately needed to be healed.

"Well damn," she muttered, tearing her eyes away. "Guess I'll have to get my kisses somewhere else. And suddenly I'm not feeling very wanted. You want me to skip out, J? Leave you to your sugar?"

"Actually, I have to be at a race in an hour and I'm thinking it would be best if you both came along." He looked down at Lana and cupped her cheek with his hand. He had no doubt the suitcase meant a hell of a lot more than she was letting on, and her lack of trust hit him hard. But he wasn't about to walk away. Not when she was in danger. He would tease it out of her, and then he would find whoever had scared her and pound the crap out of him.

"Rex made it clear last night that he's not backing off," he said to Lana. "And now you've got me worried that something else is going on. I don't want to leave you alone but I have to race. Jackie can come and keep you company. If someone is after you, you'll be safer with Hades."

"Now there's an irony," Jackie said. "Safer with a gang of outlaw bikers."

"You could tell me what's going on..."

Lana stiffened. "It's nothing. Really. And don't even think about trying to pry it out of me."

Christ. Didn't she understand he *had* to know, just like he *had* to breathe? A danger so great she had packed a suitcase and prepared to run was a danger he needed to know about.

"Thanks for the offer but we're staying in tonight." Lana pulled away. "I've had enough of bikers. And it's probably better if we don't spend too much time together."

"What?" Jackie's voice rose in pitch. "We're staying in instead of going to watch a gang of bikers racing their crotch rockets around a track? Are you crazy? It will be one hell of a party."

"Jackie!"

"Give us a moment." Jackie gave James a reassuring wink before dismissing him with a flick of her fingers.

James walked through the living room and over to the window. He spotted Kickstand outside, guarding their bikes. Good kid. Too bad he'd fallen in with the wrong crowd. He would get a wake-up call when his biker worship got him five to ten in the local penitentiary, and he hadn't even been involved in any major crime. James sighed. Maybe he could save Kickstand too.

After five minutes, Jackie raced past him. "We're coming. Back in a minute. Stay out here." She returned a few minutes later with an armful of black leather.

Five minutes became ten, became twenty. James paced across the living room. If they didn't leave soon, they would be late. Rex wouldn't be pleased. And the way things were going between him and Rex, he couldn't afford another black mark against him.

Finally the bedroom door opened. His breath caught in his throat and his eyes widened.

Lana and Jackie had kitted themselves out in black leather from their stiletto boots to skintight pants, corsets to fitted jackets. Lana's glorious red curls spilled around her shoulders and over the creamy expanse of the swell of her breasts.

And he'd thought the milkmaid costume was hot...

No way was he allowing her at a Hades gathering dressed like that. No fucking way.

Jackie grinned at his scowling face. "Gotta dress the part. I keep some spare disguises in my trunk. This outfit was from the time I had to crash a *Grease* party. Lana's got her own reasons for having a closetful of leather."

Lana winked and posed for him. "What do you think?"

Christ have mercy. She was beyond tempting. "Change. Now."

Her face fell. "I thought leathers were appropriate attire for your old lady."

"Not those leathers." He struggled against his stirring lust. "They're too...tight and...leathery."

Lana's eyes sparkled with amusement, and she sauntered over to him, all fire and curvaceous charm. "I can move just fine. You want me to go with you, then this is what I'm wearing. If not, Jackie and I know a club where they appreciate a girl in leather."

James's scowl deepened. The thought of other men

watching her, touching her, set his blood to boil. A low growl escaped him and Lana's lips curled into a smile. "Does that mean I'm coming with *you*?"

He clenched his jaw and took a slow, deep breath. He didn't want another fight. Too much was happening: Rex, the weapons, the DEU not having his back, Bones and his suspicions. Too many things to worry about. He needed to know he had one thing under control. He needed Lana soft and sweet in his arms. And if that meant letting her parade around in skintight leather, he would choke back his jealous, protective side and keep his mouth shut.

But only once.

And he would make sure Ryder, Kickstand and Jackie stayed with her. Maybe Claw as well. Slider was always on the ball. And Spook...

And maybe he could find a burlap sack to put over her.

"That means you're going to pay for the stress you're going to cause me." He pressed a kiss to her forehead and clasped her hand. "Let's go. We brought extra helmets for the race. Might be a bit big but they should do the trick."

"We?" Jackie raised an eyebrow.

"Kickstand is outside. I had just planned to stop in for a few minutes before heading off to the race. You can ride with him."

Jackie grinned. "Oooo. The little golden boy. I'd like to get my claws into him."

"Last I heard you were with Ryder." James ushered them out and locked the door. Lana huffed and glared at his key. Well, she could huff all she wanted. No way was he giving it up. He needed to know he could get to her if she was in danger.

"It was just one night," Jackie groaned. "Seriously, have you never had a one-night stand?"

He shot her a warning glance and followed Lana down the stairs. As if he was going to answer that question with Lana nearby. Especially after last night.

"I think what James is saying is maybe Ryder thinks differently," Lana said over her shoulder. "And if he does, then he has to say it's over. In the biker world, if the guy doesn't say it's over, it's not over, and no one else can touch you until he does."

James frowned. No way was Lana getting this biker information from television.

"Jeez Louise." Jackie slapped her head. "I thought bikers were supposed to be anarchists, flouting the law, thumbing their noses at societal conventions. I'm beginning to think they have more rules than the real world has laws." She waved to Kickstand as they crossed the street and then blew him a kiss. "As you know, I'm not one for rules."

"Unfortunately, Kickstand has to be or he'll never get his patch," James said. "Talk it out with Ryder. He's not an unreasonable guy." Ryder had only briefly mentioned Jackie, and he had no idea what his friend thought of what had happened between them.

He helped Jackie mount up behind Kickstand and then held out a hand to help Lana.

"Babe. On the bike."

"Where did you get the V-Rod Muscle?" She ran her hand over the artwork on the back fender—an exact replica of the Hades patch. "Where's your Rocker?"

Hell, she even knew her Harleys.

"This one's better for speed."

"He won it in a poker tournament." Kickstand grinned. "He beat out everyone in Hades until it was just him and Bones left. Bones was out of cash but he thought Ice couldn't beat his straight flush. So he threw his bike into the pot."

Lana's hand flew to her mouth. "No." She looked over at James. "What did you have?"

"Royal flush."

Kickstand bounced on his seat, clearly eager to finish the story. "Bones accused him of cheating or counting cards. They had a big fight. Ice won. Bones never forgave him. He's hated him ever since. Bones went trunking the next day and got some cash to buy a new bike but it wasn't the same. He'd modded this one out and got that fancy artwork on the rear fender..."

Lana tilted her head to the side and studied the V-Rod. "It's a nice bike but pretty heavy. Might not be a match for the crotch rockets."

"You can judge for yourself when we get there. We're already late but we should still make the first heats." James circled his arms around her waist and lifted her onto the bike before swinging his leg over and taking his seat. He pushed in his earplugs and tugged on his helmet. Then he twisted around to give Lana a hand with her helmet.

"You weren't planning to stay more than a few minutes at my place tonight, were you?" she said as she snapped the strap into place.

His stomach clenched. *Fuck.* Last thing he wanted her to know was why he had gone to her apartment or what had changed his mind.

"James?" She tilted her head to the side and gave him a questioning look.

He tapped his helmet, pretending he hadn't heard her and then turned away to start the engine.

Some questions were better left unanswered.

Chapter Fourteen

The ride was torture.

Without the benefit of rear grab handlebars, Lana was forced to hold on to James for the entire trip. Already hot from his heated response to her leathers and the press of his muscled back against her breasts, the throaty rumble of the motor between her legs was almost as good as her rabbit vibrator, and far more arousing. By the time he reached the abandoned Surrey airstrip, she was almost ready to beg him to take her. Preferably over his mouthwatering bike.

The V-Rod Muscle was an exquisite piece of engineering. Built to Harley standards, but designed for speed, the V-Rod quickly changed her mind about its ability to keep up in a race against lighter, faster bikes when it roared down the Fraser Highway, leaving Kickstand to eat its dust.

Sex throbbing, pulse pounding, she slid off the motorbike after they pulled to a stop at the far edge of field and considered finding somewhere private she could relieve the ache between her thighs. She was so close to orgasm all it would take was the lightest of touches...

"Don't even think about it," James said softly, coming up behind her.

Lana whipped around, eyes wide, cheeks aflame. "What are you talking about?"

His eyes darkened. "I know that flush on your cheeks, babe. And I know what it means when your eyes turn that particular shade of green. I'll take care of you when I'm done tonight. He slid his hand between her thighs, cupping the curve of her sex, his touch at once possessive and arousing.

Shocked, aching, confused, her voice caught in her throat, "James..."

"You want me to stop?" he murmured, his hand still gently stroking over her leathers.

Desire raged through her like a tidal wave, sending her body from hot to raging inferno in a heartbeat. Where was her resolve? He was supposed to be out of her system. A distant memory. But the minute he'd walked into her apartment, she couldn't deny the sexual chemistry between them. She suspected he'd intended to end whatever was between them, but something changed his mind, and part of her—the stupid part—was glad he'd had a change of heart.

"No," she breathed, "but...I thought we decided not to do this anymore."

"If you want me to take you home after the race and walk away, I will." He pressed the heel of his palm over her throbbing clit. "But I won't pretend it'll be easy."

"How about we go home now? Or over there in the trees?" she said, her voice thick with desire. "Actually, I'm almost at the point where I don't care if anyone sees us. How about here, now, over your bike?"

He pressed harder, his palm tracing a slow, agonizing circle around her clit. Her body tightened. Her sex squeezed. She gripped his shoulders and teetered on the edge of climax.

Then he walked away.

A thin whine escaped her and James grinned over his shoulder as he headed across the field to the dimly lit racetrack.

"Bastard," she shouted, dipping her head so he couldn't see her smile.

James spun around to face her and winked. "You have no idea."

Half an hour later four motorcycles lined up on the tarmac

behind a chalky white starting line. Cars dotted the runway, their lights illuminating the worn pavement of the rough oval the bikers had created for the race. Hay bales were stacked in the corners and stolen traffic cones marked the edges of the track.

The summer air was fresh and warm, and the bonfires from the kindling-filled barrels in the spectator's area scented the air with the faint fragrance of cedar. Save for the orange glow of the city far in the distance, there were no lights visible from the field. No highways. No cars. No houses. No towers. They were in their own dark, dangerous world lit by fire and moonlight and the warm yellow glow of headlights.

The Hades crew had come prepared to party. Pickup trucks filled with beer kegs and snacks dotted the field. Bikers and their old ladies greeted Lana with warm welcomes and plastic cups filled with warm beer. While James prepped his motorcycle, Lana chatted with the people she knew and made a few new friends. Although a part of her was still wary about being around the bikers, she didn't feel like she was acting a part. Here, tonight, she was Ice's old lady and the knowledge warmed her from head to toe.

Of course he had put a watch on her. She was acutely aware of Ryder shadowing her every move. Kickstand had intervened when a drunken Diesel had fingered her curls. Spook and Slider flitted in and out of the crowd, appearing instantly at her side if anyone so much as brushed against her shoulder. She felt perversely safe.

Except from Rex.

Although she had only caught a glimpse or two of his blond ponytail and broad shoulders over the course of the evening, she felt his eyes on her everywhere she went. Had he recognized the tattoo? Jackie had put enough doubt in her mind to keep her from running, but she couldn't afford to totally drop her guard.

She patted her pocket, checking to make sure her new

minicam hadn't fallen out during the ride. Jackie, a self-taught electronics expert, was still trying to retrieve the pictures of Rex and Portia from her lipstick camera. If Jackie hadn't pointed out the race was yet another opportunity to get the pictures she needed for Angel, Lana would never have come. Not even for the chance to dress up in leather. But now that she was here, she was glad she had listened.

Lana joined a group thronged around Bones's pickup truck. Always the life of the party, Jackie was at the center of the crowd, laughing it up with Diesel and Tally. Ryder leaned against the tailgate, arms crossed, watching her, his eyes glittering with amusement. Every so often Jackie would glance in his direction and give him a shy smile.

Lana's heart gave a hopeful squeeze. Maybe it wasn't a one-night stand after all. Maybe Jackie had finally found *the one* she had always talked about finding.

Bones called the next heat, and Lana and Jackie ran over to the track to watch James race against Rex, Dawg and Punch. As they eased their motorcycles to the starting line, Jackie sighed.

"I'm not so keen on this lineup. I mean, Ice looks hot. But the others...meh. Maybe you should just tell me who wins and I'll go get another beer."

Lana laughed. "The race will be between Rex and Ice. Dawg and Punch are riding stock crotch rockets with a lot of fairing but no real staying power. Dawg's Honda VFR is good for speed but not against James's modded V-Rod or Rex's brand-new Kawasaki Ninja. Punch's weight will slow him down on that Ducati."

Jackie shook her head. "You sure can talk the talk. All these years you've been holding out on me. Don't tell me you can ride too, because I used to have a motorcycle, and the idea of the two of us blazing through the mountains in our leathers makes me all warm and fuzzy inside."

She gave Jackie a half smile. "I can ride."

"Damn girl," Jackie shrieked and threw her arms around Lana. "We better get in some new cases. We've got some motorcycles to buy."

"Maybe you'll have a guy to ride with." Lana grinned and nodded toward Ryder standing not more than twenty feet away and engaged in a heated conversation with Bones.

Jackie blushed and looked away. "Maybe you will too."

Biting her lip to repress a smile, Lana ran onto the track. She handed James the green panties he had caught in her room. "For luck," she whispered. James tucked them into his jacket, and then he pulled her against him for a long, deep kiss. The crowd cheered and Lana's cheeks heated, but for the first time she didn't mind the bikers' attention. She was Ice's old lady and she'd done what old ladies do.

After Lana returned to the safety of the field, Portia, clad head to toe in red leather, waved the checkered flag and the race began. Rex had the inner curve. Good for psychology but sometimes bad on the knees, depending on how far he was willing to angle. James matched his speed and after one lap they'd left Dawg and Punch behind.

Ryder joined Lana and Jackie as the racers started the second lap. "Four laps to go. Winner of this heat advances to the quarterfinals. Been a long time since anyone challenged Rex. He buys a new bike for each race, but Ice's V-Rod is heavily modded. It'll be close."

Lana gave him a sideways glance. "Did he ask you to watch over me?"

Ryder laughed. "No, darlin'. He didn't have to ask."

They watched the racers round the oval a third time. Dawg and Punch were now almost a full lap behind Rex and James. The roar of motors drowned out the excited murmur of the crowd. Lana's pulse raced and her mouth went dry. And to think she had almost missed this.

"I'm surprised there aren't any dirty tricks," Jackie said.

"We don't mess around on the bikes. We run our races with gentleman's rules." Ryder absently tucked Jackie's hair behind her ear and rested his hand on her shoulder. Jackie shot Lana a curious glance and her lips curled into a smile.

Lana caught a flash of red near the track and spotted Portia, looking furtively from side to side. Portia's arm jerked up, and the beam from one of the vehicle headlights illuminated a cluster of sparkly objects flying through the air. They hit the ground in James's lane just as Rex and James rounded the corner for the last lap.

"*Stop!*" Lana bolted across the field but even as her feet pounded across the grass, she knew she was too late.

James's front tire hit the objects and blew with a loud bang. The motorcycle somersaulted, throwing James over the handlebars and into a stack of hay bales at the corner, and then slid to a stop at the side of the racetrack. Dawg and Punch pulled their motorcycles to the side and ran over to help him.

Heart thudding in her chest, Lana reached the hay bales just as they tugged the helmet off a motionless James.

Lana's heart skipped a beat. *Nonononono.*

"Ja...Ice." She corrected herself quickly as she ran her hands down his body. "Talk to me."

"Roxie," he moaned. His hand waved through the air and she grabbed it and held it to her chest.

"I'm here."

"I need..."

A crowd had gathered around them, and Ryder and Kickstand struggled to hold the concerned onlookers back.

"What? What do you need?" Her throat tightened. Where would they get an ambulance out here? If he was seriously injured, how would they transport him in a pickup truck? Did anyone know first aid?

"I need you to lie on top of me and give me a kiss." He pulled her over his chest, cupped her face between his hands

155

and kissed her. Hard.

The crowd cheered. Lana pushed herself up, straddling his hips and glared.

"Jerk." Her hand sailed toward his cheek, but he caught it easily and pressed it to his lips.

"I thought you were seriously injured," she shouted, as her adrenaline found an outlet. "You scared me half to death."

James grinned. "I am seriously injured and there's only one cure."

Another attempt at a slap.

Another catch and kiss.

Lewd comments and catcalls echoed around them. Ryder and Kickstand dispersed the crowd. Rex joined them and helped James to his feet.

"What happened?"

"What happened?" Lana jumped up and rounded on Rex. "Portia threw something on the track. I saw her do it." She let loose a string of swear words in biker slang that would have sent her mama to her grave if she hadn't already died twenty years ago.

A hand clamped over her mouth and Jackie whispered in her ear, "If you are concerned he might have seen the tat, letting him know you can talk the talk might just jog his memory in the wrong direction."

Jackie dragged Lana backward and away from the shocked bikers. "I'm just gonna take Roxie and wash her mouth out with soap."

"How long were you with Levi?" Jackie asked when they were out of earshot. "You know more biker cuss words than most of the bikers here."

"Four years." She trembled as adrenaline continued to surge through her body.

"It took you four years to escape?" Jackie's voice rose in

disbelief.

Lana shook her head. "It took me three years to escape. The first year wasn't so bad. Levi was the leader of a small motorcycle club in Kelowna. I was sixteen and had dropped out of school. He was charming and exciting, although very insecure about me. He had big dreams. He convinced me to go with him to Seattle so he could pledge himself to a US motorcycle club. They used me to test him, and he did nothing to protect me. I realized then he'd never really loved me. And then they wouldn't let me go..."

She choked on her last words and Jackie wrapped her arms around Lana. "I'm so sorry, honey. I didn't mean to bring it all up."

"What's going on?"

Lana startled at the sound of James's voice directly behind her. She spun around and grimaced when she saw Rex beside him. Had they overheard?

"You need to come with us, babe. We're going to church."

"Church?" Jackie gave him a quizzical look. "You're going to church? Now?"

"Full-patch meeting," James said. "It's a cross between a courtroom, where Rex is law, and a board meeting where everyone gets a vote. Prospects, mamas, old ladies and guests aren't invited."

Rex studied Lana for a long moment. "But you are. I'm sure you know why." His cold, calculating smile sent a shiver down her spine.

Had she given herself away?

Rex held court beside the starting line and banished the nonpatch members to the far end of the racetrack. James gritted his teeth as Lana repeated her allegations. He knew damn well she wouldn't have accused Portia if she hadn't been

100 percent sure. But if Portia swayed the vote, Lana would have to pay the penalty for falsely accusing her. He couldn't let that happen.

After Lana finished talking, she answered questions from the group. How far away was she when she saw the objects? Did she see Portia throw them? Did she have any reason to be angry with Portia? Could she have made a mistake?

In answer to the last question, Lana pointed to the tack-studded tire and a handful of tacks she had picked up off the track on the way to the meeting. Hard evidence.

Lana's forthright answers and her willingness to admit to the occasional uncertainty garnered her many nods and smiles. Still, sweat trickled down James's back despite the cool breeze, and his heart thumped in nervous anticipation of what Portia might say.

"Don't worry." Ryder came up beside James and clapped him on the back. "No one's gonna back Portia over Lana. They know what Portia's like. They know the truth."

In the end, Ryder was right and Portia was banished from the club.

"You should be thanking me instead of condemning me," Portia spat after Rex told her to leave. "I was helping you win the race. I was showing you how much I care. You didn't have a chance against Ice."

Wrong thing to say. Rex's face turned multishades of purple.

"Get her out of here," he bellowed.

Portia spun around, turning the full force of her fury on Lana. "You fucking bitch. You were angling to be mama from day one. Well, it isn't all it's cut out to be. You're going to pay for this. You're going to be damn sorry you messed with me." She stalked over to Lana, hauled her elbow back and threw a punch at Lana's jaw.

James was running before his conscious mind had even

processed he'd moved, but by the time he reached them, Portia was on the grass with a furious Lana twisting her arm behind her.

"Never. Touch. Me. Again," she growled.

James gently pulled her away and Ryder escorted Portia to her motorcycle. The crowd booed, disappointed they'd been denied what had promised to be an exciting fight.

"You okay?" James slid an arm around Lana's waist and pulled her into his chest. More for his sake than hers. He was still riding high on the adrenaline rush from the accident and the overwhelming fear that she could have been hurt. He wanted nothing more than to take her away and hide out with her until he could be certain the world was safe again.

Damn protective instinct. He was in too deep and drowning fast.

Lana gave a noncommittal shrug. "Sure. I took a self-defense course and I've dealt with worse...in the bars with Jackie."

James frowned. Her slight hesitation suggested she'd encountered worse somewhere else. Yet another secret he would have to tease out of her. Why had none of these things come out during the six months they were together?

James nodded to the crowd heading back to the racetrack for the quarterfinal heats. "You won yourself some fans."

"I was a bit worried at first. I felt like I was Alice in Wonderland and any minute Rex was going to yell 'off with her head'."

He cupped her head and brushed a kiss over her hair. "I might have had something to say about that."

Lana looked over at the V-Rod and sighed. "I guess we'll have to catch a ride with one of the drivers. Your V-Rod doesn't look like it's going anywhere."

"Unbelievably, it's just cosmetic damage to the fairing, and Diesel has my spare tire in his truck. We might not look pretty going home, but we'll make it there."

No damn way was he waiting for a ride. His body burned with the need to hold her. He wanted to check every inch of her skin for bumps and bruises, assure himself she was okay. But more than that, he needed to be inside her to soothe the ache in his soul.

Mine.

While James and Kickstand fixed the tire and ran an engine check, Lana ran to find Jackie and make sure she had a ride home. No problem there. She had bikers falling all over themselves begging for the honor, Kickstand salivating at her feet and Ryder watching from the shadows.

Lana wove her way back through the crowd and into the parking area. A shadow crossed her path and she startled when someone caught her by the elbow.

"Hey, let go." She tried to pull away and looked up, only to see Rex's grim face.

"Wildcat. Been waiting a long time to get you alone." He tightened his grip, spun her around and pushed her up against a pickup truck, caging her with his body. For a long moment he just stared at her, gnawing on his bottom lip as if trying to make a decision.

The cloying stench of stale beer and pot assailed Lana's nostrils and she turned her head away and stared out over the empty field. Where was James? Or Ryder? Even Kickstand had abandoned her. What had happened to her League of Shadows?

"Can I do something for you?" Lana cringed the second the words left her mouth. Wrong thing to say.

Rex's eyes gleamed and he smiled. "You can and you will. I'm just trying to decide what you'll do first."

Lana swallowed. "Um...Ice is over there. Waiting. If I don't show, he'll come looking for me."

Rex trailed his finger up her throat, tilting her head back when he reached her chin. His eyes were black holes in the night sky. "We've played this game before, wildcat. We both know how it will end."

"With me leaving?" she squeaked.

"With you in my bed."

Lana's hands clenched and unclenched down by her sides as she tried to stay calm, but her heart pounded so hard against her ribs she thought they might break. "I'm flattered by your attention. But I thought you and Ice sorted that out. I'm his old lady."

"You have a choice," Rex murmured in her ear, his rasping breath hot and harsh on her skin.

"I choose Ice," she blurted out.

"That isn't the choice I'm offering." His voice took on a sinister tone. "And I think you know what I mean."

She drew in a ragged breath. "I have no idea what you're talking about."

"Oh, I think you do." He took a step back and Lana slid away from the vehicle and forced herself to walk—not run—away.

"Think about it," Rex called out. "There are far worse places to be than in my bed."

Lana's breath caught in her throat and a burst of adrenaline shot through her veins. Suddenly she didn't care about posturing or playing Ice's old lady. She didn't care if Rex knew he'd scared her. She didn't care about anything except getting the hell out of there.

Without a moment's hesitation, she kicked up her heels and she ran.

Chapter Fifteen

Lana rested her cheek against James's broad back as he raced the V-Rod through the night. Only the dim orange glow of streetlights and a sliver of crescent moon lit their way. The cool evening breeze tickled a path through the seams in her leathers, chilling her even more than she had been after her encounter with Rex.

Although she had thought she'd left the biker world behind, it had clearly left an indelible imprint on her soul. She'd slipped right back into the patter and the politics, as if she'd never been away. Big mistake. It had been easy to hide her past from James when she wasn't immersed in it. But now she'd raised his suspicions. And then there was Rex.

The motorcycle slowed and Lana peered around James's shoulder as he pulled off the road and drove toward a small grassy square almost totally hidden within a copse of trees. He parked out of sight of the road and tugged off his helmet. Lana followed suit.

"Why are we stopping?"

"Up here." He patted the seat and Lana maneuvered herself around his hips until she was straddling the bike in front of him.

"We're gonna play a game," he said coolly. "It's called ten questions. I ask. You answer. Usually the game is played with twenty questions, but I don't think I'll be able to hold out that long with you looking at me like you're needing something I'm burning to give."

Lana swallowed hard. She didn't know what secrets he was after and she sure as hell wasn't going to volunteer them.

Maybe a diversion...

She leaned up and brushed her lips over his. "I was kinda hoping we were stopping in the dark, romantic moonlit field for another reason," she breathed.

His gaze dropped to her mouth and his hand slid around her waist. She knew that look only too well. Maybe she would get away with no questions at all.

"In time." The heat dimmed in his eyes. "But I've been getting the feeling I don't really know you, and that problem needs to be remedied before I tie you to my bike and make you scream with pleasure."

"Modest."

"Always."

She bit her lip to suppress a smile. "Too bad it won't work. Tying girls to your bike is nice in theory, but not in practice."

James raised an eyebrow, and she sighed and patted his thigh. "You would have to balance me and the bike and..." she blushed, "...you know...perform."

"Never had a performance issue, babe. No matter where I was or what I was doing."

Lana snorted. "Good to know."

James gave her a curt nod and then settled her farther back on the seat. "Question one: How is it you know so much about bikers?"

Damn. She wasn't being seductive enough. She unzipped her jacket, dragging the zipper inch by inch over her chest as she considered her words. No lies, but lots of omissions. "I used to go out with a guy who was a biker. It was a long time ago."

James's eyes fixed on her hands as she pulled the jacket apart. She cupped her breasts over her leather corset, offering them up for his touching pleasure.

"I know what you're doing." His voice was hoarse, husky with need. "You're trying to distract me."

Lana glanced down at the bulge in his leathers. "Seems to be working."

He caught her hand as she reached down to touch him and shook his head. "Question two: the suitcase. It's been burning a hole in my brain. Who were you running from?"

She gritted her teeth and tried to think of something that wasn't a lie but that wouldn't send him raging on a suicide mission down to Seattle. "I thought I might have been recognized from the time I went out with the biker. I wanted to leave that...embarrassing part of my life behind me so desperately the thought of seeing anyone from those days freaked me out and I wanted to get out of town. Jackie convinced me I was overreacting."

She nibbled his bottom lip and frowned when he didn't open for her. Come on. She wasn't that bad at seduction.

James stiffened and pulled away. "Not done yet, babe. Dinner first, then dessert. Question three: What aren't you telling me?"

Lana groaned inwardly. She should've known. He wasn't one of the Lower Mainland's top homicide cops without reason, and she was already well acquainted with his interrogation techniques. But right now he would be expecting evasion, so she would give him honesty.

"Yes, there's more. But you don't need to know more. That Lana is gone. That past is past."

Well, not total honesty. Her past was still inked into her skin. She knew, without a doubt, she could never tell him what the mark meant. Aside from the utter humiliation, she might put him in a position that could compromise his assignment—or even his life—if he decided to jump on his motorcycle and ride down to Seattle, spoiling for a fight. Not only that, but Rex's comment had raised her uncertainty again. Had he seen the mark? Recognized it? Was the choice he offered really a threat?

She eased herself closer to James's broad, muscular chest

and leaned up to nuzzle his jaw, scratchy with a five o'clock shadow. James hissed in a breath, but this time he didn't pull away.

"I'm not done with the questions." His low, husky growl betrayed his desire.

Hands on his shoulders, she trailed her tongue over the seam of his lips. "I'm done with the answers."

"Babe." He grunted his disapproval and Lana sighed.

"Okay, one more."

His gaze slanted down at her. "Question four: What happened when you went to find Jackie? Something or someone scared you. I could see it in your face and your heart was beating a mile a minute."

Easy question. Easy to tell the truth. She stroked the soft curls at the back of his neck. Two years ago she would never have been able to imagine James with long hair. Now she couldn't imagine him without it.

"Rex caught me. He said he wants me in his bed." She shrugged off her jacket, thrusting her breasts out as it slid over her arms. Leather hit grass with a soft thud.

"He must have said something else," James grumbled. "You were shaking when you came back to me." Tension suddenly gripped him. His arm around her waist tightened. "Did he touch you? Hurt you?"

"That's two more questions, five and six. You're going to run out soon. But the answer to both questions is no. If you don't believe me, you can check out the situation for yourself." She unlaced the corset and shrugged it over her head, dropping it on the grass beside her jacket. The cool air on her bare skin made her shiver, but the heat in his gaze warmed her to her toes.

"James?"

"God, you're beautiful." He bent down and drew her nipple between his lips.

Success! Crisis averted.

Lana sucked in a sharp breath as the firm pull of his mouth sent waves of heat through her body. "Are we done with the questions? Please say we're done."

He switched to the other nipple, teasing her with his teeth until her brain fuzzed with lust. A moan escaped her lips and his arm locked around her, pulling her into his chest. She could feel his erection through his leathers, hard as steel and pressed tight against her pussy.

"Question seven..." he murmured against her ear, "...what else did Rex say?"

Noooooo. Her head fell back and she groaned as he sucked and laved her nipples into tight peaks. Unable to think, much less come up with a lie, she blurted out the truth. "He said he was giving me a choice and you weren't one of the options."

James froze and, quietly, he asked, "What did he mean by that?"

"I honestly don't know. And that was question eight."

He smoothed her hair from her face. "I'll deal with him, babe. You won't have to worry about him again."

Lana shuddered at the undertone of menace in his voice. "You're not going to...you know...hurt him, are you?"

His jaw tightened. "I'll do what I have to do to keep you safe."

"And how will you keep me safe if I do this?" She lay back over the gas tank and reached over her head for the handlebars. Her back arched up over the cold metal surface and her hair tumbled down the sides of the motorcycle like a waterfall.

A sound erupted from James's throat—a cross between a choke and a groan. He smoothed his hands down her body, in and out of her curves and around her breasts. "Do you know what it does to me seeing you like this?"

Lana gave him a half smile. "After spending years surrounded by pictures of women and motorcycles, I have some idea what turns a biker on. And I have made a very careful study of you." A cool breeze brushed over her bare skin, making her shiver. "Bikers especially like to see a woman lying naked across a motorcycle."

James's eyes darkened and he feathered his fingers over her exposed belly. "My woman. My motorcycle." He gave her a look that was nothing short of carnal. "You want to play, babe?"

Her insides turned liquid. The first and only time they had played together had been the most intense sexual experience of her life. Although she hadn't been able to handle his gentle restraint of her hands after Oktoberfest, tonight she was feeling brave. "Yes, James. I want to play. And that was your last damn question."

Still, he didn't move. His lips twisted to the side and he studied her, considering. "I thought you didn't want this," he said cautiously. "Last time you said it was a mistake. I don't want you to feel that way again. If this isn't right for you, if I'm not right for you, we should wrap it up and go home."

Her stomach clenched. "I was scared, James. I was scared you would hurt me again, so I ran away. And I think I was right, because when you came to my apartment tonight you weren't planning to stay. But something changed your mind, and when I saw you lying on those hay bales I changed my mind too. Tonight I've gone from thinking my life was over to spending another night with a motorcycle club. I've suffered through your near-death experience, an *Alice in Wonderland* kangaroo court and an altercation with Rex. It all makes me think I'd rather have a little piece of you and risk getting hurt again, than not have you at all."

A slow grin spread across his face. "Off the bike."

She mocked a frown as he pulled her up. "Shame. I was hoping we could do it here after all."

He dismounted the bike and helped her down, then shrugged off his pack and tugged out several coils of soft rope. "You okay with this?" he asked, dangling them over her head.

Lana stared at the ropes. It had been so long. And the last time...the first time...the only time... Did she trust him enough to do this?

She studied him—silent, patient, waiting for her answer. Although he still had the same dry sense of humor, he'd lost the edge that had kept him up every night worrying over his latest case. He had been seduced by the outlaw biker ethos, taking to the freedom from social constraints as if he'd been born to it. He wore his leathers like a second skin, rode like there was no tomorrow and talked the talk better than she ever did. The biker world had unleashed the wild side she'd only glimpsed when they were together two years ago. Exciting. Dangerous.

James touched her cheek and smiled, all crinkled eyes and boyish charm. "It's up to you, babe. I'm just as happy to fuck you the old-fashioned way."

Lana snorted. "So romantic. When you put it that way, how can I say no?" Her evening had been full of risks. Why not take another?

James's eyes glittered in the moonlight. "Romance has nothing to do with how bad I want to be inside you."

"James?"

"Babe?"

"Best keep quiet. Now is not the time for crude biker charm."

Chuckling, he tossed his jacket on the ground and then knelt in front of her. With practiced ease, he unfastened her leather trousers and slid them over her hips, greeting each inch of exposed skin with a feathered kiss. Then he eased her down.

"I don't suppose you have any other clothing, maybe even a picnic blanket." She tried and failed to repress a giggle. "Although I'm nice and cozy on top, my ass is on the grass and it's not feeling the love."

With a snort of laughter, James stripped off his shirt and tucked it underneath her. Then he eased her arms over her head and tied her wrists together. "If you move, you'll be a sorry girl."

"The kind of sorry I like?" She looked up at him, a dark shadow in the night.

"The kind of sorry that happens when you move and I tie you to a tree instead."

She sighed a dejected "oh" and then yelped when he delivered a stinging slap to her thigh.

"Of course the kind of sorry you like," he rumbled as he bent her legs one at a time and positioned her feet in the grass. "Now open for me."

Softened by liquid lust, Lana dropped her knees to her sides, her body arching upward to take the strain. Apprehensive anticipation ratcheted through her. She was totally open to him. Vulnerable. Her body and her heart...her soul.

James's firm hands traced lazy circles along her inner thighs, moving closer and closer to her throbbing center. He leaned forward and pressed a soft kiss to her mound, his breath teasing over her swollen clit. Lana moaned and rocked her hips, seeking more than just his breath.

"Stay still," he warned, "or I might have to restrain your legs too." His fingers stroked through her folds, parted her, and then he pressed one finger inside.

Her hips lifted and she gasped, her muscles tensing as she fought the urge to wail and thrash around.

"Not easy keeping still, is it?" His thumb moved over her clit, spreading her moisture around and around in maddening circles, but never where she needed it to be.

"I need to move," she whispered.

"Not allowed, babe. Keeping still focuses the mind, heightens your pleasure. All that energy has to go somewhere."

He thrust a second finger inside her, hard and deep. Her strangled cry only seemed to encourage him. He added a third finger, stretching her, filling her, until she was stiff and trembling and willing to answer any question, do anything, if he would just give her release.

Which, apparently, had been his plan all along.

"What aren't you telling me?" He withdrew his fingers, leaving her aching with need.

Through shallow breaths, she groaned, "You only had ten questions."

He leaned over and drew a nipple into his mouth. His hot, wet tongue sent her right to the edge, and she stifled a groan of frustration. "Now. Please. Now."

His eyes darkened and he licked his lips. "Soon. You need to answer the bonus questions first."

He continued to tease. His fingers curled inside her again and stroked along the sensitive tissue of her inner walls. Then he really began his assault, alternating the stroke of his fingers inside her with the lick of his tongue on her nipples, teasing her until she was trembling violently.

And then he stopped. "I'm waiting."

Lana's blood pounded in her ears. Her sex ached. Her clit throbbed. Her body was taut as a bowstring. She had wanted to play, but not this game.

She gritted her teeth and stared up at the sky, letting truth drop from her lips like a falling star. "Fine. You want it. You get it. What I'm not telling you is that I still don't trust you. Despite everything, I think you'll hurt me again. Probably worse than last time. Whatever took you away from me before is still with you. I saw it in your eyes when you came to my apartment this evening. I can hear it in your voice. I can feel it when you touch me. Something is holding you back. But I want you anyway. Life is too short. You could have died in that motorcycle accident..."

Or Levi could be coming for her.

Just the thought of Levi chilled her blood and her arousal plummeted. Suddenly the restraints became unbearable, frightening, taking her back to a night she would have cut off her own arm to be free.

"Untie me. Let me up." Heart pounding, she lowered her hands and tried to sit up. "James. Please."

"Shhh, babe. It's okay." He unfastened the ropes and then lay beside her, pulling her into his chest, his hand stroking gently down her back.

For a long moment she didn't speak. Just lay beside him, listening to the steady beat of his heart, soaking in the warmth of his hand. Finally her pulse slowed and her throat loosened. "I'm really sorry."

James traced lazy circles over the curve of her ass. "For what? I'm the one who tied you up."

"For ruining everything. For freaking out. For telling you how I felt. For being naked in the grass in the middle of nowhere and still being unable to get your pants off."

He nuzzled his way through her curls to her ear. "You want my pants off, babe?"

Lana's body went from dejection to shocking arousal in a heartbeat. "God yes. I feel very naughty lying naked in the grass in the dark. I could be persuaded to do all sorts of kinky things. But just...not with my hands restrained."

Before her brain had even registered that James had moved, he had flipped her over, tugged her ass up in the air and spread her legs with a thick thigh.

"All fours," he rasped as he smoothed his hands over her rounded cheeks, sending little quivers of lightening straight to her core.

Lana pushed herself up and bit her lip as she listened to the sound of a belt buckle being undone, a zipper pulled down, boots and clothing thudding on the grass.

And then the *unsaintly* crinkle of a condom wrapper.

Moments later, his bare chest was pressed tight over her back, his hands on the grass beside hers, his cock, thick and heavy between her thighs.

"This is new." She wiggled her bottom against him and giggled when he growled. "Kinky."

"I aim to please."

"Although, this isn't really the kind of kinkiness I had in mind. To be honest, I don't even know if it makes the kinkiness cut."

James chuckled. "Resources are limited, as is my self-control. Right now, this is the best you'll get. After we take the edge off, I'll take you over to the trees and show you just how kinky I can be."

Lana turned her head and kissed his cheek, wiggling against his hardened length. "A little helpful advice. Your aim is off. Too far outside. I think you should go left and try for a central position. Once you're in, you'll score big."

His body shook with laughter. "Whose game is this anyway?"

"Yours, I hope."

James licked his way around the curve of her ear, his breath hot and moist on her skin. "Mine."

His hand slid over her hip, dipping into her center and then out to spread her moisture over her clit. Her eyes slitted closed at the startling sensation and the heady feeling of being totally surrounded by his heat and his intoxicating scent of fresh soap and worn leather.

"Not wasting any time, are you?" she mumbled between panting breaths. "No buildup. No teasing. No foreplay."

"What do you think we've been doing all evening? Every time I looked at you in those leathers I wanted to throw you down on the grass and take you right there. And then you…on the motorcycle…" His breath caught. "I need to know you're ready for me because you're gonna take me deep, and you're gonna take me hard, and you're gonna take me rough and dirty. And when you come baby, you're gonna come screaming my name."

Lana sucked in a sharp breath. She'd thought watching James on the racetrack, his taut, muscular body wrapped over one thousand pounds of speeding metal, was as good as foreplay could get. But his words took her arousal over the top.

His gentle touches became firmer, more insistent. Lana's body tensed, spiraling near and nearer to her peak. "That...would...be...now," she rasped.

James pulled away, and then his hands were on her hips, digging deep. He slid through her wetness, pulling her back as he pushed inside, until he was deep, deeper than fingers could go. Lana's eyes watered as the overwhelming fullness eased into exquisite pleasure.

With a groan, he moved within her, sending tremors through her body. Then he eased out and thrust back in. Her sex clenched around him and she gritted her teeth against the urge to scream or whimper or both.

Holding her steady, he pounded in and out, surging like the tide within her, filling her ear with whispers of all the things he wanted to do to her—dirty things, naughty things, wicked things. Each thrust took her closer and closer to the edge, until she was coiled tight and ready to explode.

"Now," she growled.

With a chuckle, he slid his hand over her hip, seeking out her swollen clit. One stroke. Two. A pinch. And then the world sheeted red as pleasure surged through her body like white lightning, spreading outward to her fingers and toes.

Before the waves subsided, James tightened his grip on her hips and hammered into her until he became impossibly hard, swelling against her sensitive tissue. With a low groan, he came inside her in long heated jerks.

For a long moment he rested on top of her, his body like a warm blanket. Finally he eased out and knelt behind her, pulling her back into his chest. Lana turned and rested her cheek on the soft mat of hair and listened to the drum of his heart as she soaked up the comfort of his embrace.

"How did you find this place?" she said softly. "It's so beautiful. Quiet. Peaceful. Private. It's like a little oasis in the middle of nowhere."

He stiffened and his arms tightened around her. "Christine, the woman in the picture, was a recreational pilot. We came out to Surrey quite often so she could keep up her flying hours. We flew over here one time and it stuck in my mind."

Lana looked up at his stark expression. "How did she die?"

Although his gaze slanted down at her, his lips stayed closed. After the intimacy they'd shared, his silence hurt, but then she hadn't shared her past with him—at least not the things that mattered.

She rested her hand on his chest. "I'm sorry. I shouldn't have asked."

He drew in a ragged breath and stroked his hand down her hair. "I want to tell you. It's just...hard. But you should know because she's the reason I left and why I don't know if this can work."

Lana's blood chilled but she forced herself to stay calm, still. Listen. Not one of her strongest abilities.

His voice rough, he said, "She was my partner when I was a beat cop, and then my lover. And then we got engaged. It was against the rules, but we thought we would sort it out after we were married."

"I can't believe you broke the rules," Lana said lightly.

"First and last time. I learned my lesson the hard way." His voice tightened and on impulse Lana turned and wrapped her arms around him.

"Keep going."

His fist clenched and unclenched against her back. "One morning we were getting ready for patrol and she got a text. I picked up the phone to hand it to her and saw who it was from.

He was a homicide detective who'd been fired for...unethical behavior. He wasn't a friend of ours and no longer part of the department so I read the text."

Lana's heart squeezed and she inhaled sharply. She didn't need him to tell her what it said.

"He was married." James's voice broke. "He had kids. That made it ten times worse for me. There aren't many things left in the world that have meaning, but to me marriage is one. I didn't ask Christine to marry me lightly. I thought of it as a lifetime commitment, an enduring partnership and an unbreakable bond. You don't run away from a marriage. If something is wrong, you try to fix it. You don't break the trust."

Lana's stomach clenched and nausea roiled in her belly. He could not have said anything to make her feel worse than she did right now.

"I didn't tell her I saw the text," he continued. "I asked her if she was having an affair. She lied to me. I didn't pursue it. I wanted to give her time to think about it. I trusted her to tell me the truth." His arms squeezed Lana tight, and she closed her eyes to fight back the tears of her own betrayal.

"You can't stand lies," she whispered, more for her benefit than his. Lost in his memories, he didn't respond.

"Just before noon we were called out to an abandoned building. Someone had reported a fire. Christine raced inside and ran up the stairs. Protocol was for us to go together. One on point and one as backup. I told her as much, but she was still angry at me for accusing her. She said she needed space. She went up alone."

His voice caught in his throat and for a moment Lana feared he wouldn't be able to continue.

But he did. Gritting his teeth, he said, "It was a trap. Retaliation by a drug gang for a bust that had happened a few days before. They wanted to kill a few cops to send a message. Didn't matter who we were. I had to fight four of them off before

I could get to the stairs. But by then it was too late. They'd been waiting for her."

"Oh God." Her arms tightened around him. "Oh, James. I'm so sorry."

James drew in a ragged breath. "I blamed myself. I knew better than to get involved with my partner. We couldn't be objective, professional. If she hadn't been angry she would've waited for me, let me take point. I would've been the one to die. That bullet was meant for me."

A chill shot through Lana's body. Suddenly, the grass that had seemed so soft prickled her skin and the cool air became cold. "She made her choice."

"Easy to hear. Hard to accept." He kissed her forehead. "I knew I couldn't go through that again, losing someone I cared about. I thought it would kill me. And I cared about you…"

"So you left," she whispered, "sooner rather than later."

He rested his chin on her head. "I was offered the assignment and I jumped at the chance. There was an undercover operative already in place, although the DEU didn't tell me who he was, and he'd come up with a story to get me in that night. I watched you sleep for hours and tried to decide if I should wake you. In the end I took the coward's way out. Probably the first time in my life. I didn't think I would be able to go if I had to look into your eyes and say goodbye. And I was worried you would change my mind. You can be very persuasive."

Lana gave a low laugh. "I could say the same about you."

He pulled back and cupped her face between his hands. "I told myself it was better that way and I was saving you from getting hurt later on. But really it was about me protecting myself. I'm sorry, for all that's worth now." His lips brushed over hers and then he kissed her soft and sweet.

"You grovel well," she murmured, trying to lighten the mood. She needed time to process what he'd said, instead of reacting immediately as she usually did. "I want to hear more groveling."

His eyebrow lifted. "Groveling is done. I believe you told me you could be persuaded to do all manner of kinky things in the dark, and since this may be our last night together, we'd better get started."

Last night together? Lana didn't think so. If she was willing to risk her heart, he damn well better be prepared to risk his. He had run out on her once already, but time had passed and he'd changed. They both had. Hopefully his old-fashioned attitudes had changed too.

Turning to face him, she wound her arms around his neck. She would make this a night he wouldn't...couldn't forget. A night that would leave him wanting more.

"So...about those kinky things..." she whispered.

Chapter Sixteen

Bubbles "Angel" Bodine was a rough woman. Five foot nothing, with a tough, wiry frame, overprocessed, bleached-blonde hair, perma-tanned skin and piercing blue eyes, she sucked up all the air in Lana's office and replaced it with nicotine fumes. She dressed biker. She looked biker. And when she leaned forward to rasp out her demands with an irritated growl, Lana wondered why Angel had bothered to have *Ima Biker Bitch* tattooed across her highly visible and very generous cleavage.

"Where're my pictures?" Angel pulled the client chair closer to Lana's desk.

Lana swallowed. "I got pictures of Rex with Portia, but unfortunately I dropped the camera and I haven't been able to retrieve them yet."

"*Portia?* That little two-faced slag has been after him since day one. You know how she got to be Hades's mama? One day she called all the brothers down and lined them up…"

"Actually, I don't need to know." Lana threw up her hands in a defensive gesture as if she could physically ward off Angel's words. "And it doesn't matter. She's been banished from Hades for throwing tacks onto the racetrack during a race."

Angel snorted a laugh. "I taught her that trick, but I also taught her not to get caught. She's stupid, as well as a fucking whore."

Lana bristled at Angel's language. Not that she wasn't prone to swearing herself, especially when out drinking with Jackie, but she had limits and denigrating other women was one of them.

"I gotta get those divorce papers filed," Angel said. "Rex is driving me fucking crazy. He hauls his sweaty carcass into my bed every night and tells me I gotta do my wifely duty. Wifely duty, my ass. There's no fucking wifely duty when he's been parading his dick around the Lower Mainland. You know what he gets when he wants 'wifely duty'? He gets a frying pan to the head. I keep it under the pillow for when his one-eyed dog comes sniffing around."

"Um...I don't really..."

On a roll, Angel ignored her. "He's been no husband to me. He turned my greenhouse into a grow-op. Ripped out my petunias and replaced them with weed. Every flowerpot, every window box, every houseplant—weed, weed, fucking weed. My momma had a birthday and I had to give her a weed bouquet. I mean, don't get me wrong. She likes a good joint before bed, same as anyone, but I would have liked to give her something with more color."

"Sure. Color is good."

"So you got anything new for me? Or do I gotta slap your face to wake you up and tell you to call me when you've got something for me to see?"

Lana swallowed hard. Although she had no great affection for Angel, she didn't want to lose a paying client. And Angel had paid. First the retainer, and then the monthly bill, and then her expenses. No questions asked. "Actually, I have a lead about a new woman..."

She hoped Rex had a new woman. Kickstand had assured her Rex hadn't been alone in his office last night or the night before, and while on guard duty he'd caught a glimpse of a tall redhead in a red dress leaving the clubhouse in the early hours of the morning.

"New woman?" Angel shrieked. "Bastard's desk is still warm and he's already got a replacement. No big surprise there. Can you imagine what it's like being married to that two-timing scumbag? I got this voice from screaming at him all the time.

'Where you been all night?' 'Who the fuck were you with?' 'Why you got lipstick on your dick?' Doc says I cracked my voice box from all the yelling, and a couple of ribs too. You know what else I got from him and his wandering dick?" She scratched down below. Lana's stomach clenched.

"Um...not really information I need for the case."

Angel looked her up and down. "Pretty little thing like you musta had your share of salami. I'm sure you know what it's like."

Cheeks burning, Lana cleared her throat. "I'm sure I can guess."

Angel gave her a few ideas of places to look for Rex and his new woman, and they chatted about the new greenhouse she was planning to set up once the divorce settlement came through.

"My baby girl is going to want for nothing," Angel said as she shrugged her leather jacket over the six-inch shoulder pads on her bright orange, Harley Davidson brand spandex dress. "When the divorce is done, we're going to move to a small town where she'll never see a biker as long as she lives. She'll go to the best schools and have nice friends. Somewhere pretty and wholesome. Maybe Kelowna."

Lana's stomach heaved. "Definitely don't move there. Lots of bikers. Too many."

Angel grunted and followed Lana into the reception area. "Like you would know anything about bikers. You look so sweet I wanna lick you all over. And lookit the fancy digs you got going on here."

Lana smiled at the compliment. The renovated boutique architectural loft in the heritage building in Yaletown hadn't been her first choice when she and Jackie decided to merge their PI practices, but, the minute she'd seen the exposed brick, high wood-slat ceilings, skylights and reclaimed fir flooring, she had been sold.

Derek, her houseboy/receptionist/wannabe PI raced around the glass reception desk to hand Angel her bill. Angel gave his young, lean, muscular body a slow perusal and grunted her approval.

"Is he man candy or does he actually work?"

Derek grinned. "Man candy. All the way."

Lana snorted a laugh. He knew the score. Jackie made no attempt to hide the fact she'd hired him for his blond-haired, blue-eyed surfer-dude looks and nothing else. And nothing else was what she got. He was totally incompetent, lacking in any semblance of office management skills, but utterly charming with the clients and devoted to his bosses.

"Well, you got something right," Angel said to Lana. "I'll bet he keeps you busy after hours."

She reached for the door just as a key scraped the lock. Derek and Lana shared a glance. Aside from Jackie, visible through the glass wall of her office, they were the only two people with keys.

The door swung open.

At the sight of a biker-booted foot, Lana sighed. She should have known. Who else would make an unauthorized and illicit copy of her office key?

"What can I do for you...Ice?"

James removed his glasses, then leaned against the doorframe, arms folded, one leg crossed over the other. He met her gaze and winked.

A thrill of excitement coursed through Lana's veins. So the night in the field wasn't their last night together after all. He'd come back for more. *Lana Parker is a sex machine!* She pumped an imaginary fist in the air and chalked one up to the seduction techniques she'd learned in romance novels.

Angel coughed nervously and James turned his gaze on the open-mouthed, wide-eyed, stiletto-booted woman in front of him.

"Angel."

"Ice? What the fuck are you doing here?" Angel bristled and her face reddened. "Did Rex send you to spy on me?"

James stared at her until she looked away. He was in full-on intimidation mode, and in those tight leather pants, Hades vest, black T-shirt and dark glasses, he didn't even have to try. The do-rag covering his hair only added to his unshaven appeal. He was badass and Lana wanted him. Badass bad.

And from Derek's red face and panting whimpers, so did he.

"Well fuck," Angel muttered. "I'm doing it for my baby girl, Ice. You know things aren't good between Rex and me. You know about all the girls he takes into the office. I want her to have a normal life and that means I need to keep Rex the hell away from her. I know I'm no saint, but I'll do right by her. You know I will."

Lana cringed at the begging tone in Angel's voice. So unlike her. But she was clearly scared of James...Ice. For the first time, Lana wondered how he'd earned his road name.

"I didn't see you here," James said quietly. "I walked into this office and I saw a redhead and..." he glared at Derek, "...I don't know what the fuck you are...looking like some kinda pumped-up, pimped-out GQ model...but you better start packing your bags because you're not staying either."

He turned back to Angel. "You got five minutes to get the hell outta Dodge before I open my eyes and see someone I shouldn't be seeing in a PI's office."

Angel's jaw tensed and she gave him a curt nod. "I owe you one."

"Yes you do. And now you have four minutes and twenty-seven seconds left."

Angel hurried to the door and paused to look back over her shoulder at Lana. "You call me when you got the goods. I'll mail the payment to you."

And then she was gone.

"Interesting woman." Derek shuffled closer to Lana, and then his eyes fixed on James. He pressed his lips to Lana's ear. "Interesting man."

James's gaze flicked from Derek to Lana, and back to Derek. "What's this?"

"He's Jackie's."

"He's leaving."

Lana groaned. "Lighten up. He's harmless and not my type. I like brooding, dark, dangerous bikers who tell me it can't work between us, fuck me senseless in a field and then show up at my office with an unauthorized copy of my key to mark their territory."

Derek chortled. James scowled. Jackie looked up from her desk and winked through the glass.

"I didn't say it couldn't work." James followed Lana into her office and slammed the door behind them. "I said I didn't know if it could work."

"So...you came here to tell me you just want to be friends?" She whirled around to face him. "Is that it? Because I have all the friends I need. And I have Derek in case I need something my friends can't give me."

James folded his arms and leaned against her office door. "He's gay."

His smug attitude began to grate on her nerves and she had to remind herself that she was the one who had taken the initiative to convince him he wanted more. If not for her unrestrained, wanton, kinky behavior the other night, he probably wouldn't be here. She needed to bring him down a peg and level the playing field.

"You wish."

His eyes narrowed and he rocked his neck from side to side, puffing out his chest like he was spoiling for a fight, as he whipped off his leather jacket. "Then I'll deal with him. My girl's not working in an office with that fucking dick on legs."

My girl. Smug *and* possessive. She'd created a monster. And one who looked like he was about to beat on poor defenseless Derek. But at least she had her answer. He wanted more than friendship. And so did she.

"He's bi." Lana sighed. "And I told you, he's Jackie's." And then because she couldn't help teasing him… "Although…he's always said he would be willing to lend a hand, if you know what I mean."

"Jesus Christ." James ran his hand through his hair. "What kind of office are you running here?"

"A happy one. At least it was until you violated my privacy and made an illegal copy of my key."

"I need to know you're fully accessible."

Lana huffed a breath. "I'm not a bus, James."

But he wasn't listening. Instead, he paced around the room, pulling books from the bookshelves, studying her scenic mountain prints, tugging on the drawers of her filing cabinets and peering out her windows. He rifled through the papers on her desk, the files on her credenza, and peered into the closet full of emergency clothing and disguises. At least she'd picked the one office without glass walls. She could just imagine Jackie's laughter if she caught sight of James rummaging through her cupboards.

Lana couldn't decide whether or not she liked this territorial sniffing around her office. He seemed determined to touch and study every single thing in her room. She sat at her desk and tried to focus on her paperwork, but his constant shifting of objects, shuffling of papers and peering into corners both unnerved and irritated her. She wasn't possessive about her stuff, but she did like it untouched.

She finally snapped, "What the hell are you doing? Why don't you just piss in the corner and get it over with. Derek used that one…" she pointed to the left, "…but the one behind my desk is free."

Seemingly unconcerned by her uncharacteristically crude outburst, James thumbed through an investigative-techniques textbook. "Just getting to know you, babe."

"The usual way of getting to know someone is to take them on a date and talk, like over dinner and drinks, or hiking up a mountain, going for a walk, sitting on the beach or even white-water rafting. You don't break into the person's office while they are *working* and start rifling through their stuff."

"You want to go on a date?" He came around her desk and stood beside her, legs spread, arms folded. Her chair was low enough to position her mouth right at the bulge in his jeans. An image of James in the same position in the field popped into her head. Except she had been naked, on her knees, her lips wrapped around his...

Lana turned bright red. "Ah...no. I wasn't asking... I mean...we seem to have moved past the dating stage."

His intense gaze bore into her. Hunger gleamed in his eyes. "We had dates before," he said softly.

Lana cleared her throat and shifted in her seat. "That was...um...in the past. What we had then was different."

But was it? They'd had a few dates at the beginning of their relationship, but work pressures meant they rarely saw each other until late evening and inevitably they would wind up in bed. She'd learned more about James in the last few weeks than she had in their six months together. Now they laughed more, joked more and spent more time together. She was falling faster, deeper for him than she had before. She hoped it didn't mean she would crash harder too.

A muscle ticked under his eye and she wondered if she'd hit a nerve. "What do we have now?" There was an edge to his voice—sharp, hungry.

She lifted one of her shoulders in a shrug. "Well, we do seem to talk and hang out more, but mostly, I guess, it's just…sex. No strings. No attachments. No one gets hurt." She managed to work past the sudden lump in her throat.

James's gaze sharpened. "Just sex?"

She drew in a ragged breath. Damn her runaway tongue. "Sure. I'm okay with that. At first I thought I couldn't handle it. But I didn't have any emotional breakdowns. And, I thought, you know, if you didn't want more than that, once I was done with Angel, I wouldn't be hanging around Hades, so that would be it."

"You're done with Angel as of today. That mean you're done with me?"

She slammed her pen on her desk, frustrated at her inability to articulate her thoughts and irritated as hell he still thought she would drop the case. "As you saw, I am not done with Angel."

"You're done, babe. I should have shut you down long ago. Angel and Rex are an accident waiting to happen and I don't want you in the middle. Move on."

Teeth clenched, Lana pushed herself out of her chair and stood toe to toe with James. If she didn't take a stand, he would walk all over her. But if she did, he might walk away. She didn't want to lose him, but she didn't want to lose her self-respect. If they were going to work, they had to find a middle ground.

Taking a deep, calming breath, she said, "I like that you're protective and possessive. Frankly, it turns me on. A lot. My panties right now…totally soaked. And when you go all badass because you're worried about me, it turns me on even more."

His body stilled and he stared at her, riveted, save for his rasping breaths.

Well, at least now she had his attention.

"But this is my case. My client. My business. There is no 'move on'. There is no 'shut you down'. There is no 'you're done'. I'll do the best damn job I can for her, same as I do for other clients, and…you…will not…interfere." She punctuated her last four words with pokes to James's chest—old-lady style.

James caught her hand and brushed his lips over her knuckles. The gentle, tender gesture took the wind out of her sails and stole the breath from her lungs.

"Stop that," she whispered, but she didn't pull her hand away.

"No one has ever riled me up the way you do," he growled. "You are headstrong, stubborn, wild, relentlessly determined and too smart for your own damn good. You're hard on my patience. Hard on my mind. Hard on my heart. But you're so damn soft inside. You see to the heart of people. Accept them for who they are. You light up a room the minute you walk in the door. And you are so beautiful, so fucking sexy I can't get you out of my mind."

She looked up into eyes as dark as the stormy sea and breathed out a confused "oh."

James chuckled. "I'm saying I'm sorry, babe. I'm saying you're right. I won't interfere with your work, but I also won't sit around if I think you're in a dangerous situation. Something happens that makes me worry for your safety, I'm pulling you out. Kicking and screaming if I have to."

Her heart swelled and her lips curled into a smile. An apology and a concession. Maybe they could work after all. "I'm okay with that...I think."

"Good. Now pack up. We're going on a date." He spun her around and slapped her ass. "Get your stuff."

Lana glared over her shoulder. "Despite all your sweet words, I'm not really feeling the love for your bossy, controlling, ass-slapping self. I think you've been with those bikers too long. Or maybe you've forgotten who you're talking to. I don't like being ordered around."

His eyes flashed with sensual fire. "Yes you do."

She turned to face him, the beat of desire pulsing through her veins. "No I don't."

His hand curled around her neck and he slanted his mouth over hers. She instantly opened for him and their tongues met in a deep, wet thrust. He fisted her hair, holding her in place, taking complete control of her mouth. Passion and arousal blazed between them. A whimper escaped her lips.

"You do," he whispered, his breath hot and moist against her ear.

She melted against him. "Maybe...sometimes...in the bedroom."

"And in the office." With one sweep of his arm, he cleared her desk, scattering files, papers, pens and coffee cups to the floor. Then he cupped her ass and lifted her, laying her full out across the cool wood surface. Good thing she'd ordered the larger size desk.

"Is this just sex?"

He licked his lips as he studied her body, a predator ready to feast.

"Definitely not." He shoved her T-shirt and bra over her breasts, baring her for his viewing pleasure. Lana shivered as the cool air brushed over her skin.

"What if someone comes in?"

"I'll kill them." His deadpan delivery made her laugh, but the speed with which he stripped off her clothes took her breath away.

"So romantic," she murmured. "I've always wanted to hear a man say 'I'll kill anyone who interrupts me while I'm fucking you on your desk'."

"Well then, it's your lucky day." He leaned down and drew her nipple into his mouth. Lana gasped and arched toward him.

"It certainly is."

"So this is your idea of a date?"

Barely Undercover

Lana picked up her DSLR and attached the 300-to-500 mm lens, perfect for the dim light at Jericho Beach.

James grunted. "I thought you'd appreciate the opportunity to get the pictures you need for your case in a romantic location." He waved his arm expansively toward the windshield. "Moonlit night. Mountain and ocean views. Sand and surf. Warm summer breeze. Crisp ocean air. Rusted-out, fucking dangerous bucket of bolts..."

She chose to ignore his insulting her Jetta. "If Rex hadn't replaced you with Bones at the last minute on this deal, you wouldn't even have thought about taking me to the beach. We'd probably still be in my office."

"Or you'd be getting yourself into trouble."

She slid a hand over the bulge in his jeans and squeezed gently. "This kind of trouble?"

"You keep that up and you'll never get your pictures," he growled.

Lana leaned over and tongued his ear. "I love it when you talk dirty."

He cupped her hand, lifting it off his groin and placing it between her legs. "I love it when you touch yourself." He shifted her hand to the side and flipped up the bottom of her dress. Then he held her hand as he pressed it over the curve of her sex, gentle rubbing the palm over her clit and angling the fingers along her folds.

"I also like it when you wear dresses," he whispered in her ear. "Easier access." He slid their hands up and down, increasing the pressure with each stroke. "Next time lose the panties."

Lana gasped and her body tightened. "You're insatiable. How many times did we have sex in my office? Three? Four? Now we're on a surveillance date, for God's sake. We should be eating donuts, talking about the right lens for moonlight and discussing whether we'll have to leave the vehicle to get a good shot."

James chuckled. "I've been on more stakeouts than I can count. This is a far better way to pass the time." He pushed her panties aside and stroked their forefingers along her labia. Lana arched in the seat and rocked her hips toward the two fingers sliding over her pussy, eliciting such delicious sensations.

"You want a donut right now, babe?" His voice was low, husky, dripping with sensual promise.

"No," she breathed.

"You want to talk lenses?"

"No."

"You want to leave the vehicle?"

Her breath caught in her throat. "Yes."

James froze. "Yes?"

She pointed out the window. "Rex. On the beach. Deal going down. I think it's too dark, even with this lens."

Withdrawing his hand, James eased himself lower in the seat. "We can't risk being seen. You'll have to do the best you can."

Sex still throbbing, Lana grabbed her camera and snapped pictures of Rex standing near a log, talking to a man with a cell phone. He handed Rex a briefcase.

"Do you know what's in the briefcase?"

Silence.

"James?"

He'd stilled, his eyes fixed on the rearview mirror. "It's Bones. He's driving the white van behind us and he has someone with him. Stay low."

They shrank down in their seats as the van pulled up at the far end of the parking lot. Bones and his passenger walked to the back and unlocked the doors, just as Rex and his companion joined them. Everyone looked inside the van and a discussion ensued.

"I want to see what's in the van. Back in a moment." Lana opened the car door and slid out of the vehicle, then darted over to the snack shack and hid behind the corner.

"No. Fuck. Get back here." James's voice faded as she raced over to a large tree and plastered herself against the trunk. No cover behind the van. She would have to hide between the cars. She eased herself into the shadows and dived behind a giant black Hummer, lifted high enough she could easily fit underneath. Hitting the ground with a soft thud, she wiggled her way between the tires. Perfect. She adjusted the lens and began to shoot.

"What about the weapons?" the mystery man said.

"You'll get them," Rex snapped. "Our upgrades haven't arrived yet so I'm not ready to part with the old ones yet."

As they argued about whether Rex should keep all the money the man had given him, the van door swung open wider. Lana held her breath and pressed the shutter release.

Hands clasped around Lana's ankles, sending her heart into overdrive. She tried to kick the nasty hands away, but her body was already sliding backwards under the Hummer. Frantically she held her camera in the direction of the van and continued to shoot. When she was clear of the vehicle she flipped onto her back and glared up at a furious James.

"You totally ruined it," she growled in whisper. "I was going to get a shot of what was in the van."

"You were about to get killed. Did you think Rex came here alone? He's got twenty brothers patrolling the beach and his contact will have his own men around."

"I would've been fine. I was concealed. This is one of the occasions where you've gone too far with the whole protectiveness thing."

His eyes narrowed. "This is one of the occasions where I remove you from a dangerous situation." He reached for her hand and pulled her up. "I would advise against kicking and screaming unless you want to attract attention."

"Hey, you two. Over by the Hummer. What are you doing?"

Lana's head jerked in the direction of the voice. Two men raced toward them. Her heart took off down the speedway. "Okay then. You win. Remove me. Remove me."

James grabbed her hand and dragged her across the road and into the forest. They followed a bike trail through the bush at top speed. Branches cracked and leaves tore as their pursuers ran through the forest behind them.

"Oh God. Oh God. Oh God," she panted as she tried to keep up with James's long strides. The light faded as they ran deeper into the undergrowth. Finally, James's steps slowed. He pulled her down to the forest floor behind a dense thicket of bushes, and threw leaves over the shiny surface of her camera.

Lana lowered her head and breathed in the scent of fresh earth and decay. Her heart thundered in her chest. Feet thudded down the path and the beam of a flashlight swept over their hiding spot. Lana held her breath until she thought she might burst. Finally the steps faded away and she let go a sob.

"Shhhhh." James stroked his hand down her back. "We'll have to stay here for a bit. They'll be waiting on the road, hoping to flush us out, and it's too dark to navigate the rest of the trail without a light."

"Well, it certainly hasn't been a boring date," Lana mumbled. "Sex in the office. A stakeout. A little nookie in the car. Illicit activities in a parking lot. And pursuit by armed bikers and drug or arms dealers. You sure know how to show a girl a good time."

"It's not over." James flipped her onto her back and eased himself on top of her, holding his weight on his elbows, his weapon still in his hand. Lana wiggled and felt his erection, hard as steel, settle firmly between her legs.

"James Hunter. I can't believe you. We are *not* having sex in the forest while we're being hunted by men with guns. Who gets turned on in life-threatening situations?"

"You." He slid his hand between them and under her dress. Shoving aside her panties he pressed a finger into her center and then trailed her wetness along her inner thigh.

"That was from before," she spat out, her cheeks flaming. "It doesn't just evaporate."

James slid his finger between his lips and smiled. "It's from now."

"Like you can tell."

His hand cupped her sex again and his finger dipped inside her, just enough to tease, and then out. "Maybe you're right. I need another taste."

Heat flared through her body and she softened beneath him. "What if they come back?"

"I have my weapon ready."

Lana wiggled her hips against his hardened length. "I noticed. Good thing I'm wearing my easy-access dress."

James tilted his head down until his eyes met hers. The warm glow in their blue depths stirred the heat in her veins.

"I'm sorry I pulled you out from under the Hummer." He leaned forward and brushed his lips against hers. "They wouldn't have seen you under there. I should have trusted your judgment."

A strange contentment flowed over her skin and squeezed a drop of graciousness from her heart. "You were just trying to protect me."

When he kissed her again, something changed in the air between them. Her body still thrummed with need, and his hand still slid down her body, seeking her moist, warm heat. But something else flowed in the current, breaking down walls, joining them with an invisible bond.

Whatever it was—danger, desire, desperation—it clouded her mind and opened her heart, and for the first time she wanted to share with him some of the past that haunted her.

"You're not bad at this protection thing," Lana said. "I might hire you as a bodyguard when you're done with your assignment."

James chuckled. "You're my girl. You get my services for free."

Lana lifted her head. Darkness surrounded them like a thick black cloak, pierced only by the tiniest sliver of moonlight. "I was Levi's girl," she whispered. "And he never protected me."

"Who's Levi?" His hand stilled.

"He was the biker I told you about. I was with him for four years, from when I was sixteen. I was kind of a bad teenager, looking for trouble, and he was a badass biker who was all the trouble I could handle. I thought it was meant to be. He didn't hit me much the first year, but then we moved to the US and he joined the Wolverines."

James sucked in a sharp breath and for a second Lana wondered if she should tell him the rest. Maybe not. Maybe just one piece at a time until she knew she could trust him with the biggest secret of all.

"I know about the Wolverines." A worried crease formed between his eyebrows.

"They didn't care that I was his old lady. They...made me do things around the clubhouse and when I didn't do them right they...were violent. Levi didn't intervene. He said I deserved what I got." Lana's voice thickened with remembered pain. "Sometimes he would just...watch them hurt me. Only thing he stopped them doing was..."

A stick cracked not more than ten feet away, and a gasp broke free from her lips as she glimpsed the beam of a flashlight.

James bolted to his feet and helped Lana off the forest floor. "Looks like we'll have to continue our date in a new location."

Chapter Seventeen

"Carpe Noctem?"

Lana stared at the golden plaque affixed to the wall in the now-familiar Gastown alley. "This is where you're taking me to escape from the drug dealers? The cab we caught outside the University Endowment Lands would have taken us anywhere. You must really get off on the whole danger thing."

James chuckled. "You certainly do."

Lana's cheeks flamed at his overly accurate statement. If they hadn't been interrupted in the forest, no doubt their date would have involved even more sex in unusual places.

James slid his access pass through the reader. "I need to speak to Tony," he said. "I overheard something at the beach that could be a concern. He knows I'm undercover and he has a knack for sorting through thorny issues."

Lana shuffled her feet. "How about I just wait for you out here? My last two experiences haven't been the most positive. The first time I visited the club you interrogated me and then threw me out. The second time you riled me up so I would get thrown out. This time I'll just save you the trouble and stay out here."

"You have no problem endangering your life to get a picture for your case, but you're afraid to go into a sex club?"

She saw the challenge for what it was, but she couldn't stop her hands from finding her hips. "I'm not afraid."

"Good." He clasped her hand and led her down the stairwell and into the black-and-white-tiled reception area. Trixie hustled out to greet them wearing a barely there, blood-red corset dress lined with gold trim, red mesh stockings and red stilettos.

Lana swallowed and looked down at the little black dress she had thrown on after they had had sex on her desk three different ways. Jackie had convinced her to keep a selection of outfits at the office for various emergencies, but she hadn't been prepared for an impromptu visit to a sex club.

"I'm...er...overdressed."

Trixie gave her a wink. "Not at all. Your dress is tight, short and low cut. You just make the grade. And there's someone here tonight I know you'll want to see, so you get a free pass."

After James headed to Tony's office, Trixie walked her to the bar. Lana kept an eye out for leather jackets with Hades patches but the only leather in the club was the kinky kind.

"Katy!" Trixie called out. "Look who's here."

Lana smiled as a woman with long brown hair turned around. Katy Sinclair. Her first surveillance suspect. Her first case. The reason she'd met James.

"Lana." Katy gave her a warm smile and turned to her companion, a glamorous woman in head-to-toe leather. "This is the private investigator who saved my life after Steven had his breakdown."

They exchanged greetings and Katy and Lana chatted about Katy's new law practice, her children and their new house in West Vancouver.

"Hey, it's my favorite PI." Katy's husband, Mark, joined them from behind the bar. Also a lawyer, and James's best friend, he and Katy had met on the same case and been instrumental in putting some serious criminals behind bars. Tall, with broad shoulders, sable hair and dark eyes, Mark had been the object of Lana's fantasies until she realized he was totally smitten with Katy.

"I've been curious about the woman who managed to tame James," Mark said. "He's been quiet about you two for so long that I thought you weren't together anymore."

Lana swallowed and her cheeks flamed. "We aren't.

Weren't. Aren't. I don't know."

How humiliating. Either they were going out or they weren't. How could she not know where they stood?

Mark chuckled. "Totally understand. I lived with him for almost ten years and he still confuses the hell out of me."

Lana stiffened. She had forgotten how close Mark and James were. He probably knew James better than anyone. And there was a question dancing on the tip of her tongue.

Swallowing hard, she asked, "Did you know...Christine?"

Mark's eyes shuttered and he cast a quick glance around the club. "Yes, I knew her. What do you want to know?"

She wanted to know a million things. What was she like? Did she make James laugh? Did they have fun together? How long were they together? But in the end it was all the same question.

"Did he love her?"

Mark studied her for a long moment and then his eyes softened. "Why do you ask?"

Lana looked down and twisted her hands in her lap. "He said he asked her to marry him, and it wasn't a decision he made lightly because to him it was a lifetime commitment. I just thought...it was a strange statement. He didn't say he loved her and wanted to spend the rest of his life with her. He talked about getting married like he was entering into a contract."

"Sounds like you have your answer," he said softly. He put his arm around Katy and gave her a squeeze. "When we got married it was for love, and nothing else."

"I know. I watched you for weeks." Lana smiled at their obvious affection. "I was there from the beginning. I saw you fall in love." At the time she'd thought she had the best job in the world. If she could live vicariously through other people's relationships, she wouldn't long for her own. But in the end, Katy and Mark walked away with each other, and Lana was still alone.

Katy's eyes teared and she squeezed Mark's hand. "It wasn't an easy road."

"But you knew," Lana persisted. "You knew from the beginning it was something special. Something worth the hardship of the bumpy road."

"I knew the minute I laid eyes on her." Mark leaned over and kissed Katy on the forehead. "I would have walked through hell to make her mine. Almost did."

Katy shuddered and Lana gave her a sympathetic glance. They had both almost lost their careers and their lives in the pursuit of justice.

"Is James here tonight?" Katy took a quick glance around the club. "I didn't see him come in."

Mark snorted. "He's here, but in disguise. We'll have to pretend we don't know him."

Disguise? Not once since they'd met again had she thought of James as being in disguise. He wore the biker persona as easily as he wore his low-slung jeans. But Mark was right. When his assignment was over, he would hang up his leathers, return the motorcycle and become James Hunter, crusty cop, once more.

A bruise of sadness formed in her chest. She would miss biker James. The new James was spontaneous and unrestrained. Possessive and protective. He laughed more, lived more.

Did he love more too?

"I thought you said she hated you."

James leaned back in his chair and looked around Tony's office—anywhere except at his all-too-intuitive friend seated behind an enormous glass-and-oak desk. Sleek, modern and sophisticated, Tony's office was a reflection of the man, lacking only the enigmatic quality that made most people wary of the club's owner.

"Maybe not as much as I thought."

"So what's going on with you two?"

James drummed his fingers on his thigh. "I didn't come here for a psychological analysis. I came here because my life is in danger and the DEU is doing dick-all about it. I need some advice. My relationship will be neither here nor there if I'm dead."

"You have a relationship?" Tony stroked his nonexistent beard.

"I didn't say that."

"You did. You said you had a relationship. Not that I needed to hear it from you. I could see it the minute you two walked into the club. Body language. Powerful tool in a psychologist's arsenal." A grin split his face. "I can say with 100 percent certainty, she doesn't hate you. At all."

James shrugged. "She doesn't want to have a relationship. She doesn't trust me because I messed her around so bad. She wants to keep it casual."

"What do you want?"

James stood and paced around the room. He'd asked himself the same question one hundred times since he'd reconnected with Lana. Finally he shrugged. "I don't know. I guess that works for me. No one gets hurt. I don't wind up in the same situation I was in with Christine."

The words didn't ring true, even to him, and suddenly he didn't want to be having this conversation. He spun around to face Tony, knowing as he did it was the wrong thing to do. "Are we done now? Can we talk about the more serious issue?"

"We *are* talking about the more serious issue."

Unnerved by Tony's steady gaze, James stuffed his hands in his pockets. "You should have stayed in psychology, indulged your need to analyze people and spared your friends." He knew he was being defensive. Hell, his back had been up since Tony mentioned Lana, but he didn't need help with her. He just needed time to sort things out in his head, and he couldn't do that when he was concerned about his cover.

Tony raised an eyebrow. "Practicing law gives me plenty of opportunities for psychological analysis, and the club even more so. My friends get my help, even when they don't think they need it. And as for me, it was time for a change. New scenery. New people. New career."

"Most people only make one life-altering change at a time," James said bitterly.

Tony's eyes shuttered and his hand clenched on the desk. "I'm not most people."

Now there was an understatement. Cloaked in an aura of danger and mystery, with a commanding, physical presence, Tony could control a room with only a glance. Even James knew better than to challenge him, although right now, with anxiety pumping through his veins, he couldn't help but try again.

"How about you help me figure out how to convince the DEU to return the weapons cache? Leave me to handle my own damn nonexistent relationship."

"You're about to lose the one thing in the world that means something to you and you don't even realize it," Tony replied coolly.

"My life."

"Roxie."

Tony's mild, unthreatening tone belied the danger inherent in the fact he knew Lana's real name, a name she had said she'd never used since moving to Vancouver. James's teeth gritted together and his skin prickled. Maybe Tony wasn't the friend James had thought he was.

"That's not her name."

"It's the name she was given at birth."

Heart pounding, James leaned over Tony's desk, dropping his palms to the cool surface. "I don't see how that was information you needed to collect for the club."

Although James had breached Tony's personal space, Tony didn't move.

"I collect information on everyone who comes into the club, and especially on anyone who manages to sneak in not once but twice. She's intelligent and resourceful, as well as beautiful. And I'm guessing her kink—and yes, I know she has a kink—is a result of some past trauma, a way of finding control in a situation where once she had none."

James's vision sheeted red. If Tony had been any other man, he would have grabbed him by the shirt, hauled him over the desk and tossed him into the wall before wiping that damn knowing smile off his lips. But something held him back. Whether it was Tony's utterly calm demeanor in the face of James's anger, or the sense Tony was more than he appeared, he didn't know.

Still, his overwhelming urge to protect Lana in the face of a threat needed an outlet. With a low growl, he swiped everything off Tony's desk, taking what satisfaction he could in the sound of pens and books hitting the floor.

Tony snorted a laugh and leaned back in his chair, folding his hands behind his head. "And there, my friend, is the answer to your relationship problem. It's not casual at all. Not in the least. You're in so deep you're drowning."

In response to James's quizzical look, he continued. "I highly doubt you would have reacted like that if the object of my inquiries had been Katy, or Trixie..." he tilted his head to the side and said quietly, "...or even Christine."

Hands trembling, blood still pounding through his veins, James could only stand and stare. Tony was right. He'd never felt this way about Christine. Affection, yes. Respect, definitely. They'd shared similar values and interests. They'd agreed on most things and rarely fought. Being with Christine had been easy, comfortable. He had thought it was enough to sustain a marriage. But in the end, it wasn't enough for her. And if he was honest with himself, it hadn't been enough for him. He needed more. Fire. Challenge. Sass.

"You played me," he said as he collapsed into the chair across from Tony's desk.

Tony smiled. "I helped you. No thanks necessary. Now that we've sorted out that problem, you mentioned an issue with the DEU refusing to release a cache of weapons?"

James scrubbed his hands over his face. Although Tony had been cleared to know about James's assignment, he couldn't give him too many details, certainly nothing regarding Bones's suspicions about his identity or the possible DEU mole. But after overhearing Rex at the beach, he was damned sure Rex had purchased some new weapons and was looking to offload the existing cache on his buyer. Which meant he would be asking James for his weapons in the next few days and the DEU wouldn't give them up. No way could he involve Ryder again.

He gave Tony the basic info and twisted his lips as Tony steepled his fingers.

"I can see both sides." Tony sighed and shook his head. "Despite my formidable powers of persuasion, I don't think even I could get past the bureaucracy. Still, something doesn't sit right with me. With your distinguished career, one would think they would bend over backwards to keep you safe. Why hang you out to dry? And why now?"

"So I'm screwed."

"You could pull out."

James shook his head. "I can't quit before the raid, otherwise two years of my life was for nothing. Problem is, I've given them at least four good raid opportunities and each time something went wrong. I'm running out of time."

A frown creased Tony's brow. "Something else is definitely going on. They aren't that incompetent. They have two years of wiretap evidence—more than enough to get the convictions they need. The raid would just be the icing on the cake. They should've pulled you out a long time ago."

"I can't just walk away," James said. "Hades is totally corrupt. Drugs, weapons, executions... You name it, Rex is involved. A lot of lives would be saved if they go down."

Tony pressed his lips together. "Can you give me a few days? I have a few friends in high places. I might be able to find something out."

James gave him a puzzled look. What friends in high places? How could he possibly gain clearance for the information even James couldn't get? He threw out a little bait. "Very few people have access to that information."

"Not a problem," Tony assured him. "Leave it with me."

James hesitated and then pushed himself out of his chair. He didn't have much time and if Tony thought he could help, who was he to question him? "Thanks. And...I'm sorry about...earlier." He waved vaguely at the mess on the floor.

Tony held up a hand and grinned. "Nothing more than I expected. You'd be surprised how many times my desk has been swept clean."

Halfway across the room, James stopped and turned. "If something happens to me..."

"Nothing will." Tony's smile faded. "But if it makes you feel better, you can rest assured I'll look after her."

"So, what do you want to do while you're waiting for James?" Trixie settled herself on Katy's vacant seat and waved goodbye to Katy and Mark as they left the club. "I would offer you a tour but you've been here twice already." She winked and Lana's cheeks heated. Her two illicit visits to the club clearly hadn't been forgotten.

Biting her lip, she pointed to the ornate wooden doors leading to the private members' area at the back of Carpe

Noctem. "I've never been in there. Maybe I could..."

Trixie smiled and cut her off. "You have a dark side after all. Master Tony won't mind if you have a little peek. Actually, he even suggested it."

Moments later they were standing on a balcony overlooking a softly lit, circular, sunken room. Twice the size of the club proper the members-only area looked more like a private fitness club than Sex Central. Polished hardwood floors gleamed under the bright lights overhead. Thick area rugs in red and beige complemented the soft leather furniture and warm wooden tables in the seating areas. Except for the terrifying equipment scattered around the perimeter, it was almost inviting.

Sensing Lana's trepidation, Trixie immediately launched into an explanation of the various pieces of equipment: slings, sawhorses, benches, a St. Andrew's cross...The list went on and on. But before Lana could ask any questions, Trixie was called away, assuring Lana as she left that there would be no problem if she wanted to stay and watch the couples scening.

Sweat trickled down Lana's back as she gazed out over the floor. She'd heard about places like this, but had never realized all her secret fantasies could be lived out in one room.

In one corner, a woman knelt on all fours on a padded bench, her arms and legs secured with cuffs. A man wearing black leather pants and a leather vest selected a wide paddle from a rack on the wall and then spanked her, gently at first and then with increasingly firm strokes. Lana's blood heated. Although the woman's body shuddered with each blow, her eyes were half-closed with desire. The man said something and she looked back over her shoulder and laughed.

Lana's tension eased. She'd heard more laughter than screams since she stepped through the door. Maybe BDSM wasn't all about power or pain. Maybe it was about having fun too.

She closed her eyes and imagined herself in the woman's place. Hands and feet restrained. Ass in the air. The swish of the paddle before it made contact with flesh. And behind her, James. It had to be James. She couldn't imagine anyone else with the force of will to even get her down the stairs.

"You like the idea of being restrained on the bench," he whispered in her ear. A statement, not a question.

Lana startled at his sudden presence behind her and then blushed, embarrassed at her obvious reaction. "Where did you come from?"

"Hell. But now I'm back. I didn't expect to see you in here."

She gripped the railing in front of her. "I was...curious. Trixie said Master Tony wouldn't mind if I watch for a few minutes as long as I don't go down onto the floor."

"First time for everything," James muttered under his breath. "He's causing all sorts of trouble today."

Lana gave him a sideways glance. "So...you play here?"

"Sometimes."

Her heart stuttered in her chest. "With someone...special?"

He peeled her fingers off the railing one by one and brought her hand to his lips. "No."

"Why not?" Her already heated body flamed as he kissed his way down her arm to the sensitive crease of her elbow.

"I never met anyone I wanted to bring here." His lips travelled higher, over the strap of her sleeveless dress to nip the sensitive tendon between her neck and shoulder. A soft, breathy moan escaped her lips.

"Not even Christine?"

He hesitated for the briefest second, and then stepped closer, his fingers curving over her left hip, his lips brushing over her ear. "No, babe. Wasn't her thing."

She bit her lip, unexpectedly shy and embarrassed in front of the man who had stripped her naked on her desk only a few hours ago. "Were you...going to bring me in here?"

His hand slid over her hip to squeeze her ass while with the other he pulled her against him. Highly aroused, partly entranced, she was only vaguely aware of the fact they were on a balcony and clearly visible to everyone below.

"I hadn't decided, but I should've guessed you would find your way here. You have a nose for trouble."

Lana trailed her fingers down his arm, admiring the corded muscle, imagining how it would flex if he held a paddle in his hand. Or a flogger. *Oh God.*

"James? Would you..." Her words caught in her throat as he smoothed his hand down her spine, making her arch toward him and sending a ripple of pleasure through her body.

"Anything." His hands were everywhere now, as if the room had somehow inflamed his desire. He caressed her back, gently at first, and then he kneaded his way down to her ass with firmer strokes. A groan escaped her when he buried his lips in the sensitive juncture of her neck and shoulder, his breath hot and heavy on her skin. Their hips melded together and she could feel his erection hard against her stomach.

"I'm not into the lifestyle but I enjoy playing with the right person," he murmured against her heated skin.

A thrill of fear jolted her body and a low moan escaped her lips.

"That excites you." His voice dropped to a low, husky growl.

"I...don't know. It's only something I've read about. Imagined." She looked up at him and her brow creased. "Maybe I like it in theory but not in practice."

James laughed and kissed away her frown. "You won't know until you try. Other than the bench, what else interests you?"

Her insides turned liquid, but her answer came without hesitation. "That...post."

A shiver ran down her spine as she pointed to a tall polished wooden pole with black leather cuffs hanging from a chain clipped to an eyebolt at the top—so similar to the pole that Fang, the Wolverine leader, had chained her to after one of her more daring escape attempts. And yet, when she thought of James restraining her on the post, it wasn't fear that made her shiver, but something else.

Therapy, Jackie would say.

"Do you want to try it?" he asked quietly.

Her mouth went dry and she had barely squeaked out a "yes" before he was leading her down the stairs.

By the time they reached the post, she was trembling so hard she almost welcomed the support of the cuffs as James buckled them to her wrists. Grabbing the loose end of the chain, he pulled her hands up over her head, leaving her enough slack to just touch the ground with the balls of her feet.

"That will definitely keep you out of trouble." The warmth in his eyes and his wicked smile drew some of Lana's tension away.

"If that's what you think, then you don't know me very well." She forced a grin. "I could cause trouble even if you tied my feet too."

He cupped her jaw with his warm palm and brushed his lips over her cheek. "Maybe we'll try that next."

A couple stopped in front of them. The man dressed in leather pants and a vest gave her a wink; the woman wearing a green and gold corset dress smiled. They twined their arms around each other as if settling in to watch the show.

Lana's stomach twisted in a knot and she squeezed her eyes shut. Waves of nausea roiled in her stomach. Maybe this wasn't a good idea. Letting James restrain her when they were alone together was one thing. But this public display, so like what she had endured at the Wolverine clubhouse...

Memories rose like bile in her throat. Hands touching, punching, pinching, squeezing, slapping, stroking. Restrained, alone, there was nothing she could do to stop them. Levi's cold laughter. Fang's angry growls. They kept her for the entertainment value as much as for doing the clubhouse chores.

Her lungs constricted, her body prickled with heat and her pulse raced. She tried to open her eyes but icy black claws threaded through her vision. She heard a whimper and realized it was her own.

"Look at me."

Her head jerked up at James's sharp command, and she fought back the blackness to look into his steel-blue eyes, calm and safe. And then he said the words that sent the memories away.

"Do you remember your safe word from when we played together that one time before?"

"Thrash," she whispered.

"Works the same here. Say the word and we stop. In the end, you control this, babe. Nothing happens that you don't want. Just keep your eyes on me and breathe slow and deep." He trailed his finger along her jaw and down her throat. Lana took a few deep breaths and the darkness began to recede.

I control this. I can make it stop.

"Better now?" He inched his finger down to the swell of her breasts and lightly caressed her heated skin. Fire replaced the ice in her veins, burning a trail down to her core.

She nodded, not trusting herself to speak.

James looked over his shoulder and jerked his head at the couple. The man nodded and they walked away. Lana breathed out a sigh and she managed a half smile.

"Ready to play?" he murmured.

Emboldened by the power she'd never had with Levi, she answered quickly, "Yes."

He slid his hand into the low V of her dress and gently palmed her breast, stroking the soft swell with his thumb. "Your body likes being restrained. I can see it in the flush of your cheeks and I can feel it here." He ran his thumb over her nipple, already painfully hard.

Lana struggled against the restraints as his touch unleashed a firestorm of desire through her veins.

"Be still." His sharp tone locked her in place.

Bracing himself with one arm on the post, he leaned closer and pushed down her clothing, releasing her breasts from their restraint. When his lips found her nipple, a zing of sensation flashed straight to Lana's clit and her hands yanked against the chains.

"Oh God."

James chuckled. "No, babe. Just me."

With calm deliberation, he tormented first one nipple and then the other until her breasts swelled, the nipples tight and throbbing. Pressure built inside her, a deep aching need, and she moaned and writhed, straining against the chains, arching her body toward him, desperate for more.

"You have the most amazing breasts," he murmured as he pulled away.

Lana groaned when he covered her up. "Apparently not amazing enough."

James smoothed his hand down her stomach, leaving a trail of fire in his wake. He rested his palm over her mound, his fingers barely brushing over where fingers should do more than brush.

Panting, she stared up at him, willing him to touch, to take, to rip off her panties and plunge his fingers inside her aching center.

Instead, he kissed her. His lips crushed hers, claiming her with a passionate intensity that took her breath away. His tongue dove into her mouth, possessive and demanding, and he deepened the kiss until her bones turned liquid and she sagged against the restraints.

"You're doing well, babe." The raw sensuality in his voice

almost made her come right then. With a light stroking tease of his hand, he reached under her dress, parted her legs and pressed his palm, warm and firm, against the curve of her sex.

Lana's head snapped back at the delicious heat of his hand over her barely there G-string panties, and a thin whine escaped her lips.

"Keep going, should I?" He gave her a wicked smile and shoved her panties aside, then slicked his finger along her wet folds. Fire swept through her body, incinerating everything in its path.

"Are you still afraid?" With one finger he stroked up and around her clit, then down through her wetness, and up again, barely brushing over the throbbing bundle of nerves begging for attention.

"I'm afraid you'll stop," she panted.

His lips curled into a sensual smile. "I can go all night. Or I can stop and leave you hanging. Or I can make you come in front of everyone here. I can make you scream your pleasure, and you can't do anything about it."

Moisture flooded her sex at his carnal words. She strained against the cuffs, and her inability to move, her vulnerability, started a shaking deep inside her. Did she truly trust him to keep her safe?

A disturbance at the door drew her attention away from his steady gaze. A verbal altercation. Shouting. Yelling. A crease formed between her brows. The voices were familiar.

Seconds later, an angry Rex pushed his way into the room, Angel by his side. Two bouncers grabbed them and hauled them back. Even as her face heated in embarrassment, Lana's heart sank. They were back together. Angel wouldn't need her anymore.

James shifted his position, hiding her from Rex. "That's my fault," he muttered. "I should never have organized a meeting here. Rex liked it so much he pestered Tony for a membership.

Tony only gave in because he figured the club's surveillance system might catch something that would help put Rex behind bars faster." He stroked a finger over her cheek. "Don't worry. He won't get down here. You're safe."

The door slammed open again and Lana heard the rough growl of Rex's voice and the high-pitched rasp of Angel's tirade of verbal abuse.

And then she heard another voice. A cold, cruel, sharp snarl that cut her to the core. She sucked in a sharp breath and her body tensed, as it had been conditioned to do.

No.

"We have an important guest," Rex shouted. "I want to show him around."

The other voice again. A man. Louder now. More insistent. Angry. Her lungs seized. Terror spread icy tendrils through her veins. She knew that voice. She heard it in her nightmares. She heard it on street corners and in restaurants, in coffee shops and bars. And always her heart would pound and her eyes would widen, and she would fight the urge to run.

Run. She needed to run.

Lana yanked on the cuffs but they held fast. Body trembling, heart hammering, pulse racing, she forced her words through a rapidly tightening throat. "Let me go, James. Let me go."

James's eyes widened and his face creased with concern. "What's wrong?"

"Thrash," she screamed as a scorching tide of terror crashed through her body. Her eyes fixed on the partially open door, her ears attuned to only one voice. His voice.

"Thrash," she screamed again. And then she just screamed the word over and over because, although James moved fast, he wasn't fast enough. And the door was opening; a hand was creeping around the corner. A big hand. With a big ring. The head of a Wolverine.

And then she was free.

Arms banded around her. Strong. Safe. But there was no *safe*. Not from Levi.

Tears burned her eyes as she remembered the thud of fists on her body, the burn of ropes whipping across her skin, the sting of a palm hitting flesh, the utter helplessness of having nowhere to go and no one to help her. A sob rose in her throat. She pushed James away and ran toward the welcoming red neon sign marking the emergency exit.

"Lana."

She hit the door running. An alarm went off but she didn't stop. Couldn't stop. She ran and she ran and she ran. Then she threw up and ran some more.

Chapter Eighteen

"Jackie. Open the fucking door. I know she's in there."

James pounded on Jackie's apartment door, determined to break it down if it didn't open in the next thirty seconds.

"Quiet down," she shouted. "You'll wake my neighbors. I waited a year to get this place. I'm not about to be kicked out because you can't wait long enough for me to undo the lock. And don't even think of breaking down the door."

Finally, the door opened and a furious Jackie glared at James. "Like I told you earlier when you called, she's not here. But feel free to come in and stomp around and check for yourself." She stepped to the side and James stormed into her tiny apartment.

"What happened here?" He looked around at the piles of clothes, pizza boxes, disguises and half-open suitcases.

"Nothing happened. I live like this," Jackie huffed. "I'm not a clean freak like Lana. I like things to be relaxed."

James gritted his teeth. "I could search through this place for a week and never find her."

"You're a smooth talker, J. I can see why she fell so hard for you. You keep buttering me up like that and I'll be kissing your shoes in no time flat. But you don't have to worry about sullying your hands with my filth. Like I told you, she's not here."

The knot that had formed in James's gut when Lana had run out of the club tightened. After spending the night looking for her, he'd come to the conclusion she had to be hiding out at Jackie's place. He had been so certain of the fact, for a moment he felt utterly lost.

"Did she call you?"

"Yeah, she called me," Jackie said. "She was totally hysterical. She wouldn't tell me where she was. All I got from her was you took her to some club and she ran away. What the hell did you do to her?"

James gritted his teeth and shrugged off the question that had tormented him all night. If she wasn't here, where could she be? With the help of Tony, Ryder and Kickstand, all bases had been covered: apartment, office, local restaurants and bars. He had her car keys so he knew she was on foot. Jackie had been calling Lana's friends and acquaintances until she'd suddenly cut off all communication without a word of explanation. How could Lana not be here?

For the first time in his life he didn't know what to do.

Jackie tilted her head to one side and studied him. Her face softened and her voice dropped to a quiet murmur. "Okay. I can see you're worried and pretty beat up. I'll tone it down. You need anything? Glass of water? Something stronger?"

He shook his head. "It's my fault. I shouldn't have taken her there. I should have asked her more about her past. I pushed too hard and something set her off." He paused. "Maybe it was Rex. He was trying to get in."

"She's not that scared of Rex." Jackie wove her way through the clothes and boxes piled on the floor. "Not scared enough to run. Only one guy I know she would run from, but he's somewhere in the US."

"Levi?"

"She told you?"

James nodded. "Not everything. We were interrupted."

Jackie walked over to the window and stared out into the night. "She thought she'd been recognized last week and he would be coming for her. That's why she had the suitcase packed. She ran from him once before. Took her three years to escape. Any chance she might have been right? Do you think he's in town?"

A chill raced down his spine. Why hadn't he even considered she would've had to run? Abusers rarely let their women walk away. But why would Levi be in Vancouver? Would he still be hunting for her after so many years? If so, how did he find her? Or was he here by chance, perhaps to form an alliance with Hades? It didn't make sense.

"If Levi is here, I haven't heard about it." He brushed his thumb over his bottom lip as he considered the possibility. "If he did come to the Lower Mainland, he would've had to stop at Hades to pay his respects. And if he showed up at the clubhouse, Rex would be shouting it out to the world. The Wolverines are a very powerful West Coast club. And I only saw Rex and Angel at Carpe Noctem, no one else." His voice broke. "It was me, Jackie. It was my fault. I just can't do right by her."

She looked at him aghast. "It has nothing to do with you...I'm sure of it."

"Easy to say. Hard to believe."

His cell buzzed against his hip and he sighed heavily before he accepted the call.

"Bones."

Bones didn't waste time on social niceties. "We need you at the clubhouse right away. We've got an unexpected drop tonight at Kirkland Island. Rex wants the inner circle on the pickup team. You need to come in for a briefing."

James scraped a hand through his hair. For the first time in his life he wasn't going to do his duty and it didn't even give him pause. "Tell Rex I can't make it. Roxie's missing and I'm trying to find her."

"You want me to tell Rex you can't make it because you're chasing after your old lady? You got a death wish? I'm telling him you'll be here within the hour. Don't be late."

The phone went dead.

James stared at his cell for a full three seconds then threw it as hard as he could against the wall. The impact made a satisfying crack and the phone fell to the ground.

"Fuck." He sank into a chair, his head between his hands. The DEU would have heard that call and no doubt would be calling his broken phone to ask why he'd refused Bones's request. It was a perfect setup for a raid. Isolated island. Inner circle together. Hard evidence of drug smuggling.

Openmouthed, wide-eyed, Jackie asked lightly, "Bad news?"

"That was Bones. I'm supposed to meet the inner circle at the club and then head out to Kirkland Island tonight. I told him I couldn't make it, but it's something I've been waiting for a long time. Something that could bring down Hades for good."

Kneeling in front of him, Jackie gently stroked a hand over his bowed head. "Look at me."

He lifted his head and his stomach clenched when he saw the guilt on her face.

"You go do what you have to do," Jackie said quietly. "She's safe."

James froze, his breath leaving him in a rush. "Where is she?"

"She doesn't want you to know. She thinks it's better that way. Safer for you."

He cursed softly. "She's trying to protect *me*?"

Tears glistened in Jackie's eyes, and she squeezed his hand. "She has to leave and she doesn't know when she'll be back, if ever. She said you would understand that sometimes it's easier to just disappear than say goodbye."

Bile rose up the back of his throat. Nothing could have cut him more deeply. His actions coming back to haunt him. Pressing his fist to his chest to stem the ache in his heart, he forced himself to be calm.

"He's here, isn't he? Her old boyfriend. Levi."

Bottom lip quivering, she said, "To be honest, I don't know. She wouldn't tell me, for the same reason she won't tell you. Maybe it is him. Or maybe it's like you said and what happened at the club triggered some bad memory." Her voice cracked and tears spilled down her cheeks. "Whatever the reason, she's not sticking around. She's done with Vancouver. With us. Unless...you want to go after her? You, of all people, would be able to track her down."

Her words hit him like a punch in the gut and his throat tightened. He'd failed. In the end, he hadn't been able to mend the rift between them. She still didn't trust him. Leaving her two years ago had been the biggest mistake of his life.

Voice thick with regret, he shook his head. "I won't go after her, Jackie. She doesn't want me. She knew I would have protected her and she chose to run instead. And if I did something wrong, she didn't trust me enough to tell me. If she needed my help, she didn't feel she could ask."

Jackie gave him a warm hug and a sad smile. "Well then, you might as well go finish your assignment, J. Take Rex down. I know in my heart he has something to do with this. She had no problems with anyone until the day he grabbed her in that club. Make him pay."

He rose from the chair and threw Lana's car keys on the table. "And then what?"

"Then I guess you're back to where you started."

"Is he gone?"

"Yeah, he's gone." Jackie leaned out the window and helped Lana off the fire escape. "It went even worse than I expected. In fact, I have to say that was the most gut-wrenching conversation I have ever had in my life, and I've had a few. To put it bluntly, he was sick with worry and beyond despair, and he walked outta here a desolate man."

A dark tide of emotion swept through Lana, sending waves of nausea roiling through her stomach. The last thing she had wanted to do was hurt James.

"Are you still going to leave?" Jackie's bottom lip quivered, and for the first time Lana realized she was hurting her friend too.

"Levi is here. I heard him when I was at the club. He was with Rex. At first I thought maybe I was imagining it, but then I saw his hand and he was wearing the club ring. He'll be looking for me. I don't have a choice." She grabbed an empty shopping bag from a pile on the floor and headed into the kitchen.

"There has to be another way," Jackie whined. "What will I do without you? Who's going to be my wingman on surveillance missions? Who's going to dance with me on the tables in the bars? Who's going to feed me sympathy and Oreos when my relationships sour? Who's going to stop me from manhandling Derek? Who's going to look after me?"

Tears welled in Lana's eyes and she wiped them away with her sleeve. "You don't know what they did to the people who tried to help me. The guy who helped me escape had to leave the state, dye his hair and change his name. I'm not dragging anyone into this. Not you. Not James. You don't need me. The past is so far behind you it's ancient. You'll be fine." She opened a cupboard and peered inside. "Okay if I take some snacks for the road?"

"Take what you want. I'm going to pine to death anyway," Jackie snapped, her eyes glistening with tears. "But have you thought about your clients...Angel?"

Lana gritted her teeth and tossed a few granola bars in the bag. Tempting as it was to ask for help or even take Jackie with her, she couldn't take the risk. Levi was her problem alone. And the only way she knew how to deal with him was to run.

Her chest tightened at the thought of moving again. New city. New job. New friends. New life. She would be back to jumping at every shadow and peering into every corner.

Trusting no one. She would spend her nights tossing and turning, terrified every creak meant Levi had found her. After coming so far, she was back to the beginning again.

"If you manage to pull the pictures off the lipstick camera, you can send them to Angel." Her voice wavered. "But I think she and Rex are back together. You can tell my other clients I had an emergency and had to leave town. I already did briefing notes for you. Somehow I knew it would come to this."

"He loves you." Jackie's voice broke. "Don't do this to him. Don't do this to yourself."

He loves me. Lana rolled the unfamiliar concept around her mind. No one loved her. Not since her mother died. Not her father. Not her brothers. Boyfriends had come and gone until Levi. But he had never loved her either. And neither had James. She had let herself forget how she felt the morning she woke up and found him gone.

"How can you leave without saying goodbye?" Jackie threw open another cupboard and absently tossed a few boxes of JELL-O powder and Hamburger Helper into Lana's bag. "Why won't you give him a chance to help?"

"Because he'll go after Levi and get killed, and if he doesn't die, they'll go after him." Lana closed her eyes and sighed. "The Wolverines aren't ordinary bikers. They make Hades look like pussycats. Someone cuts them off on the road, they burn the guy's car...with him in it. Someone steals something belonging to them, they cut off the guy's hands and feet, and toss him in the lake. A biker from another gang tried to help me escape, and they shot up his house. He and his family only survived because he had a safe room and after that they had to leave the state. Every time I ran away, I was beaten and chained up as punishment. And Levi was worse than most of them."

"Wait." Jackie raced past Lana and plastered herself against the door. "You're my best friend. I love you to bits. I'm there for you, no matter what. But I think you're making a mistake. James is one of the toughest guys I know. He's like a rock…ice. Probably how he got his road name. But if you leave, you'll break him. And you'll lose the best thing that ever happened to you."

"How can I *not* leave him?" Lana's voice cracked, broke. "I have to protect him. Not only that— his biggest fear is that he falls for someone and loses them. If I stay, his worst nightmare will come true. I can't do that to him."

Jackie sagged against the splintered wood. "It's too late. You already did. He thinks he lost you because of what happened at the club. He thinks it's his fault."

Nausea roiled in Lana's belly and the shopping bag fell from her hand, hitting the floor with a loud thunk. "Oh God. That wasn't it at all."

"Then tell him and at the very least say goodbye. Give him a choice, a chance. He's got to go to Kirkland Island tonight with Rex and his inner circle on some kind of secret mission, but if you hurry you could probably catch him at the clubhouse before they leave."

Lana sucked in a sharp breath and her blood turned cold. "James is going to Kirkland Island?"

Jackie shrugged. "He got called to help on some last-minute deal that he thought could close off his case. He was going to blow them off to look for you but I…I told him you were safe and he should go. He was so desolate. I was worried about him. He didn't even crack a smile at the chance to shut Hades down for good."

Lana's hand flew to her mouth. "He can't go, Jackie. It's a trap. They're going to kill him. They must have found out he's a rat."

"Oh God." Jackie's breath caught in her throat. "You should have told him."

A sob escaped Lana's lips. "I did."

James parked his Rocker at the edge of the marsh and

waited for Ryder to join him. Although the sun had set hours ago, Kirkland Island was abuzz with the croaking of tree frogs, the barking of sea lions and the odd squawking of the many birds that inhabited the tiny island between Richmond and Delta on the South Arm Marshes. They dismounted, clipped their helmets to their seats, and followed Rex, Punch and Dawg down a small dirt hill to the beach. Bones and Diesel silently fell in behind them, packs on their backs.

"I have a bad feeling about this," Ryder said quietly.

James had had a bad feeling since he'd walked into the clubhouse. The feeling had become worse when Rex insisted they go to the storage locker where James said he'd hidden the weapons. And he'd had to fight the overpowering instinct to run when he opened the staged locker to reveal empty gun cabinets, broken locks and a fake letter from the DEU inviting Hades to the police station to retrieve their lost property. Best ruse he could come up with, given the time. Rex had said nothing and James still didn't know if he'd bought the story or not.

Despite his misgivings, he had to stay with the group as they headed out to the island. Not only would his abrupt departure have aroused their suspicions, the DEU needed him here. After leaving Jackie's apartment, assured of Lana's safety, he'd made the call. His handler had promised the raid was finally going to happen. In a dual attack, one team would raid Hades and the second would raid the Kirkland drop site. He could only hope they got there before Rex shot him in the head.

Gravel crunched underfoot as they walked single file on the path through the marshy swamp. As he followed Ryder's broad back, James wondered if his friend would try to defend him if Rex called him out as a rat. Even together, they wouldn't have a chance against five armed men. He had given Ryder's description to his handler, with instructions that he shouldn't be arrested but, now, considering both risks, it might be better to get Ryder out of the way.

He waited until they were out of earshot of both groups and

then clasped Ryder's shoulder. "Maybe you should go back and keep watch."

"Fuck that."

"Seriously. You should go watch the bikes. Keep an eye out for the police. We don't all need to be on the beach."

Ryder rolled his eyes. "Seriously. Fuck that."

They reached the sand and picked their way through stones and washed-up logs, giant pieces of sea kelp and the remnants of picnic lunches. The air was cool and crisp and thick with the scent of brine. James reached behind himself and checked for his weapon. Ryder did the same.

Rex stopped near an outcropping. Together with Punch and Dawg he turned to face James and Ryder. James glanced quickly over his shoulder, taking note of where Bones and Diesel were positioned. He would have cover if he could make it back to the thicket of trees they'd passed on their way down. But he would have to be fast.

For the longest time nobody moved. Blood pumping hot and fast, James's every muscle tensed for flight. He licked his lips and imagined he tasted Lana, sweet and sensual. He pictured her laughing, her green eyes dancing and her hair a wild tumble around her face. He felt her soft curves beneath his palms, heard her moans of pleasure in his ears, breathed in her scent of wild flowers.

His heart squeezed and ached. What the hell had he been thinking when he told Jackie he wouldn't go after her? If he made it off this beach alive, he would find her, and when he did, he would never let her go.

Rex's gaze stayed on him. James caught the glitter of anticipation in the black depths of his eyes, and something else. Something deadly. He took a deep breath and reached for his weapon.

The thudding of helicopter blades cut through the stillness.

"Here they are." Rex broke their connection and looked up

into the sky. "Bones. Diesel. Get the money ready. They'll drop a bag and half the load. Empty it out. Put in half the cash. They'll send down the rest of the kilos and we'll send up the rest of the money."

James staggered backward as his breath whooshed from his lungs. Maybe it wasn't a hit after all.

At a shout from Rex, he joined the others to help with the switch. Suddenly an air siren wailed and the roar of a motor cut through the sound of the helicopter's blades.

Anticipation ratcheted through him. This was it. The beginning of the end.

"Fuck. Coast Guard. Pack it up," Rex yelled.

Coast Guard? James turned to the water and startled at the glare of headlights as a boat raced toward them. Who the hell had called the Coast Guard? Where was the DEU?

Bones and Diesel grabbed the packs, and they raced up the beach as the helicopter disappeared into the night.

James took a last glance over his shoulder as they dove into the bushes. He caught the sweep of the Coast Guard's searchlight and the blare of a siren. What the hell was going on? Why would they send the Coast Guard, knowing the bikers would easily be able to flee by land?

Something didn't add up.

Again.

Chapter Nineteen

"Ice. You got a call."

Ryder held out his phone and James frowned. Who the hell would be calling him at Hades's clubhouse on Ryder's phone? Not for the first time that evening did he curse himself for breaking his cell. He couldn't call the DEU to find out why the raid hadn't happened, and he couldn't meet his handler because Rex had instituted a lockdown until he figured out who had ratted them out to the Coast Guard.

"Who is it?"

A slow grin spread across Ryder's face. "Someone I'm damn sure you want to talk to. She got my number from Jackie."

Swallowing past the lump in his throat, James took the phone and dashed up the stairs to his room. Slamming the door behind him, he pressed Ryder's cell to his ear.

"Babe…"

"James." Her relief was almost palpable. "I was so worried. I couldn't leave until I knew you were safe. But I didn't know who to call." Her voice came out in a rush and before James could take a breath, she was talking again.

"I tried the DEU, but they said you didn't exist. So I called Tony because you said he knew you were undercover. He told me he had some information that made him wary of calling the DEU or the police, but he had a friend in the Coast Guard. So we called them instead. I wanted to go to Kirkland but he wouldn't let me. He said it was too dangerous." A raw, guttural sob escaped her lips. "I thought they were going to kill you and I thought…"

He knew what she'd thought. Hell, he'd thought about it

too. "It wasn't a good day to die," he said softly. "I'd decided to go after you. There was something I'd forgotten to say."

She drew in a ragged breath. "What?"

His gut clenched as he imagined telling her what he should have said, instead of walking away two years ago. But he couldn't do it over the phone. He needed to see her, hold her. Show her his feelings went beyond words. "I'll tell you when I get there. Where are you?"

"I'm at my office." Her voice was barely a whisper.

"I shouldn't be here much longer. Rex is trying to find out who sent the Coast Guard, but if Tony was involved he'll hit a dead end pretty fast. Can you wait for me?"

"I'll wait."

James sagged against the door as the tension he'd been carrying with him since she'd run from Carpe Noctem eased. She was safe and she was waiting for him. Emotion overwhelmed him and for a moment he couldn't speak.

"James?"

"Yeah, babe. I'm still here."

"I need to tell you something."

Overwhelmed by the sudden urgent need to see her, he grabbed his pack and threw open the door. He was done with the DEU. Done with the assignment. And Rex could fucking go to hell. He was leaving now and no one was going to stop him.

"Tell me when I get there," he rasped. "I'm on my way."

"Well, look who's running away."

James spun around, only three feet from the front door, to see Bones and Diesel standing behind him, guns leveled at his chest.

"Rex wants to see you." Diesel jerked a thumb behind him.

Bones smirked. "He wants to see you pretty bad."

They flanked him through the clubhouse as he made the march down to Rex's office. The inner circle was seated in a semicircle around the room, faces grim. Bones slammed the door behind him and took up a guard position.

"We've got some unfinished business from the beach." Rex leaned over his desk. "Usually I don't like to bring shit into the clubhouse, but since we had to break the rule to bring back the drop..." he pointed to the cocaine-filled backpacks lined up against the wall, "...I don't see why we shouldn't break the rule about getting rid of rats."

James's pulse pounded in his temples, and he pulled up a mental picture of Rex's office. Thirty-five square feet. Small bathroom at the back. One door now guarded by Bones. Three windows along the side, now guarded by Punch, Dawg and Diesel.

Five against one. Six, depending on which way Ryder would swing. All armed.

Bad odds at the best of times.

His heart stuttered in his chest. He should have told Lana over the phone what he wanted to say. He should have told her he loved her. He should have said goodbye.

"I just called you a rat," Rex growled. "You got nothing to say? No denial? No defense? No explanation?"

Adrenaline pumped through James's veins, forcing his body into hyperawareness. He felt his every rasping breath, heard the scrape of every chair and the slide of every weapon leaving a belt or holster. He tasted the bitterness of betrayal on his tongue. He saw Rex's anger and Ryder's calm confidence. He smelled the acrid odor of death.

"Jesus Christ, Rex. You don't crap in your own nest. We can't off him here." Ryder leaned against the wall, arms folded, weapon hanging loose between his fingers. "You need to take him off Hades's property. If the police ever raid, they'll bring dogs. No matter how much you clean, the dogs will smell the blood. Then they'll be all over this place with a fine-tooth comb. They'll find things you didn't even know were hidden. We'll all go down, and for what? For a fucking rat?"

"He's not worth it," Bones said. "Let's take him out to Gunn Island, or Williamson. They're both isolated and restricted to the public. You already took a risk bringing the kilos on site. We gotta dump them before we do anything else. And our guests should be back soon. You don't want a mess."

James's heart hammered in his chest, and he forced himself to look anywhere but at Ryder. His friend was on his side, but even two against five were bad odds in such a tight space.

Rex looked from Ryder to Bones. Then he studied James for a long moment. "You would've made a damn good biker, but you'll make an even better dead rat."

He leveled his gun and smiled.

Lana paced up and down in front of her office window. She'd called James almost three hours ago. Where was he? With Levi in town she couldn't wait much longer.

The wind whipped around the building, rattling her windows. He'd better hurry. If it started to rain he wouldn't be able to ride and they would have to run away in her Jetta.

A half smile curled her lips. Wouldn't that be the ultimate irony? The car he despised would save yet another life. This time, hers.

She still couldn't believe he was coming to help her. Even after she'd run away. Nothing she'd done had put him off. He had trusted her with his heart, how could she do any less for him?

A thud sounded at the door and a gasp broke free from her lips. Breathless anticipation ratcheted through her as she ran into the foyer and threw open the deadbolt. Only then did she remember.

James had a key.

The door slammed open. Lana staggered back, her breath catching in her throat as she came face-to-face with her worst nightmare.

"Levi." Her horrified whisper brought a cruel smile to his thin lips.

"Hello, darling."

Lana's stomach clenched violently. She willed her feet to move, but fear and shock had frozen them in place. Even after so many years, she couldn't look at him without a painful tightening in her chest. His beauty—sharp and sensual—had not diminished with age. Black hair, steel-gray eyes, sharp cheekbones, a narrow jaw and a cruel slash of a mouth. With his pale skin, his incisors shaved to points in tribute to Fang, he resembled a gothic vampire. But he was no comic book villain. Tall and muscular, his corded forearms covered in tats, he'd dished out his strength frequently and always with a side helping of bruises.

"Did you miss me, Roxie?" He struck her across the face, the blow so hard her head snapped to the side.

Lana stumbled away and fell to the ground. Ears ringing, she could just make out Kickstand's angry shout as he raced into her office and crouched protectively by her side.

"You told me you were friends. You can't touch her. She's Ice's girl."

"She's no one's girl." Levi kicked her in the ribs with the hard tip of his biker boots, and she instinctively curled up, trying to protect herself from the sharp, familiar pain.

"She's my wife."

A hushed murmur swept through the crowded Hades clubhouse as Levi dragged Lana into the center of the empty lounge. The main floor of the clubhouse had been cleared of furniture for the extraordinary visit of the Wolverines. James counted at least twenty Wolverine patches in the crowd. A large contingent for an insignificant city, but a small group in the packed clubhouse.

Every full-patch member, prospect, old lady and Hades affiliate had been called to witness Rex's biggest triumph. The return of a runaway slave to one of the biggest, most powerful motorcycle clubs on the west coast. The reward was substantial. The accolades impressive. But the goodwill Rex had bought Hades was priceless.

James couldn't decide whom to kill first.

Hands cuffed behind his back, ankles tied together, flanked by Ryder and Bones, James growled his anger and frustration. Ryder glanced over and frowned, warning him to keep quiet. If not for the timely arrival of the Wolverines, Ryder might not have been able to convince Rex to hold off the execution. He shouldn't be pressing his luck.

Claw and a sheet-white Kickstand stood beside Ryder. Tears streaked Kickstand's face. Horrified that Rex had used him to lead Levi to Lana on the pretense of reuniting two old friends, he'd begged Rex to release him from his pledge to the club. Rex had promised him his patch instead.

Rage thrummed through James's body when Levi forced Lana to her knees and fisted her hair, holding her in place.

"Which one of you is Ice?"

James forced himself to keep his gaze on Levi, and not Lana on the floor, head bowed under the pressure of Levi's fist.

"I'm Ice."

"I heard you were fucking my wife."

Wife? The word cut James like the sharpest knife. Had she married the bastard? Was he sleeping with another man's wife? She knew how he felt about marriage and she'd slept with him anyway? Betrayal hit him like a punch to the gut. She'd lied like

Christine had lied.

"I didn't know she was your wife." His low, cold voice betrayed no emotion as he turned his gaze to Lana. "Why didn't you tell me?"

She didn't look up. Instead, she moaned softly, and the utter despair and hopelessness in her voice diluted his bitterness to a dull ache.

"Answer him." The icy tone of Levi's words stung James's flesh. "Tell him what a bad wife you were, running away and hiding from me all these years." Levi yanked Lana's head back and James looked at her aghast. Eyes swollen, lip split, face covered with cuts and bruises. But what made his heart ache most was the desolation in her eyes, dark without hope and bleak without her fire.

"Answer him, dammit." Levi struck Lana across the face and her head snapped to the side.

Protectiveness surged through him. How could he condemn her for running away from Levi? He suspected she'd only touched on the abuse she'd suffered during her years with him. Theirs wasn't a marriage to be saved; it was a marriage that should never have happened. A marriage to be forgotten. Abandoned. Just as she had done. She'd left Levi to start a new life, heal the scars...and James had just added another.

"Fucking bitch." Levi kicked her thigh. "I'll make you talk when we get home. Or, better yet, I'll let the brothers convince you to talk."

Hot, hard rage suffused every cell in James's body. Suddenly it didn't matter that she was married, or that she hadn't told him the truth. He was done with rules and rigid, meaningless personal codes. He'd been so focused on the past he couldn't see his future standing in front of him. It was time to leave the path and follow his heart. Follow his fire.

"You're not looking very apologetic." Levi turned his gaze on James. "Maybe you don't understand. Not only did you fuck my wife, you fucked the property of the Wolverines."

He lifted Lana by the hair and spun her around. She moved like a rag doll, limbs limp, body swaying. Levi yanked up her shirt and shoved her jeans low enough to give James a clear view of her tattoo. The tattoo she hated. The tattoo he had kissed.

"Same mark we use on all Wolverine property," Levi said. "Equipment, furniture...slaves." He kicked Lana's knees and she dropped to the floor.

James's vision sheeted red. He yanked at the cuffs, pulled against the hands gripping his arms, his body shaking with the effort to get free. Two minutes. That's all he needed to wrap his fingers around the throat of that soulless bastard and make sure he never hurt Lana again.

"Looking at her now, you wouldn't believe it took eight guys to hold her down," Levi said with a smirk. "She fought like a fucking wildcat. Bit a chunk out of one guy's arm and nearly tore the balls of another one. But they finally got her pinned and I marked her myself. My initiation into the Wolverines."

Rex motioned Bones over to the side and blood pounded through James's veins as he sensed an opportunity to escape. Frantic, he looked over his shoulder. He'd never asked for help, but he was asking now. Voice cracking, he rasped, "Ryder."

"Son of a bitch," Ryder muttered behind him. James felt a tug on the handcuffs and the soft scrape of metal on metal as Ryder worked the lock, stepping between James and the rest of the inner circle to keep his activity hidden from view.

Levi spun Lana around again and pushed her to her knees. She wilted to the floor, her hair drooping over her shoulders.

She's lost hope.

Because of me.

Fury poured from James's heart, his rage directed not just at Rex and Levi, but at himself and his inability to see what really mattered.

Levi thanked Rex for finding his property and directed one of the Wolverines to hand over several packages of neatly stacked bills to Bones. "American dollars," Levi said. "They're worth more than your plastic play money."

While Bones counted the money, James motioned Kickstand over and leaned down to whisper in his ear. "Something happens to me, I need you to give Roxie a message. Go grab a pen and get back here quick."

Kickstand dashed away and Levi announced an affiliation between the Wolverines and Hades, and the establishing of a new drug-trading route between the two clubs. James's heart pounded. He was having a hard time concentrating. All he could think about was getting free of the goddamn handcuffs and getting Lana out of Hades. Once they were on his bike, he would drive until he ran out of road. And then he would keep her safe until the last breath left his body.

A breathless Kickstand returned with a pen, his face twisted by remorse. James dictated the message letter by letter and Kickstand wrote it on the underside of his arm.

"I'll make sure she gets it. You can count on me, Ice."

"I know I can. And if you have any sense, after you deliver the message you'll get the hell out of town and away from Hades."

Business concluded, Levi yanked Lana to her feet. "Say goodbye to your Iceman, Roxie. You'll never be seeing him again. It's time to go home."

"No." With a shriek, Lana suddenly spun, breaking Levi's grip on her hair. She shoved her hands hard into his groin, and when he doubled over, she kneed him in the chin. Levi's head snapped back; he groaned and staggered to the side. But before Lana could run, the Wolverines descended on her, pinning her arms and forcing her to her knees in front of an enraged Levi.

"Fucking bitch," Levi screamed. "You know better than that. Looks like we'll have to teach you to behave all over again." He drew his leg back for a kick and a white blur shot across the room and forced itself between them.

Kickstand.

"Don't touch her," he shouted. And then to Lana, "I'm sorry. So sorry."

James roared and threw himself forward. The ropes around his legs caught and he fell to his knees. Ryder yanked him up, murmuring in his ear that he would have the cuffs off in less than a minute.

Levi laughed and plowed his boot into Kickstand's side, over and over again. Despite James's exhortations to get out of the way, Kickstand stayed between Levi and Lana, taking the blows that surely would have broken her ribs.

Grumbles in the clubhouse turned to yells and shouts. Although they couldn't defend Lana because she was marked as Wolverine property, Hades couldn't allow the disrespect done to their prospect. Within seconds, a full-scale brawl erupted. The clubhouse filled with the sounds of breaking glass and splitting wood, shouts, grunts and moans. Sharp and tangy, blood scented the air.

Anxiety ratcheted through James. He couldn't see Lana. Or Levi. Or even Kickstand. He howled Ryder's name just as the lock clicked. The cuffs fell to floor and within seconds he'd untied his feet.

Fury wiped everything from his mind but the instinctive need to find Lana. He forged a path through the crowd, pounding on anyone who dared get in his way. He didn't ask himself how they would escape two gangs of bloodthirsty bikers. He had no plan. He knew only that Levi intended to take her away. And damned if he would let that happen.

"Quickly. My bike's over there."

Kickstand half pulled, half dragged Lana across the parking

lot, clutching his side as they wove their way through the neat rows of motorcycles.

Thunder boomed in the distance and a cool breeze sliced through Lana's thin cotton shirt, sending a wave of goose bumps over her skin. Thick black clouds choked even the light of the moon and they had only the dim orange glow of the perimeter lights to guide them to Kickstand's bike at the far end of the parking lot.

"You're hurt." Lana gently touched the side of his shirt as he pulled out his key. He hissed and pulled away.

"No worse than you. But we have to hurry. It won't take them long to realize you're missing."

He slid an arm around her waist to help her up and pain sliced through her ribs. Dazed, exhausted, her body bruised and broken, she could barely walk, much less hold on to Kickstand if he planned to drive any faster than a slow crawl.

As the motorcycle roared to life, she glanced back at the clubhouse. Already bikers were spilling into the parking lot. Her heart skipped a beat when she thought she recognized James, but then she remembered the confusion and pain in his eyes, the shock and anger in the taut lines of his face when Levi told him she was married.

James wouldn't be coming for her this time. Not after she'd lied to him and betrayed him just as Christine had done. Not after she had kept secret the one thing that meant the most to him.

"There they are." Shouts from the door. The thud of feet on pavement. The crack of a gun.

"Fuck. I forgot the helmets. Let's hope we don't meet a cop." Kickstand revved the engine and peeled away.

Lana clung to his back and squeezed her eyes shut. "I hope we do."

"Don't even think about starting that bike."

Rex pointed his weapon at James and walked toward him. "Get off nice and slow. I don't want your blood messing up the parking lot."

James shot one desperate glance at Kickstand's disappearing taillights and dismounted his motorcycle. Bones came up behind him and pressed the barrel of his gun to James's head.

"I shoulda killed you earlier, instead of listening to fucking Ryder," Rex drawled. "Although, seeing your face in there was almost worth it. Can't believe you didn't recognize her tattoo. All the US motorcycle clubs with slaves use the same mark, except they change the club initial. If you'd been a real biker, you would have known that."

"And if you'd been a real man, you would have walked away when she rejected you, instead of taking your revenge by selling her like a piece of property," James spat out.

"She *is* property."

"She's gone," James said coolly. "The Wolverines will hold you responsible. If you don't find her, you'll pay the price. Personally. Maybe they'll tattoo their mark on your ass and use you as a replacement."

"I'm gonna fucking enjoy every second of your death," Rex snarled.

James caught movement in the shadows behind Rex and then a flash of white teeth when Ryder grinned. Damn Speedy Gonzales. He must have run around the entire building to take up a position behind Rex.

"You fucked up," James said, stalling for time as Ryder crept up behind Rex. "You can't handle the Wolverines. Once they find Lana, they'll rip you to shreds. Maybe they'll even do it now."

As if on cue, Ryder slammed the butt of his gun into Rex's head.

Taking advantage of Bones's moment of confusion, James

knocked the gun from Bones's hand and spun around to face his assailant.

With a roar, Bones leaped for the gun, but James met him with a full-body slam. Bones reeled backward and into a motorcycle. It tipped to the side and the entire row toppled like dominos.

"Looks like you'll be taking Kickstand's place," James muttered.

Bones jumped to his feet and drove his fist into James's stomach. "Fucking rat," he grunted. "We trusted you. Treated you like a brother, and you betrayed us. I knew from the beginning something was off about you, but fucking stupid Rex wouldn't listen."

James stepped to the side just in time to avoid another blow. "You're still pissed I won your bike."

"Fuck you."

They traded kicks and punches, hammering, thumping and pounding on each other. Bikes fell, the fence groaned, and a trash can went flying. Finally, James forced Bones against the wall and let loose a one-two punch that snapped Bones's head to the side and sent him sagging to the ground.

"You know what?" He bent down and grabbed Bones's hair, yanking his head back until their gazes locked. "You were right. I counted the cards."

One last punch and Bones was out cold.

A gun clattered across the pavement. James spun around to see a disarmed Ryder drop to one knee under the force of Rex's blows. Damned Rex must have one hell of a hard head.

"It's me you want," James yelled as he stalked across the parking lot. "Come and show me what you've got. Let's have a real fight. I won't be pulling any punches this time."

With a roar, Rex turned and rounded on James, closing the distance between them faster than James would have thought possible for a man his size. Rex's momentum carried him forward and his giant fist slammed James back against the concrete wall, lifting him off the ground. James fought his way free, but just as he dropped to the ground, something whacked against his head. In the split second before he lost consciousness, he thought of Lana.

He'd lost her at the very moment he knew he had to have her. And if she didn't get his message, he would lose her forever.

Chapter Twenty

"Don't even think of telling me I can't come." Jackie tossed her hastily packed bag of random disguises into the trunk of her car and slammed the lid. "This is my car. Only I drive my car. And since you need a ride, seems to me I'm coming along."

"What about our business?" Lana winced as she followed Jackie to the front of the vehicle. "Who's going to look after our clients?"

Jackie gave her a wicked grin. "Derek will keep them happy until we get this sorted out. I fixed your camera and sent the pictures to Angel, so you don't need to worry about her."

A smile ghosted Lana's lips. "I do have to point out I am being pursued by armed and dangerous bikers. You're putting yourself in a life-threatening situation."

Jackie's face softened and she stroked a finger over Lana's bruised cheek. "You don't have to tell me, honey. I can see it for myself. But I put up with a hell of lot worse than Levi when I lived on the streets. He doesn't scare me."

"Nothing scares you," Kickstand muttered. "You should've been the Hades prospect, not me."

"Are you coming with us?" Lana still couldn't believe the risks Kickstand had taken for her. Rex would see his actions as a betrayal. Banishment was the least of the punishments Kickstand would face.

He shook his head. "I've got things I gotta do."

"Why did you help me?" Lana asked softly. "I mean...the repercussions..."

He shrugged. "I owed you. Not just for the time you warned

me about the colors, but because it was my fault the Wolverines found you."

"You were just following orders," Lana said softly.

"I shoulda thought it through. I mean, why would someone like you associate with the Wolverines? You're sweet and funny and kind, and you treated me with respect. You aren't like the other old ladies. When I find an old lady, I want her to be just like you."

Lana frowned. "You're staying with Hades? Do you think that's safe?"

His face fell. "Nah. I'm not staying with them. It's not what I thought it was—money and glamour and riding kick-ass bikes with the guys. I didn't sign up for the murder and drug running and selling women as slaves. I don't want to wind up in jail. You must think I was pretty naive."

"I think you're a hero." She gave him a soft kiss on the cheek.

He swallowed and his cheeks reddened. "I don't know how you married Levi, knowing what it was like to live the biker life."

A cold ache seeped into her bones. "I didn't have a choice. The day after they marked me, Levi found out the mark meant I could be shared around. He didn't care what they did to me or what they made me do, but that was a line for him. I had been his since I was sixteen. Marrying me was the only way he could keep me for himself. Bikers have a strange code of honor."

"What?" Jackie jumped out of the car and grabbed Lana by the shoulders. "You married the bastard? Why didn't you tell me?"

Lana shrugged as the memories rose like bile in her throat. Levi storming into their room at the Wolverine clubhouse and dragging her semiconscious body off the bed. His hands rough on her cut, bruised skin as he hid the rope burns on her wrists and ankles with bandages. A painful truck ride later and they were at the local marriage registry. Dazed from pain, her voice raw from a night of screaming, she couldn't even call for help.

"The house mama held a gun to my back, concealed in a bouquet of flowers, and his buddy stood between me and the door. Levi had to hold me up because I was in so much pain I couldn't walk. I couldn't even say the vows. My wedding clothes were a T-shirt covered in bloodstains and a pair of torn sweats. They paid the registrar a small fortune to look the other way."

Kickstand scratched his head. "Ice know all this?"

"No. And he never will. Marriage means something to him. He'll think I made him betray his beliefs. He'll never forgive me for lying." Tears welled up in Lana's eyes as she rounded the car and pulled open the door. She should've been honest with him from the beginning, but the temptation of being with him again had proved too strong.

Kickstand grabbed her arm before she could slide into the seat. "I think you're wrong. He gave me a message for you in case something happened to him. I'm guessing now, with the Wolverines *and* Rex wanting him dead..." He choked on his words and then took a deep breath. "I think you should have the message now. He said to make sure you knew he sent it *after* he found out you were married."

A trembling formed deep within her, working its way from her core through her limbs. "What did he say?"

James awoke to a loud crack and a sharp pain burning across his cheek.

"Wake up, sunshine." Ryder peered down at him and frowned. "You need me to slap the other cheek?"

Still groggy, James pushed himself to a sitting position against the wall. "You fucking touch me again and I'll rip off your hand."

"Finally. Back to normal." Ryder squatted against the wall across from him, his hands dangling between his legs. "I was beginning to wonder if Dawg had caused some permanent damage when he hit you over the head with that metal pipe. You've been lying there moaning for a couple hours."

James frowned. "Where's here?"

"Storage room at the clubhouse. You'll notice the lack of windows, the steel fire door and the interesting fact that Rex's secret drug stash is missing. I guess he and the boys didn't want us to overdose since they're planning to torture and kill us. Not as much fun when the victim doesn't know what's going on and can't feel any pain."

"Sorry I dragged you into this." James rubbed the lump on his head and stared up at the naked bulb overhead. Maybe they could use the wires to pick the lock.

Ryder snorted a laugh. "I'm not. Best time I've had since joining the fucking club."

"I gotta get out of here. Find Lana." James pushed himself to his feet and staggered as a wave of dizziness hit him.

"Easy there." Ryder jumped up and eased James back down to the floor. "You got hit by the pipe *after* Rex smashed your head against the wall. You've probably got a concussion. You need to chill for a while."

"Chill?" James shook his head in disbelief. "Rex is coming to off us. Lana is out there being hunted by Hades *and* the Wolverines. And you want me to chill?"

"We've got some time," Ryder said. "They were planning to finish us off in the parking lot but Angel drove up. You should have heard her. Seems she'd hired a PI to follow Rex around, and she'd just received an email with pictures of him and Portia. She came here on a fucking tear, shouting the place down. Even the Wolverines were afraid of her. She grabbed the metal pipe out of Dawg's hand and chased Rex into his office. Bones and Dawg didn't want to do anything without Rex, so they locked us in here."

Amused, James said, "She owes me a favor."

241

"Well, call it in. She's the only person besides Rex who has a key."

Kickstand pushed up his sleeve and showed Lana the message on his arm. "It's in another language. I think it might be German."

Hands trembling, Lana traced the letters of the three words penned on Kickstand's arm.

Ich liebe dich.

I love you.

A ball of warmth formed deep inside her chest, flowing through her veins like liquid heat. He forgave her. He loved her. For real.

"What does it mean?" Kickstand lowered his arm.

Lana smiled through her tears. "It means I have to find a guy named Hans and thank him for the German lessons. And it means you have to find Ice and tell him where we're going to be since he doesn't have a damned phone." She grabbed an old receipt from her purse and scrawled down an address. "This is a motel between Kamloops and Kelowna. Tell him I'll be waiting. But…be safe. The Wolverines and Rex will be after you too."

Kickstand's bottom lip trembled. "What if he didn't…?"

"There is no *if*," Jackie barked. "That Ice is a survivor. He'll probably have wiped the floor with the Wolverines and is now working his way through Hades."

A smile ghosted Kickstand's worried face. "You're right about that. I'll find him. Don't you worry."

Jackie blew Kickstand a kiss as she slid into the driver's seat. "You know where we are. You're welcome to join us too. Nothing more fun than being on the run from a sadistic, ruthless motorcycle club times two."

Kickstand grinned. "Nothing except leading them in the

wrong direction."

"Get the fuck outta my way. I'm getting my boy outta there."

James and Ryder shared a glance as Angel's harsh voice pierced the thick steel door and echoed around them as if she were standing in the room.

"Imagine listening to that every day," Ryder muttered. "I'd hide in my clubhouse too."

Low murmurs outside and then a thud. And then Angel's shrill voice.

"Rex is having a rest, courtesy of this here pipe. So the answer is no, we're not going to wait for him. And unless you're feeling tired too, I suggest you get the fuck outta my way."

Ryder and James plastered their ears to the door, unable to tear themselves away from the train wreck on the other side.

Voices. Low. Urgent. *Crack!* A grunt.

"Don't tell me I don't got any say," Angel shouted. "Last I heard, I was still married to the cheating bastard, which makes me the number one old lady in the club, which makes you dirt under my fucking shoes. See these shoes? He bought 'em for me as an apology for fucking the babysitter. They look pretty but they got steel toes. You know why he bought 'em with steel toes? So I could kick losers like you in the balls and cause some permanent fucking damage."

Thud! A long, low pained groan.

James winced. Beside him, Ryder grimaced and the color drained from his face.

"You sure it was a good idea calling out for her? What if she's pissed at us too?"

"I told you," James said, with a confidence he didn't feel in the least. "She owes me a favor."

"She doesn't owe me." Ryder paced his way to the back of the room. Away from the door.

James gave a harsh laugh. "She's half your size. Maybe even less."

Ryder shook his head. "Size means nothing. She scares me. Just like black widow spiders and scorpions scare me. They're so small you can't see them coming, and by the time you do, it's too late." He drew a line across his throat. "You're dead."

A key rattled in the lock and the door swung open. Angel stomped into the room, a metal pipe in one hand and a key in the other. Her fluorescent-pink spandex dress reflected off her scowling face, brightening the room.

She poked a finger into James's chest. "Been hearing things about you, Ice."

James backed up to the wall. Ryder sidled toward the open door.

Cowardly bastard.

"Been hearing you're a rat. If you are, you're a bad one. Woulda made my life a whole lot easier if you'd put that fucking bastard in jail. Just went to the doctor this morning and guess what that dickwad brought home from Seymour Street?"

James could guess what Rex had brought home from Vancouver's red light district and it wasn't something he wanted to discuss with Angel. Especially now.

Ryder snorted a laugh and Angel whipped her head around and glared. "Shut your fucking mouth, Ryder. Show some respect. I know about you too. I've been keeping quiet about you, but if you push me I'll open my mouth and it won't be for the sweet treatment you've been begging for since the day we met."

James sucked in a sharp breath. What could Angel possibly have on Ryder? He rode cleaner than anyone in the club. Maybe...too clean.

The sound drew Angel's attention. She didn't look like

herself today but he couldn't put a finger on what was different.

"I know you're fucking my PI. She did a damn fine job. Got me some good pictures and musta taken a big risk to get them. You mess her around and you answer to me."

"It's not me you should worry about. It's Levi." Even as the statement left his lips, rage coiled around his chest so tight he could barely breathe.

Her face tightened. "Yeah. Claw told me what happened at the meeting. I went after Levi, but he'd already gone. I told the boys, he shows up here again, they call me." She paused. "You going after her?"

"The second you let me out of here."

Angel's face softened and James realized what had changed. She wasn't wearing any makeup and without it she looked...young. Probably late twenties. And attractive. How did she wind up in a biker gang? And with Rex?

Maybe the same way as Lana. Young and innocent and desperately searching for someone to love her.

He must have been staring because Angel fisted his shirt and pulled him down toward her.

"Why you lookin' at me like that?"

He swallowed hard and gave her an honest answer. "You're very pretty without all the makeup."

Myriad emotions crossed her face—surprise, regret, pleasure and...displeasure.

Then she slapped him.

At least she'd picked the other cheek. Now they both burned.

"You coming on to me when your girl is out there being chased by a pack of fucking Wolverines? She's a sweet girl. She's got a good heart. I told you not to mess her around. I'd leave you locked up in here to think about your behavior, but someone needs to save her. That's you."

She turned and scowled at Ryder. "And, you, since you got nothin' better to do with your time than stare at me with your mouth hanging open like a panting puppy."

"Yes, ma'am." Ryder gave her a salute and a wink.

She pinched his ass as she headed out the door. "Cheeky. You bring her back and maybe I'll give you that sweet treatment after all."

James and Ryder followed her out, stepping over a groaning Dawg, an injured Punch and an unconscious Bones. Angel looked back over her shoulder and flipped back her long blonde hair.

"We're even, Ice."

He nodded. "We are."

She pressed her lips together and then her face softened. "Don't let them take her. I hooked up with Rex when I was only seventeen. Biggest mistake of my life. This world, it beats the hell out of a girl. Sucks up her sweetness and spits her out the other end with nothing left but bitterness in her heart. The minute my baby girl was born I knew I had to get her out of here, and I knew I would do anything to make that happen. And that was just Hades. Those Wolverines…"

James's throat tightened. "I know."

She drew in a ragged breath, her face tightening once more. "If you know, then why are you standing around gawking at me? Go!"

"They aren't going anywhere." Rex stepped into the hallway, arms folded, a trickle of blood on his temple and a scowl on his face. "They betrayed Hades. They pay the price."

"For the love of…" Angel cut herself off when Rex walked toward them. "You got one hell of a hard head, Rexy. Most men would have been out a coupla hours after getting hit with this here pipe. Maybe it's been all that coke you've been snorting or all the girls you've been fucking. You're too stupid to know when it's best to stay passed out."

"Only one girl I wanted," Rex snarled. "Wasn't you."

Unperturbed, Angel gave a bitter laugh. "I heard you were sniffing around my PI and she wouldn't have you. So you decided to give her up to the Wolverines. Isn't that right? If you couldn't have her, no one else in the club could have her? You're pathetic. And you know what I'm thinking? I'm thinking the reason you didn't stay down is because the wrong person hit you with the pipe."

She tossed the pipe to James and gave him a wicked grin. "Let's see what you got, Ice. If you can't knock him out longer than I did, I'll take that damn pipe to your head next."

James hefted the pipe and stalked toward Rex. "Go home, Angel. By the time I'm done here, there won't be any pipe left to play with."

Chapter Twenty-One

The heart-shaking roar of a motorcycle engine wrenched Lana from sleep. She shook Jackie awake and raced to the window of the tiny motel hidden away in the Rocky Mountains.

"Is it Levi?" Jackie ran around the room, still half-asleep, stuffing clothes in her backpack, her long dark hair a tangle around her face.

"I can't tell. It's too dark," Lana whispered.

"How did he know where we are?"

"Maybe it's not him." She dared to hope, but practicality reared its ugly head. "We have to be prepared to escape on foot. Our car will be blocked off once they enter the parking lot."

Jackie tugged a hoodie over her pajamas. "Excellent. I've always wanted to run aimlessly through a cold, dark forest in the middle of the night, being pursued by crazed Wolverines. Can't have too many experiences in this life, I always say."

Lana peered out the window again and her heart skipped a beat. "There's only one guy and he's parked beside your car."

"If he puts a scratch on that paint, I'll kill him," Jackie grumbled. "I just had it redone. Cost me every penny I made on the Pomeranian case."

"He's heading to the front desk. We can sneak out now." Lana grabbed her backpack and pushed open the door.

The phone rang, the sound jarring in the quiet of the night.

"He's calling." Jackie's eyes widened. "Very thoughtful. I thought he'd just bust down the door and drag you out by the hair. But I guess he wants to be sure you're properly dressed for your kidnapping. Are you going to answer it?"

Heart pounding, Lana lifted the receiver.

"Babe..."

"James." Her heart swelled in her chest and a grin split her face. "It's James," she whispered.

Jackie raised an eyebrow. "I gathered that from the breathy sigh and the stars in your eyes. He's like a white knight riding his silver steed into the mountains to rescue his damsel in distress. What I wouldn't give for one of those." Her face fell and for the briefest moment Lana thought she caught a glimpse of regret in Jackie's eyes, but it was so fleeting she could have imagined it.

Footsteps hammered down the wooden walkway in time to Lana's beating heart. She pulled open the door and threw her arms around James's neck as he stepped into the room.

"You came."

"Of course I came," he murmured. "You're my girl."

"Did Kickstand call you?" Jackie asked. "Is he okay? I got the feeling he was about to do something stupid."

James kicked the door closed and wrapped his arms around Lana. "He called Ryder. And Ryder was with me. We had just dropped Rex off at the hospital. Someone beat him up pretty bad with a pipe. He's got a coupla broken limbs and a concussion. Maybe a broken nose and a few broken ribs. Lots of cuts and bruises. Internal injuries..."

"Hmmmm." Lana looked up and raised an eyebrow. "Sounds like someone was pretty pissed at him."

James brushed a kiss over her forehead. "Someone was. A man sees his girl being abused and sold to a bunch of fucking Wolverines, he gets a bit annoyed. A man gets annoyed, he has to do something about it. Someone puts a pipe in his hand and pushes him in the right direction, he knows what to do."

Lana bit her lip to repress her smile. "I'm surprised he's alive."

"That's Ryder's fault."

249

"Where is Ryder?" Jackie peered out the window. "I thought he'd be with you."

James sighed. "Kickstand gave us your location and then said he was going to lure the Wolverines away. Ryder's gone after him. Once he catches up to Kickstand and knocks some sense into his head, they're going to meet up with us."

Jackie's face fell and she sighed. "Oh. Great. The more the merrier. No better way to keep a low profile than by travelling with three bikers."

Lana gave her a puzzled frown from the safety of James's arms. Were things not going well between Jackie and Ryder? She'd been so caught up in her own problems she hadn't even asked.

"You okay?" she said softly.

Jackie gave a noncommittal shrug. "Hell yeah. Now that you two are together again, all is right with the world."

James tossed Jackie a set of keys. "Got you a room. Two doors down."

"Oh." Jackie's mouth turned down. "Lana and I usually sleep together. Naked. Are you sure you…"

"Jackie."

Her eyebrows shot up at Lana's warning bark. "I meant to say, how thoughtful and considerate of you to send me packing without so much as even a 'hello' or 'thank you for saving my girl'." She gave Lana a wink, grabbed her bag and dashed out the door.

James pulled Lana into his chest and buried his face in her hair. But she couldn't enjoy the moment. Regret gnawed at her. Now that he had forgiven her, she wanted to come clean. She wanted him to know everything. And if he walked away afterward, well, then it was never meant to be.

"James?"

"Yeah, babe?"

"I need to tell you something." And before he could stop her, she did. She told him about being sixteen and so deeply lonely Levi had seemed like a savior. She told him about the abuse and the day she'd been marked. She told him how being with the Wolverines had brought out the worst aspects of Levi's personality. She told him about the wedding she didn't want and how she'd escaped.

"I'm sorry I wasn't up-front about everything," she said quietly. "It was a part of my life I wanted to leave behind. I couldn't divorce him without letting him know where I was. And I was afraid to tell you. I didn't want to lose you. But you were always so rigid in your beliefs. I was worried marriage meant marriage to you, regardless of the circumstances."

"Not those circumstances," he murmured. "And you didn't consent. The marriage is invalid. You can easily have it annulled."

Lana sucked in a breath, but couldn't meet his gaze. "I'm not legally married to him?"

"No, babe." His voice was almost a whisper.

She felt a weight lift off her shoulders. A taint removed from her soul. Relieved of a burden she'd carried far too long, she found the courage to ask, "You didn't know I didn't consent to the marriage, so why are you here?"

He tilted her face up and gave her a puzzled frown. "What do you mean?"

"Are you here because I'm in trouble and that's what cops do?"

Cupping her face in his hands, he brushed his lips over hers. "I'm here because there is nowhere else I'd rather be."

Lana's throat tightened with emotion. His tender words and his gentle kiss awakened something deep within her—a flame she had thought long since beaten out of her by cruelty and betrayal and self-doubt.

He kissed her again, so soft and sweet—the last of her

resistance crumbled.

"I love you," he whispered. "I should have told you a long time ago."

James deepened the kiss, trying to convey the intensity of his emotions. He wanted her to know nothing could shake his feelings for her. Not Levi or her past. Not her propensity to rush headlong into danger or to sass him every opportunity she got. They were fire and ice, and they burned bright together.

She yielded with a soft whimper. The embers of his desire flared as she pressed her soft, sweet body against his.

"I want you."

His cock hardened in an instant. "You can have me. Every bit of me." He tangled his fingers through her hair, marveling at how the wild curls could be so soft to touch. Like silk. Leaning down, he cupped her chin and angled her head for a kiss. A deep kiss. A possessive kiss.

Mine.

"I want to mark you, baby," he growled. "Make sure anyone who sees you knows you're mine."

"Hell yes," she whispered. Despite the bruises covering her body, she wanted James's mark. Something to wash away Levi's stain.

He tilted her neck to the side and feathered kisses down the column of her throat. Then he placed his lips to the side of center and sucked.

Lana drew in sharp breath and moaned. He increased the pressure, drawing her skin between his teeth until her hands fisted his hair and her breath came out in short pants. When he finally lifted his head, he saw his mark, red, already turning blue, on her skin. He grunted his pleasure even as Lana rubbed her hot body against him.

"Beautiful." His deep, husky growl betrayed his desire.

He slid an arm around her waist, intending to lift her and carry her to the bed, but Lana slipped out of his grasp and backed up to the door. She raised her hands over her head, grabbing the sturdy coat hook above her.

"I want this," she whispered. "Like we did in the club. I want you to touch me the way you would have if I hadn't heard Levi and run away."

James stilled. "He was there?"

"I heard him and saw his ring. That's why I ran. It wasn't because of you."

His heart squeezed in his chest. She hadn't run from him. Not only that, she trusted him. Trusted him to keep her safe. Stunned, overwhelmed, he could do nothing but stare.

"James?" Her voice, raw and vulnerable, shook him to the core.

A surge of protective feelings washed through him, and he covered her small, tightly clenched hands with one of his. "I thought I'd pushed you too far. I don't need this. In the end, it's just a game. And you're hurt."

Her lips curled into a shy smile. "A very enjoyable game. And I'm not hurt *everywhere*. Take away the pain, James."

Hunger coiled in his belly driving away his own aches and pains—a hunger that wouldn't be satisfied with a gentle hug or a sweet kiss. He wanted more. He wanted everything she was offering. Lana, body and soul.

"Hold still." He unbuckled his belt and slid it off, taking care not to let it crack. In under a minute he had her hands secured to the hook, her body stretched until the balls of her feet just touched the ground.

She looked up and met his gaze. A storm of emotions raged through her eyes—fear, passion, desire—mimicking the emotions deep inside him.

He slowly pushed up her lacy little tank top, imagining her bound to the post at Carpe Noctem, in that skintight black dress and her damned sexy boots. Then he cupped her breast, gently kneading the ripe, warm swell. "I would have started here."

She arched her back, thrusting her breasts up and out as she let out a long, low moan. He teased her nipple with his thumb and forefinger, pinching and rolling until it hardened into a tight peak. Her hips undulated in time to his strokes and he released her breast to tease the other until she panted and groaned.

Damn. Why had he agreed to this? He wouldn't be able to last. He should have taken off the edge before he subjected them both to such sweet torment.

Sliding his hand over her belly, he feathered his fingers over her mound and cupped the curve of her sex over her silky pajama shorts.

"Next I would have stroked down here." He pressed his lips to her ear. "But first, I would have stripped off your panties so I could feel you hot and wet against my hand."

Her body stilled, eyes wide. "Please."

It was all she had to say.

Once he had her bared below the waist, her triangle of golden-red curls glistening with her need, he pressed the heel of his palm against her clit and slid his fingers through her folds. "Next, I would have touched you like this. And there was nothing you could have done about it. You were available for my pleasure and my pleasure alone."

She gave a strangled cry and moisture flooded her sex, trickling over his fingers. Heat flared deep within him, a rush that spread through his body. His cock pressed painfully, insistently against his fly. But this wasn't about him. It was about Lana and the part of herself she had long denied. The part he wanted to set free.

"What would you have done next?" she breathed, rolling her hips against his hand.

"This."

He bent down and drew a rosy nipple into his mouth. Lana sucked in a sharp breath and yanked against the belt.

"What's your safe word?" he murmured against her soft skin.

"Rocker."

His lips curled into a smile. His bike meant something to her. Something safe. No way could he give the bike back to the DEU when he handed in his notice. And he *was* handing in his notice. He was done with police work. Done with an organization that didn't have his back. Done with banging his head against a wall in the pursuit of justice.

"Good word."

"Good bike."

Laughing, he teased her other nipple until her breathing quickened and he could feel the violent thudding of her heart beneath his lips.

He ran a finger through her folds. So wet. So hot. So ready. He slicked her moisture over her clit, and she groaned and tilted her hips toward him.

"Everyone would have been watching us." He kept his voice deliberately low, forcing her to still to hear his words. "They would have seen your beautiful body stretched out for my pleasure. They would have seen my hands baring your breasts for my mouth. They would have seen my fingers stroking your sweet pussy."

A groan rose from deep within her throat, and her head fell back against the door.

"And they would have seen me do this." He thrust two fingers deep inside her and covered her mouth with his, swallowing her gasp. He slicked his fingers in and out, curving them to rub against the sensitive inner walls. Her wet, heated response drove him right to the edge.

He stepped back, heaving rasping breaths as he fought for

control, but it was almost impossible with Lana restrained and trembling before him. Her breasts rose and fell with her rapid breaths; her nipples peaked with arousal; the down between her legs was a burst of flame in the dimly lit room. There was so much he wanted to do with her but, right now, he wanted her with an intensity that took his breath away. For the first time ever, he couldn't hold out.

"And then I would have done this," he growled, his voice hoarse with raw lust.

James shoved down his clothing and sheathed himself, then released Lana from the restraints. Muscles taut, blood pounding in his ears, he lifted her and pushed her up against the wall, ignoring the residual aches and pains in his battered body. Her legs curled around him and he wasted no time burying himself inside her warm, wet channel.

Her pleading whimper almost made him come right then. But he wanted her with him. Needed to hear her moans of pleasure. He slid his hand between them and found her swollen clit.

One touch and she stiffened in his arms. She was so close, panting, her muscles taut, her sex clenched around him. He circled and stroked, spreading her moisture, teasing her until her moans became one long whimper.

Finally, he pinched her nub with a firm, gentle pressure. "Come for me," he whispered.

Her body arched like a bowstring and then she flew, her shriek piercing the night air, her sex spasming around him, pulling him deep.

No longer able to hold back, James gripped her hips and drove himself into her core, thrusting inside her hard and deep. Her legs tightened around his waist. Her teeth sank into his shoulder. Her muffled shrieks rose as he pounded his need into her warm, wet sheath.

Mine.

She shattered around him, called his name. The pulse of her sex sent him over the edge and his climax erupted from him in long, exquisite heated jerks.

When his heart stopped pounding, he leaned his forehead against hers and brushed kisses over the freckles dusting her cheeks.

"And then would you have done that?" she murmured

A smile ghosted his lips. "No. I would have teased you for at least another hour until you were begging me to take you. And then I would have taken you home and fucked you all night long. Some things aren't meant to be shared."

Lana lifted an eyebrow and her green eyes glowed warm and deep, like an emerald sea. "When can we go back?"

Lana awoke to the rumble of thunder. The warm body next to her shifted. James tightened his arm around her waist.

"Shhh. Sleep. Still dark out," he mumbled.

"I heard something."

"Storm." He nuzzled the back of her neck. "Maybe we'll be stuck here for the rest of the day. Can't ride in the rain."

The sound grew louder and a gasp broke free from Lana's lips. "Motorcycles." She wiggled from James's grasp, raced over to the window and pulled back the curtain. High above them, on the road winding down the mountain toward the motel, she spotted a blaze of headlights.

"Fuck." James came up behind her and pulled the curtain closed. "Get dressed and get into the car. I'll get Jackie."

Lana's heart pounded against her ribs. "Maybe it's Ryder and Kickstand and a few buddies."

James tugged on his jeans and T-shirt, and tucked two handguns in his belt, covering them with his leather jacket.

"Not on those bikes. The Wolverines all brought cruisers. I

know the sound."

Hands shaking, Lana threw on her clothes and raced for Jackie's car. A minute later, James and a pajama-clad Jackie ran across the pavement toward her.

"The keys," Jackie yelled. "I left them on the table beside my bed." She ran back to the room just as eight Wolverines swept into the parking lot.

Nonononononononono. Lana's breath hitched and her vision sheeted white. God, would it never end?

James pushed her toward Jackie's room. "Go inside with Jackie."

"I can't leave you out here alone," she said, shaking him off. "They're coming for me. I won't let you die on my account."

"Babe. Go inside with Jackie. Try to get out the back and into the forest. Run east but stay out of sight of the highway. I'll find you." He drew his weapons and Lana's blood chilled.

"Don't do this, James. There's no point. You don't have a chance. There're eight of them and only one of you."

He shifted his stance and tightened his grip on his weapons. "Go inside."

"Please. I don't want to lose you again." She hated herself for begging but if logic wasn't going to move him, maybe tears would.

"I have no intention of dying today," he said, his focus wholly on the Wolverines dismounting their motorcycles in front of the motel. "You promised me a night at Carpe Noctem and I intend to collect."

Lana's heart pounded so loud in her ears she could barely hear the thud of Levi's feet on the pavement as he stalked toward them. For the first time ever, she had no desire to run. If she ran, he would come after her again and again. She would spend a lifetime looking over her shoulder, jumping at every shadow. She had to stand up to him and take back the life he'd taken from her. A life with James in it.

Quietly, she said, "I need to face him, James. I need this to end."

"Too stubborn for your own good," he muttered, half to himself. "Stay behind me then."

"You got something that belongs to me." Levi stopped in front of them and narrowed his eyes. "And to the Wolverines."

The Wolverines made a show of drawing their weapons, an assortment of Glocks and Rugers, all illegal in Canada. Lana wondered how they had managed to get them across the border.

James leveled his guns. "She belongs to no one."

Levi snorted a laugh and then snapped his fingers. Two Wolverines dragged a rider off the back of one of the motorcycles and marched him across the parking lot. One of them tugged off his helmet and tossed it to the ground.

Lana gasped as a sliver of moonlight pierced Kickstand's blond hair and illuminated his battered face.

"He should really be dead." Levi forced Kickstand to his knees and pointed a handgun at his head. "He thought he could outrun us on his piece-of-shit Sportster."

"No." Lana took a step forward. "He isn't part of this. Leave him alone."

Levi's lips curled into a cruel smile. "Not part of this? He tracked us down and told us he knew where you were. Led us on a wild-goose chase around the city until Hang Nail..." he nodded to the tall, burly biker beside him, "...decided to have an intimate conversation with him. Guess what Hang Nail discovered? Boy was telling the truth. He had a piece of paper with this address on it and your name. Must just have a bad sense of direction." He thumped Kickstand on the head with the butt of his gun and Kickstand shuddered.

"What do you want?" James's deep voice, confident and powerful, rang out across the parking lot.

Levi's gaze flicked to him. "A trade. Your prospect for my wife. Usually I just take what I want, but I'm in a good mood since she was so easy to find. My advice? Take the deal. You don't, the boy dies, you die and I take her anyway." He pressed the gun to Kickstand's head.

"Don't do it," Kickstand said firmly. "They're gonna hurt her so bad she'll wish she was dead. He told me what he was going to do to her. Made me sick to my stomach. No one should have to go through that. Especially not after what they already did to her."

Raw hatred flowed through Lana's veins. It was time to deal with Levi. No more running. No more hiding. Regardless of what he did to her, she would survive on hate and the burning need for revenge.

"I'll go." Lana stepped out from behind James.

His arm shot out, pushing her back. "You won't."

"I can't let them hurt Kickstand. And we can't take them on. Even I know a losing battle when I see it. It's time I dealt with him and I can't do it hiding behind your back. But I'll only be able to manage if I know you and Kickstand are alive. I'll go and I'll find a way to end it, and I'll come back to you."

"Wait." Jackie raced out of the motel room and threw her arms around Lana. "Let me come with you," she murmured. "You saved me when you pulled me off the streets. I can use the tricks I learned... I could have us home in a day."

"And then he would come after me again," Lana said, gently pulling away. "I want my life back, and I want you and James in it."

"Come back safe." Jackie wrapped her arms around herself, tears streaking her face.

"Roxie. You comin' or am I shootin'?" Levi's harsh voice sent a chill down Lana's spine.

She lifted her gaze to James. Her eyes stung, but no tears fell. Crying would only make him think she didn't want to go. But she did. A perverse excitement pounded in her temples—the chance to end Levi's reign of terror and live a life without fear.

Ice glittered in James's eyes. She tried to say goodbye, but her mouth went dry and the words stuck in her throat.

He cupped her cheek with his warm hand. "I know this is something you've got to do, but I'm coming for you, babe. Nothing is going to stand in my way. I said I love you and I mean it. Nothing else matters. You aren't alone in this. Trust I'll find a way. Don't lose hope."

She closed her eyes and leaned into the warmth of his palm. More than his declaration of love, his forgiveness seared her to the core. "I trust you," she whispered.

Then she looked up and winked. "But you'd better hurry. I'm not the kind of girl who sits around waiting to be rescued."

Chapter Twenty-Two

Lana clung to the rear handle grips on Levi's Harley Fat Boy. She tried to look behind to see if James was following them, but the helmet Levi had brought for her—not out of concern for her safety but to avoid being stopped by the police—was too big. Every time she turned her head, she saw only darkness. Not that James could possibly be anywhere near. The Wolverines had slashed the tires on his Rocker and Jackie's vehicle, and had kept Kickstand as a hostage to ensure Lana's good behavior. Gentlemen they were not.

A cool breeze whipped around her, buffeting her so badly she was tempted to hold on to Levi for balance. During their first few months together, nothing had thrilled her more than racing through the mountains tucked up against Levi's broad back. But the thought of touching him now made her stomach clench. Better to fall off the motorcycle than to let him think she had even an ounce of affection left for him...her once savior, her first lover, her husband.

After three hours, Levi turned off the main highway and headed down a narrow road. The Wolverines followed behind him. Lana was surprised they had made it this far without a break. The Wolverines were all riding Harley Cruisers. Good for show and sporting around. Damned uncomfortable for a long trip.

Lana whipped off her helmet as the motorcycle slowed to a stop. Her brain ached from trying to come up with a plan. Escape was fast becoming a better option than confrontation, persuasion or even attacking Levi in his sleep. And one thing she knew for certain—escape would be exponentially more difficult once they crossed the border. She had friends here.

People she could call. Places she could go. In the US, she would be utterly alone.

Lost in thought, Lana startled when one of the Wolverines grabbed her arm and pulled her off the motorcycle. She tried to stop her sideways momentum by hooking her foot under the passenger peg, but the bolt had loosened during the ride and the peg fell into the grass with Lana on top of it.

"Get the fuck up." Levi kicked her shin and then yanked her off the grass. "We need to be quick about hiding the bikes. Next time I say to get off, you get off fast. Guess that's something else you'll have to learn when we get home."

"Vancouver is my home," she spat. She opened her mouth to mention the peg—it would be damned hard to ride pillion without it—and then closed it again. The motel was off the main highway and tucked into the base of a mountain. She didn't have any breadcrumbs with which to leave a trail, but a passenger peg might do the trick.

"Home is where your husband is." Levi twisted her arm behind her back and Lana gasped in pain.

"Don't damage her too bad." Hang Nail loosened Levi's grip on her arm. "If we get stopped by the police or the border guards, they'll ask questions. She might decide to give her friend up for a chance to escape."

"Kind of damage I plan to do while we're waiting for her fake fucking passport to be made, no one's gonna see," Levi growled. "And the border guards won't be a problem. We're not crossing through the normal route. We're taking a smugglers' trail."

A black hole tore its way through Lana's chest, sucking the air from her lungs and the hope from her heart. Every time she thought the situation couldn't get any worse, it did. Now, even her rough plan to draw the attention of the border guards to the Wolverines' illegal weapons was moot.

Levi shoved her at Hang Nail and punched a number into

his cell phone as he walked toward the motel reception area. Hang Nail gripped her shoulders hard. "Don't think about running," he growled.

Lana snorted her derision. As if she would leave Kickstand or stand a chance on foot with eight Wolverines hovering around her.

Levi returned and threw Hang Nail two sets of keys. "The Fanelli brothers said they'll be here at dusk with her passport and a trailer to load up our bikes for the border crossing. They'll take us to the smugglers' trail after the sun sets. It's just off Zero Avenue and runs the full length of Langley. The rest of the guys can cross like normal and meet us in Blaine."

Hang Nail frowned. "Why can't we take our bikes?"

Levi clamped a hand around Lana's neck and shoved her in the direction of the motel. "There's a huge ditch between the two countries. Too wide to jump with our Cruisers. It's heavily policed but the Fanellis know where and when to cross on foot."

"So we have some time to kill." Hang Nail and Levi exchanged a glance that chilled Lana's blood.

Levi laughed. "You and the boys can keep the prospect entertained. I'm going to reacquaint myself with my wife."

"Don't forget. No visible marks," Hang Nail called as Levi dragged her to the motel.

Levi's gaze found hers and he snickered. "Not a problem. Hidden wounds hurt the most."

"What's taking so long?" Jackie tapped her spoon on the table in the motel's tiny coffee shop. "Why didn't we just steal a car and chase after them? Why do we have to wait for Ryder? We could go and buy a car or go to an auto shop and get new tires. I would even take a bus. They could be in the US by now."

Jackie's anxiety was fuel to James's fire. Not for the first time in the last hour did he wonder if he'd made the right choice to wait for Ryder. What if Levi hurt her, touched her or…worse. He slammed a mental wall down and pushed the betraying thoughts away. If he didn't stay clear and focused, he would be no use to anyone, especially Lana.

"They can't cross the border during the day," James said. "Especially at a border crossing. Too risky. They'll have to lie low until dark and my guess is they'll find somewhere else to cross. We can't take them on alone. We need help and firepower. The Wolverines aren't going to hand her over without a fight. Ryder said he would meet us here. I believe him. I've already called the local police and they're on the lookout too."

Jackie snorted her disdain. "Seriously? You're gonna put Lana's life at risk because you're that sure Ryder will show? Didn't he also tell you he was going after Kickstand? He hasn't answered any of my texts or calls, so he's already zero for one hundred in my book. And I'll tell you something else. He's not who he appears to be. You sleep with a guy and you get some insight into who they really are. Ryder has a whole lot of mystery going on."

"I'll take your word for it." Although he wasn't one to talk relationships, he was perversely glad for the distraction of Jackie's conversation.

Jackie lowered her eyes and stared down at her lap. "It's over between us," she said quietly. "I didn't tell Lana because she's got enough stress in her life. He's a great guy. Nothing like the bikers I knew. We got along well. He wanted to take things further. But…" she picked up her coffee cup and took a sip, "…he wasn't *the one*. Sounds stupid, I know."

"Doesn't sound stupid at all." James glanced down at his watch and drummed his fingers on his thigh under the table. He would give Ryder thirty more minutes and then they would head into town and rent a car. Thirty more minutes of distraction. "So, tell me about *the one*."

Jackie shrugged. "I don't mind playing around, but…I had a couple of bad experiences before I met Lana. Life's too short to put up with that crap. If I'm gonna open myself up, then I need to know I've found *the one*. Someone who lights up my life and makes my heart sing. All that stuff. So that no matter what life throws at us, I'll know, in the end, we'll wind up together. I told that to Ryder. He was cool with it."

James raised an eyebrow. "You weren't his *one* either?"

"I'm thinking not. And that's a good thing." Jackie glanced up at the clock and then dialed Lana's number for the umpteenth time that morning. When she didn't get an answer, she dropped her phone on the table with a sigh. "Let's go, J. I can't take it anymore. I've been doing my best to keep us distracted, but I'm too damn worried. And if something happens to her while we're sitting around, I'll never forgive myself."

James nodded and waved the waitress over. Fuck the thirty minutes. Jackie was right. They had to get a move on.

"Did you know?" Jackie asked softly as James tossed a wad of bills on the table. "Did you know right away Lana was *the one*?"

James met her curious gaze full-on steady. "Yeah, I knew. But I was too afraid to accept it. And look what happened. I almost lost her. I might lose her still."

They slid out of the booth and wove their way through the empty tables to the door.

"You won't lose her," Jackie said over her shoulder. "If she's *the one*, you'll wind up together, no matter what. That's how love works."

James's throat tightened. "Didn't take you for a romantic."

"Didn't take you for one either, J, but here you are, ready to risk your life to get my girl back. Doesn't get more romantic than that."

A thunder of motorcycles echoed in the valley as they stepped out the door. Jackie took an involuntary step behind James, and he reached for his gun. If Rex's boys had found them, they'd better not get in the way. James had Angel's number and he knew what to do with it.

Sunlight glinted off the lead motorcycle as it swooped into the parking lot. James threw an arm up to shield his eyes and recognized Ryder's bike as it pulled to a stop.

"Ryder," he said over his shoulder, his tension leaving his body in a rush.

Jackie stepped out from behind him and frowned at the sea of motorcycles in front of them. "Who does he have with him?"

Ryder dismounted and quickly closed the distance between them. He shook James's hand and gave Jackie a warm smile. "Sorry we're late. We've been looking for Kickstand but he disappeared. We found his bike in a field near the clubhouse, but no trace of him."

"Wolverines have him," James said. "They're holding him hostage for Lana's good behavior. They have her too."

Ryder's face tightened. "Damn. I knew we'd waited too long. Well, we're here now and we'll get them back. You have my word on it."

James surveyed the sea of black in front of him. "What is this? The guys aren't wearing their colors."

"My new club." A smile ghosted Ryder's lips. "Hades split over Rex's decision to call the Wolverines. A lot of them didn't take kindly to watching Lana being abused or to Rex's involvement in what they saw as human trafficking. Strange moral code. Drugs and murder are okay, but abusing and enslaving women are not. I convinced another eight to join my original ten." He waved his hand over the assembled crowd. "Everyone is briefed and ready to go."

"What do you call yourselves?" Jackie asked. "Right now, plain black jackets don't really scream badass bikers to me."

"We haven't decided on a name or a patch yet, so we're riding bald," Ryder said. "Got any ideas?"

"How about Hot Pieces of Ass?" Jackie murmured, looking over the vast array of leather and chrome. "You seem to have picked the best of the bunch. Something you forgot to tell me, Ryder?"

Ryder snorted a laugh. "Yeah. I forgot to tell you you're joining the club. I need an experienced PI. Part-time or full-time, it's up to you." He pointed to a tall, blond giant in the thick of the crowd. "We'll talk more about it later. We need to get on the road. Go talk to VD. He'll set you up with a jacket and helmet. I'm guessing you want to come along on the rescue mission, so you can ride with him."

"VD?" Jackie muttered as she stomped away. "All this man candy and he hooks me up with someone named VD?"

In response to James's quizzical look, Ryder said, "Viking Dan will be able to handle her. He just moved over here from Norway. Doesn't talk much, but when he does, people listen."

He pulled a leather jacket out of his pack and held it out to James. "Yours, if you're interested. I'm running a clean club. No drugs. No murder. We're about justice where the system isn't working. But we're willing to step into the gray zone. We'll hurt only those people who deserve it. We'll steal only from those who can afford it. We'll protect those who need it and help those who want it."

"Vigilantes."

"More like Robin Hood and his merry men. I also managed to bring on board a few ex-military specialists to run a Special Operations Department."

Military? Special Ops? James frowned. Who the hell was Ryder? Not an ordinary biker. Was he the deep-undercover operative who had arranged for James to join the club? The one who had called with the now-or-never opportunity? The one he'd never met?

"You forget to tell me something? Maybe that I wasn't the only rat in Hades?"

Silence.

James tried another tactic. "You're gonna mix ex-military

with Rex's castoffs? How will that work? Oil and water, my friend."

Ryder shook his head. "I'm giving them a chance to clean up their lives and make a difference. Everyone understands that any unauthorized illegal activity is a guaranteed dismissal. They get paid by the job and they don't need to worry about the cops." He raised an eyebrow and waggled the jacket. "Speaking of which...we could use someone with your skills."

James stared at the jacket and mulled over the opportunity hanging from the tips of Ryder's fingers. He wouldn't have to give up his pursuit for justice. He could still clean up the streets, put the bad guys in jail and help people who, like him, had been screwed by the system.

And if he didn't accept Ryder's offer, what then? He hadn't done anything worthy of serious discipline. Likely he would get a slap on the wrist and a yearlong posting in the frozen North. And then he could go back. Rejoin the homicide team. Return to his high-stress life of rules and order, time clocks and traffic jams. Back to a diet of coffee and donuts. Maybe the occasional night with Lana.

But if he put on the jacket, he would be crossing a line, and there would be no going back to proper law enforcement. His time would be his own. He could live free. Ride free. See Lana whenever, however and wherever he wanted.

He had wasted time considering the other option.

"Fucking embarrassing having a jacket with no patch." James took the jacket from Ryder's outstretched hand. "And a club with no name." He shrugged on the jacket and settled it on his shoulders.

"Perfect fit." Ryder slapped him on the shoulder. "And you can take Cuss's bike. He'll stay here and arrange to get your vehicles back to Vancouver."

"What's he riding?"

"Your V-Rod. He misappropriated it from Hades's lot at my

instruction. I thought you might need another set of wheels. Lucky for you, I managed to find a key."

"I'm sure you did," James muttered. "Theft and more theft. I can see we're off to a good start."

A grin split Ryder's face. "Welcome to the beginning of life in the gray zone. We're the rogues of the street."

"Rogue riders."

Ryder gave James a considered look. "Good name for the club."

"So we got a name?"

"We got a name. Now let's go get your girl."

Chapter Twenty-Three

"Move it, Roxie."

Levi shoved Lana into the drab motel room and slammed the door behind him, cutting her off from the comforting hum of traffic and the hushed murmur of voices.

Lana trembled as she turned to face Levi, her heart aching from thudding a warning she had not heeded.

For the longest time they stared at each other.

Although his face was painfully familiar, his gray eyes glittered with a cold, feverish light so unlike the warmth that had drawn her to a young, ambitious biker ten years ago. But that Levi was gone and the sooner she came to terms with it, the closer she would be to finding a way forward.

"Crazy little bitch." He backhanded her, sending her tumbling to the floor with the force of his blow.

"I've been dreaming of this moment since the day you ran out. You fucking humiliated me. Not only did I take flack for not being able to control my own wife, I lost respect. I was kicked out of Fang's inner circle. I almost lost my fucking patch." He kicked her side and then his foot came down on her chest, squeezing the air from her lungs.

Dazed, breathless, Lana fought blindly, legs and fists flailing. She made contact with something, and he swore, then pressed his weight into her rib cage.

Too hard.

Her lungs burned. The edges of her vision faded to black. Her limbs dropped heavily to the floor, and she concentrated her energy on sucking air into her chest.

And then he released her. Sweet, clean air filled her lungs in a rush, and she curled up on the floor, coughing and choking.

"I've spent a long time cleaning up your messes," he snarled. "And I'm fucking tired of it. After I was forced to apologize to the brothers, I hunted Scooter down. Didn't take much to make him scream. He bought his way into the Wolverines, but he didn't take time to learn the rules."

"Oh God." Lana's heart stuttered. Scooter had joined the club as a prospect only a few months before she escaped. A trust-fund baby wanting to rebel, he couldn't handle the violence and especially not the abuse dished out to the clubhouse slave. Underestimating their newest recruit because of his slight frame and gentle manner, the Wolverines didn't pay him much attention, keeping him around only to extort his monthly trust-fund payment. And then one day, without fanfare or warning, he wrapped Lana in an old tarp, hid her in the hollowed-out backseat of his truck and drove away.

"What did you do to him?" Part of her didn't want to know, but she owed Scooter her life. The least she could do was remember him in death.

Levi gave a rough laugh. "Question is, what didn't I do to him? He learned the hard way not to fuck with Wolverine property."

Lana's stomach clenched so violently bile rose in her throat. "You killed him."

"I would have killed him. I earned my blood patch after you left so I had the right to do it. But Fang wanted his money so he ordered me to leave him alive. I beat him up so bad he'll remember it for the rest of his life—or at least until he stops sending me his monthly payments. And it's on your shoulders. You knew better than to take that ride."

Fear slithered through her veins and wrapped itself around her heart. She'd made a colossal mistake. Levi had been cruel and abusive, but never a killer. He'd crossed the line, and from his cold, detached gaze as he talked about taking lives, she knew it was a one-way trip. There would be no talking to him. No reasoning with him. No clever plan to make him change his mind. She had been foolish and naive in the extreme.

Run. The word screamed through her head, blocking out Levi's laughter, urging her to save herself before Levi killed her too.

In one swift move, she rolled and pushed herself to a crouch, then she threw herself at him in a tackle that would have made her football-crazed father proud.

"Fuck." Levi lost his balance and stumbled back into the dresser. But he was quick. Before Lana reached the door, he grabbed her around the waist and threw her on the bed. Then he climbed on top of her, kneeling astride her hips, pinning her with his body.

"You never appreciated what I did for you." Spittle flew from his lips as he shot out his words in a fury. "I took you away from that shit-hole town we grew up in and from a family who never gave a damn about you. I helped you escape. I gave you money, a place to live and a life you loved. We were good together."

Once, she would have agreed with him just to avoid the inevitable confrontation and the consequences that flowed from it. But not now. Not after discovering there was something stronger than fear...

Don't lose hope.

"That was when I believed in you," she snapped. "After all those years of being ignored by my family, I had no self-esteem. I believed you when you said you loved me. I believed you when you said you were sorry when you hit me. I believed when you said you were going to make a success of your life. I just never realized your idea of success was running drugs and weapons for the Wolverines. I never realized your idea of love was handing me over to the Wolverines and laughing when they beat me."

Levi's lips curled into a snarl. "You were supposed to help me get ahead: give a few blow jobs, run the weapons, help with the deals. Do what old ladies are supposed to do. Instead, you kept trying to run away. If you'd kept your mouth shut and done what you were told, Fang wouldn't have had to intervene. You were the only old lady he decided to mark."

Lana shuddered. He was right. She had brought it on herself. The mark meant Levi's discipline could be collectively enforced and that she would be returned to the Wolverines if she was caught running away. It had worked only too well.

"You could have stopped him," she said. "You could have protected me."

"Jesus Christ." He raked his hand through his hair. "You still don't understand. If I had refused to mark you, I never would have become a Wolverine."

Furious, Lana struggled against the weight of his body. "You bought that membership with my blood and your soul. Was it worth it? Do you have all the money, power and glory you ever wanted? Do they treat you as a king, Levi? Because that's what you were here. You were the Gray Skull's leader. Everyone looked up to you. They respected you. Even me. And you gave it all up to lick Fang's boots."

"I fucking saved you," Levi shouted, his face red and his lips white with rage. "I married you so you wouldn't have to be the house pet. And what thanks did I get? Another fucking humiliation."

Bile rose in Lana's throat. Ten years worth of fear and anger coiled in her stomach. She clenched her fists above Levi's hands clasped tight around her wrists and willed herself to stop talking. Every instinct told her to stop. She had pushed him too far, and now that he was blood patch, she was playing with her life. But the words kept coming. Words she'd bottled up since the day they'd walked into the Wolverine clubhouse. Words she had to say, even if they were the last ones she uttered.

"Why don't you be honest for once? You married me so you

didn't have to share me. Not because you wanted to protect me. Not because you loved me. Because you're weak and insecure, and you didn't think I'd stay with you once I got a taste of someone else. You've always been insecure. You hit me at the beginning because you were worried I would leave you for someone else. You hit me in the middle because you couldn't control me. And you hit me in the end because you knew you had lost me."

"You know what your problem is, Roxie?" Holding her wrists over her head with one massive hand, Levi undid his belt buckle with the other and whipped the belt out of the loops in one long pull. "You have a big fucking mouth. You always talked too much. And you always thought you were better than me."

He cracked the belt like a whip, the sound echoing in the tiny room. "I'm gonna put an end to that right now. I'm gonna teach you a lesson you'll never forget. Then I'm gonna take my knife—the knife Fang gave me when I became full patch—and I'm gonna mark up that pretty face so no one will ever want you again. After that, you'll be damn grateful for any attention I give you."

His words had the desired effect. Terror burst from her chest and she screamed. Over and over. Until Hang Nail pounded on the door and warned Levi he was attracting unwanted attention.

Levi's eyes glittered fever-bright as he pulled the knife from his boot. "Looks like I'll have to gag you. I haven't even touched you and Hang Nail is beating down my door. Imagine how you'll scream when I cut you. We can't have someone calling the cops."

She shook her head violently. No gag. No cutting off her air. No cutting off her words—the only weapon she had left.

"If you gag me, you can't kiss me," she whispered, fighting back the wave of nausea in her gut.

Levi scowled. "Kiss you? Why the fuck would I do that?"

"Maybe you're right. Maybe there's still something left of what we had together. Maybe it got lost in the excitement of joining the Wolverines and we drifted apart. But you knew in your heart it was still there. That's really why you married me."

His expression wavered between suspicion and longing. Finally he grunted. "Don't think this will change my mind about cutting you. I can't have you running away again 'cause if you do I'll have to kill you or I'll never live it down."

Lana's stomach clenched violently as she struggled to soften her voice. "You were my first, Levi. I've never forgotten that first time. Put down the knife and kiss me like you did that day by the lake." She wiggled a little, testing his hold. His weight was like a boulder holding her down, his knees pinning her to the bed.

"You think I'm stupid?" he snorted. "I know you. The minute I put the knife down, you'll stab me in the gut. The knife stays in my hand."

Damn. He did know her well.

He leaned down and pressed his lips to hers in a hard, bruising kiss. Wet and slimy. Tasting of ashes and stinking of death.

Lana shuddered and hid her revulsion by squeezing her eyes shut.

"I'll beat you first," he mused after he pulled away. "Then I'll fuck you. Then cut you. Then fuck you again."

She forced herself to be still, think her way out. But her mind blanked, weighted under silent screams of terror. Gritting her teeth, she shut off her frantic brain and let instinct take the lead. "Oh, Levi," she breathed, opening her eyes to gaze up at him. "Kiss me again."

He stared at her, weighing her words, and then he smiled, a stark baring of stained, yellow teeth beneath the thin red slash of his cruel lips.

She knew before he even moved that the next kiss was

meant to harm. He leaned over and smashed his mouth against hers. Cruel and brutal. Teeth scraping, tongue plundering, lips bruising. She shuddered at the pain, but still she opened her mouth and let him in.

Then she bit him.

Her teeth sank through his bottom lip and he howled in pain, dropping the knife as he tried to pry her teeth away. The metallic tang of blood flowed over her tongue, making her gag. But still she held on, biting so hard her teeth scraped together through the soft flesh of his lip.

Levi screamed. He yanked her hair and punched and slapped at her head until she saw stars instead of the rage in his eyes. Only when he slid his hand around her throat and squeezed, cutting off her air, did she consider letting go. And only when her vision began to fade did she release him.

Levi shot back down the bed, clutching his torn, bleeding lip. Head still fuzzy from lack of oxygen, Lana lifted her legs to her chest and hammered them into his groin. Levi howled and fell backward off the bed.

"You're gonna fucking die for that, Roxie." He staggered to his feet and reached for the knife. "This marriage is fucking over."

James slowed his motorcycle to a stop outside the tiny motel nestled at the foot of the mountain. Viking Dan pulled up on one side, Jackie clinging to his back, and Ryder pulled up on the other.

"Last one on the list," Jackie said.

James scanned the parking lot and his heart dropped. No motorcycles. Just a few cars and a truck and trailer. *Damn it.* Where were they? Ryder's gang and the local police had checked almost every hotel and motel along every route leading to the border and no one had reported seeing a group of bikers. Did they push on? Were they already in the US? *No.* He couldn't consider failure. They had been riding longer than he had and he was already so stiff his feet were going numb. They had to have stopped somewhere.

Ryder returned from a quick reconnaissance. "Nothing. Desk clerk has only been here an hour and doesn't report seeing any bikers. He didn't have a number for the clerk who was here earlier."

Viking Dan sighed. "I guess we move on."

"Wait." James scrubbed his hands over his face. "There are no other motels for at least an hour. If it were me, this would be a good place to fuel up and lay low. It's out of the way and their legs would be hurting something fierce by now. Let's take a quick break and stretch. I'll do another walk-around."

He made a tour of the parking lot, peering into the few cars in the stalls, and then walked the perimeter of the motel, checking the grass and earth for prints. His mood darkened as he completed his circuit. Where the fuck was she? Had he totally misjudged the situation? Was Levi stupid enough to head straight to the border?

Waving at Viking Dan and Ryder to mount up, he crossed the picnic area and spotted something shiny in the grass. He picked it up and sighed. Tin foil. The remnants of someone's lunch. He tossed it in the garbage can and another glint caught his eye.

Probably more garbage.

Ryder revved his engine and Viking Dan helped Jackie onto his bike. James took two steps toward them and stopped. He had always instructed his homicide team to leave no stone unturned. Even though he was giving up that life, he couldn't turn his back on years of training. Taking a deep breath, he headed over to the shiny object just barely visible in the grass.

It was probably nothing.

"Back on the bed, bitch."

Levi grabbed Lana as she reached for the door and threw her across the bed. Her head hit the headboard with a loud crack and for a moment she couldn't move.

By the time her head cleared and sensation returned to her limbs, Levi was on top of her, his knife pressed against her throat. Blood dripped from his torn lip and splashed on her cheek, like a tear.

"I knew I shouldn't fucking trust you," he growled. "Someone betrays you once, they'll betray you again. Once you lose trust, you can't get it back."

Not true.

The tip of Levi's knife sliced across Lana's neck. Her breath caught in her throat at the sharp pain, choking off her scream. Her body shook violently with the need to writhe and twist and push him away, but with the knife on her skin, she was afraid to move. Not that she could move. Levi held her hands tight over her head, one knee pressed against her chest, his other leg pinning her to the bed.

"Now for the cheeks."

She barely heard the thud on the door for the pounding of blood in her ears.

"I fucking warned you," Hang Nail shouted. "No noise."

"Back off, Hang Nail. I've got her under control. When I'm done with her she won't be giving us any more trouble. Ever."

Levi's gaze rested on Lana, focused, intent. She looked into eyes dark as night and empty as his soul, and knew in her heart she was about to die. She opened her mouth to scream, but her throat tightened and no sound came out.

Levi slid the blade to Lana's cheek, brushing the cool steel over her heated skin. The tip of the blade cut deep and he dragged it along her cheekbone, parting her flesh with careful precision. The stinging pain brought tears to her eyes and blood trickled softly down the side of her face.

"Change of plans," he murmured. "Mark you, fuck you and *then* kill you. No more problems. No more humiliation." He drew the knife down the other side of her cheek, breaking the skin with a slow, careful stroke, drawing a strangled cry from her lips.

Her neck, her cheeks, her body—everything throbbed and burned and ached. Pain was everywhere, endless, blinding in its intensity. Hatred flared fierce inside her. And anger. Anger at what he'd taken from her as a romantic young teenager, and what he was going to take from her now—love and life and a chance at happiness.

Don't give up hope.

She clung to James's words as she clung to her life. *Run.* Her brain willed her body to move, but something else held her to the bed. Her limbs were heavy and unresponsive. Her breaths slow. And she was tired.

So tired.

No. She wouldn't die like this. Not as a victim. Not without hope. She pulled in the last of her energy, drew in a breath and spat in Levi's face.

"Do you never fucking give up?" he growled.

A thud on the door rattled the windows. Outside, a groan. A sob. Hushed words.

Levi's eyes glazed over and he pressed the knife tight against her throat. "That's the last time you ever humiliate me, Roxie. The. Very. Last. Time."

A shudder ran through her. She squeezed her eyes shut and wished she could have seen James one last time.

The door exploded inward and her eyes flew open.

James. And Ryder. Kickstand behind them. Wishes did come true.

Levi leaped off the bed, knife flashing in the air. James flew across the room and knocked him to the floor. A frenzy of punches, thuds, kicks, flying lamps, breaking glass, splintered wood, breaking bones.

Groans and whimpers.

Ryder and Kickstand pulling an enraged James away.

She watched it all through a soft haze, as if in a dream. Although she tried to move, her mind and body hit a disconnect. Dazed, confused, she tried to focus, but the world swam in front of her.

And then James was beside her. But he didn't smile.

"Jesus Christ. Look at her neck. Kickstand, get a towel. Ryder, call an ambulance."

James pulled her into his arms, his face a mask of rage and pain and...fear? "It's okay, Lana. You'll be okay. Ambulance is coming..." He choked on his words and his arms tightened around her. "I'm sorry I took so long. I should never have let you go."

"Trusted you," she whispered. "Didn't give up hope."

"You did good, babe." He pressed a kiss to her forehead.

She closed her eyes as sleep beckoned. But there was something she wanted to tell him. The words flitted through her brain, slipping and sliding as she tried to catch them. "James?"

"I'm here." His voice was distant, soft. She forced her eyes open and gazed into a stormy sea.

"Forgot...to tell you something."

Sirens. Banging. Gunshots. Crashing. Wheels squeaking. Shouting. Gasps.

"Tell me later." His voice caught and Lana frowned.

"No. Now. I might not... Please, James. Just in case."

"There is no 'might not'," he growled. "There is no 'just in case'. There is only *later*."

Her eyelids dropped and no force of will could hold them open. "I loved you from the day we met," she whispered. "I always knew you were *the one*."

Chapter Twenty-Four

James paced up and down the hallway outside the waiting area of the Vancouver General Hospital Emergency room. Jackie, Viking Dan and a bandaged Kickstand watched him from their seats in the corner. Ryder leaned against the wall nearby. Outside, a few members of the Rogue Riders patrolled the area, looking for escaped Wolverines.

Although Levi hadn't severed any of Lana's major arteries, he had come close. She had lost a lot of blood and needed stitches. Of more concern to the doctors were the injuries she had suffered from Levi's beatings: broken ribs, severe bruising and possible internal injuries.

If Levi hadn't been shot by the police as he tried to escape from the motel with two automatic weapons and a bag of cocaine, James would have gladly done the job.

"I can't sit here anymore," Jackie wailed. "I have a nurse's disguise in my bag. I'm going to put it on and sneak in."

Viking Dan put his arm around her shoulder and gave her a squeeze. "Calm," he said quietly. "The doctor said she's going to be all right."

Jackie raised an eyebrow. "I don't do calm."

He pulled her into his chest and locked her in place with a powerful arm. "You do now."

Jackie looked up at him and then rested her head against his shoulder, muttering softly under her breath.

"He soothed the savage beast," Ryder murmured to James. "Something even I couldn't manage to do. Maybe because I'm not a fucking six-foot-five, blond Viking with fucking ice for eyes."

A smile ghosted James's lips for the first time that night. "Didn't take you for the jealous type."

Ryder rolled his eyes. "I'm not jealous. I'm happy she's found someone who can manage her wild side. I'm just wondering...where's mine?"

"Mr. Hunter?" A young, harried-looking doctor joined them in the hallway. "Your girlfriend is stable and has asked—actually demanded—that you see her now. The nurse just needs five minutes with her and then you're free to go in. We'll keep her a few days just to be safe and if everything looks good, we'll discharge her."

James looked over his shoulder at Jackie. "You coming?"

She made a move to get up and then froze. "Nah. You go first. Right now I'm so mad at her for putting her life on the line I might not be able to control my mouth."

Ryder snorted. "So it can be done?"

"You keep that up," Jackie snapped, "and I won't join your biker gang, no matter how much you beg and plead. I'm already on the fence about the whole thing, seeing as you don't even have a patch."

"Design one. That can be your first job."

Jackie stared at him. "I'm a PI, not a patch designer. Do I look like I can draw? Do I strike you as the artistic type?"

"I'll help you." Viking Dan chuckled and patted her hand.

"Don't tell me that in addition to smashing Wolverine heads together, those gigantic paws of yours can wield a pen." A smile curled Jackie's lips.

"You would be surprised what these hands can do." He traced a finger along her jawbone and Jackie sucked in a sharp breath.

"Okay. Me and VD are gonna design a patch. It might take some time. Lots of time. I'm thinking something with a skull so people know we mean business, maybe some flames, knives or a sword. Something to make Hades run scared."

"Hades is gone," James said as he checked his watch. "Someone reported to the Coast Guard that Hades was involved in the illegal trade of Canadian waterfowl. Nothing riles the Coast Guard up more than someone messing with their ducks. They raided the clubhouse earlier this evening. They didn't find any ducks, but they did find five million dollars worth of coke stuffed into backpacks and a pile of illegal weapons."

After giving James the news, Tony had as good as admitted on the phone he had been the one to tip off the Coast Guard, raising yet another host of questions in James's mind about Tony's puzzling law enforcement connections. But Tony's past was a mystery for another day. Right now he couldn't think beyond getting in to see Lana.

Five long minutes finally passed. James stalked down the hallway and pushed open the door to Lana's room. Although he tried to keep his face impassive, he couldn't help his sharp intake of breath when he saw Lana lying still and quiet on the bed.

Pale, drawn and covered in tubes and wires, she was almost a ghost of herself. A thick white bandage covered her neck and smaller bandages followed the lines of her cheekbones. An IV bag dripped fluids into her arm. Monitors beeped quietly in the background. Even her hair was subdued, wrestled into an elastic behind her head.

Damned ponytail. For some reason the ponytail bothered him more than anything else.

James closed the distance between them, gently pulled out the elastic and fluffed her hair over the pillow.

"I liked it tied up." Lana's soft, raspy whisper brought a smile to his lips.

"I like you tied up, but not your hair. Some things aren't meant to be tamed."

"Still all about sex." She gave him a half smile.

"No, babe." He pressed his lips to her palm. "Still all about you."

Now that got him a grin.

He settled himself on the chair beside her bed and filled her in on the events after she'd been taken to the hospital. Most of the Wolverines arrested. Hades raided. Rex in jail. Kickstand safe. Angel happy.

Levi dead.

A shudder chased up her spine and tears glistened in her eyes. "He didn't start off bad. He changed."

"We've all changed." James brought her hand to his lips and kissed her knuckles. "Some of us, hopefully, for the better."

She smiled when he told her about Ryder's new club. "So what are they? Vigilantes? Mercenaries? Superheroes?"

"They're going to walk the gray area of the law. Robin Hood, if you're a romantic. Security consultancy, to be more accurate." He paused and took a deep breath. "I'm handing in my notice. As soon as I'm free, I'm going to join them."

Lana's eyes widened. "You? Mr. Career Cop. You're going to turn to the dark side?"

James cupped her cheek with his hand. "It's still about justice. Just going about it a different way. And it's time I left. I've done everything I set out to do. Beat cop, homicide, drug squad and undercover work. I have no aspirations to an administrative position and this last assignment took a hell of a lot out of me. And, to be honest, the biker life has a lot of appeal. Low stress. More time. And I'm keeping the Rocker."

Lana's cheeks flushed and the hint of color warmed his heart.

"Well, if things don't work out," she said, "I can always give you a job. You didn't do too badly on surveillance. A tad distracting and a bit quick to pull out the weapon, but I think we can work on it. Your car-sex techniques were beyond reproach."

"Still all about sex?"

Pressing her lips against his palm, Lana whispered, "Still all about you."

Chapter Twenty-Five

"Where are you taking me?" Jackie whined. "I thought we were going to a new club."

Lana pressed her finger to her lips as she led Jackie down the dimly lit back alley. Ahead of them, a tall, lean man stalked through the shadows. His leather boots thudded on the cobblestones. The two glowing eyes of a skull surrounded by flaming scales of justice glared into the darkness from the center of the patch on his shiny, new leather jacket.

"Hey, it's Ice," Jackie whispered. "Lookit that patch. Ryder wanted something understated but I said, 'No way. We're bikers. We have to look the part. And nothing says biker like skulls and flames.'"

Lana snorted a laugh. "James *hates* it. He wanted something with a more positive vibe."

"Viking Dan backed me up," Jackie said with a grin. "When he talks, everyone listens. What I wouldn't give to get that man into my bed."

"You haven't slept with him yet?" Lana widened her eyes. "I was wondering why you didn't talk much about him, but I was trying to respect your privacy by not asking what was going on."

Jackie blushed. "It's different. He's different. The minute I saw him...wowza. It was like I was hit by lightning. I'm not sure what that means, so I'm taking it slow. He doesn't seem to be in a hurry. All I've got so far are a few pats on the head and the occasional hand squeeze. I have to try and get off when I'm riding pillion on his motorcycle."

Laughter welled up in Lana's chest, and she tried to stifle the sound behind her hand. "Definitely not a problem I'm having. This is the first evening we've been apart in the last few weeks. James has been on a date kick. Every night, something new. And he's already got plans for when I'm fully recovered: white-water rafting, rollerblading, kayaking, skydiving, rock-climbing, extreme mountain-biking. It's like he's trying to make up for lost time."

Jackie snorted a laugh. "You're not apart. He's fifty feet in front of us. And I'm guessing you're going to be spending the evening together since you're both heading in the same direction."

A shiver ran down Lana's spine. She still wasn't sure if she was ready for Carpe Noctem. Although she hadn't told Jackie, her nightmares were one of the reasons James stayed with her every night. Nightmares of being bound and unable to move, hands in the dark, Wolverine rings and knives. Always knives.

Well…nightmares and the fact he wanted her tucked up against him every night, ostensibly so he could assure himself she was safe.

And yet, every time she thought about the club, a thrill of excitement shot through her veins. The visit tonight was her idea. Face her fears. Banish the nightmares and replace them with something else…something that made her mouth dry and her panties wet.

"Maybe we should tell him you want to spend the night with your best friend, watching TV. I can call Viking Dan and tell him not to come to the club."

"No." Lana clamped a hand over Jackie's mouth. "I'm supposed to be at the club already—awaiting his pleasure in the back room. But that last tattoo removal session took longer than I thought."

"So you're finally free?"

Lana smiled. "Thanks to Angel. She wasn't back together with Rex after all. She came to the club that night because she thought Rex was bringing someone with him. But now Rex is in jail, Angel got sole custody and I got a bonus that paid for the best tattoo removal money can buy."

They picked up the pace, trying to match James's long strides. The familiar scents of diesel, ocean mist and stale beer triggered a memory. The night James had saved her from Rex. The night she had fallen in love all over again.

"I have another surprise for him," Lana whispered as they fell into a light jog. "When I went to the commendation ceremony where he was awarded a medal for taking down Hades, I saw someone who looked familiar. It's been bothering me for days. Today, I went through my surveillance photos and I realized the assistant police chief who gave James the medal is the same man I photographed meeting Rex at Oktoberfest. He's the mole."

Jackie slowed to a walk. "Maybe you shouldn't tell James. He might decide to go back. It wasn't the organization that betrayed him. Just one man."

"He loves his new work," Lana said. "He sets his own hours, chooses his own cases and spends all day riding around on his Rocker, dispensing justice biker-style and then meeting up with Ryder for beer and barbeques."

Her foot slid on the cobblestones and loose gravel bounced off a nearby dumpster and clattered across the alley, the sound ringing in the quiet space. James stopped midstep. Lana and Jackie froze.

For a long moment, he didn't move. Then his head jerked to the side, his dark hair just brushing over his shoulders. Even in profile his rugged good looks took her breath away.

Lana pulled Jackie into a doorway and held her breath. Her new thigh-high, PVC, stiletto mock police boots were useless for surveillance, but good for getting James off. Nothing turned him on like her dirty-cop outfits and she aimed to please.

She plastered her body against the rough brick wall and breathed in soft, shallow pants. Kind of like sex. She seemed to do a lot of panting around James. But even more talking. His questions never seemed to end. He wanted to know every detail of her life, right down to her favorite color of nail polish and the grades she got in high school.

After one last sweep of the alley, James resumed his march, his long legs eating up the cobblestones until he reached the black metal door inset in the brick wall. He pulled a card from his pocket and ran it through the card reader. The door buzzed open.

"You girls coming or are you just skanking around the alley?" He looked back over his shoulder and grinned.

Damn. Caught. Her surveillance skills were getting rusty. She would need to pick up a few new cases. Motorcycles weren't cheap and with everyone and their dog now joining the Rogue Riders, she didn't want to get left behind.

Jackie cleared her throat and swanned across the alley. "For your information, we were not skanking. We happened to be coming up the alley at the same time as you, and I'm meeting Viking Dan here, just in case you were wondering." She pushed past James and stepped into the stairwell.

Lana made a move to follow her but James held her back.

"You were supposed to be waiting for me."

Undaunted by his sharp tone, Lana winked. "I have a surprise for you under my dress."

"What surprise?"

She shrugged off the trench coat she had worn to hide her risqué outfit and spun around.

Silence.

"James?"

"I like it."

Lana rolled her eyes. "Not the outfit. What's…or what's not…underneath." She flipped up her skirt, giving James a good view of her ass, a lacy black thong and a very bandaged but tattoo-free lower back.

"Christ," he muttered as he ran his hand gently over the bandage. "What if someone sees you?"

"They'll think I'm just a normal girl who hurt her back."

"You're not a normal girl. Not with that ass." He ran his hand over her cheek and gave it a squeeze.

"You looking at my ass, Officer Hunter?" She gave him a wiggle and smiled over her shoulder.

"I'm looking," he said. "And I'm liking what I see." He slid an arm around her, pulling her into his chest. Lana melted into his warmth and the comfort of his embrace.

"I'm glad it's gone," he said, nuzzling her neck. "After I knew what it was, every time I saw it, I wanted to pound on someone."

"How sweet."

"Nothing sweet about wanting to rip off a man's head and stuff his hands down his throat."

"You keep talking dirty like that and we might not make it down to the club."

"You keep talking to me in that sexy voice and I promise I'll have you down in the private members' area so fast those fuck-me boots won't even touch the floor."

Lana bit her lip to repress a giggle. "I thought our plans tonight already didn't involve my boots touching the floor."

"Babe?"

"Yeah, James?"

He swept her into his arms and kicked open the door. "They don't."

About the Author

New York Times and *USA Today* Bestselling author Sarah Castille worked and traveled abroad before trading her briefcase and stilettos for a handful of magic beans and a home near the Canadian Rockies. She writes erotic contemporary romance and romantic suspense featuring blazingly hot alpha heroes and the women who tame them.

Passion this hot should be illegal.

Legal Heat
© *2013 Sarah Castille*
Legal Heat, Book 1

Katy Sinclair made it to the brink of partnership at her high-powered law firm with hard work, dogged determination, and the ruthless self-discipline to cultivate a conservative public image. But when she follows an evasive witness into a sex club, she can't deny herself a red-hot sexual encounter with the seductive bartender who sets her body on fire. She's sure no one will ever know about her indiscretion —until she walks into the courtroom to find her dirty little secret is the opposing counsel in the most important case of her career.

As the managing partner in a struggling law firm, hot-shot attorney Mark Richards can't afford any mistakes that might cost him his biggest client. Like getting involved with his beautiful, determined opponent—the mystery woman he hasn't been able to forget. But when Katy's quest for justice leads to death threats, Mark will sacrifice everything to protect her.

Now they're risking their hearts...and their lives...in a race to catch a killer. Little do they know, the greatest danger lies closer to home.

Warning: This book contains explicit sex, light bondage, violence, murder, steamy shenanigans in the courtroom, naughty sexytimes in the boardroom, and an exceptionally hot hero with a versatile tie. Any objections will be overruled.

Available now in ebook and print from Samhain Publishing.

One night in Bangkok changes all the rules.

Black Knight, White Queen
© 2013 Jackie Ashenden

Professional chess player Aleksandr Shastin never lets emotions rule his life, or his game. Not even the unexpected death of his mentor shakes his icy control—at least that's what he thinks. Until he meets a woman in a Bangkok rooftop bar, a woman whose raw sexuality and emotional honesty find every invisible crack…and pries them wide open.

Graphic artist Izzy Cornwall fled to Thailand to escape suffocating grief and guilt after her sister's suicide. As she locks gazes with Aleks, their instant attraction sets her on fire. And the way he looks at her makes her feel what she hasn't felt in months: that she actually exists.

In the heat of a Bangkok rainstorm, their chemistry steams up what was supposed to be one night of pain-numbing passion. Neither expected that a single encounter would change all the rules, making Aleks the novice, and Izzy the grandmaster. But if Izzy wants his heart, she'll have to show him that in order to win, sometimes you have to lose.

Warning: Contains one hot, controlling Russian chess master, a heroine who's more than capable of taking him on in a game of strip chess, and a checkmate to make Kasparov proud.

Available now in ebook from Samhain Publishing.

It's all about the story...

Romance

HORROR

Retro ROMANCE

www.samhainpublishing.com

CPSIA information can be obtained
at www.ICGtesting.com
Printed in the USA
LVOW08s1442090217
523756LV00001B/249/P